DRACULA'S GIRLFRIEND?

This year, three weeks before Valentine's Day, Felicia Ames got into Sam's cab and asked to be taken to the mansion, and, just like that, Sam fell in love. She was a glowing blond model given to deep sighing and long blue gazes out the cab window. Every twenty minutes since meeting her, he had mentally proposed. Every thirty minutes, he thought about their having a child. And every forty minutes, he faced up to the terrible fact that on this Valentine's Day, sleazy Karl Richards was going to convert one more unwitting American girl into a creature of eternal darkness.

He was going to turn Felicia Ames into a vampire.

Or he thought he was, anyway.

But a hack driver named Sam McBride had different ideas.

**Other Holiday Anthologies of Horror
and Mystery from Avon Books**

13 HORRORS OF HALLOWEEN
*edited by Carol-Lynn Rössel Waugh,
Martin Harry Greenberg, and Isaac Asimov*

THE TWELVE CRIMES OF CHRISTMAS
*edited by Carol-Lynn Rössel Waugh,
Martin Harry Greenberg, and Isaac Asimov*

THE TWELVE FRIGHTS OF CHRISTMAS
*edited by Isaac Asimov, Charles G. Waugh,
and Martin Harry Greenberg*

14 VICIOUS VALENTINES

Edited by ROSALIND M. GREENBERG,
MARTIN HARRY GREENBERG,
and CHARLES G. WAUGH

With an introduction by ISAAC ASIMOV

AVON BOOKS ◆ NEW YORK

Additional copyright notices appear on the acknowledgments pages, which serve as an extension of this copyright page.

14 VICIOUS VALENTINES is an original publication of Avon Books. This work has never before appeared in book form. This is a work of fiction. Any similarity to actual persons or events is purely coincidental.

AVON BOOKS
A division of
The Hearst Corporation
105 Madison Avenue
New York, New York 10016

Copyright © 1988 by Martin Harry Greenberg, Charles G. Waugh, and Rosalind M. Greenberg
Published by arrangement with the editors
Library of Congress Catalog Card Number: 87-91628
ISBN: 0-380-75353-7

First Avon Books Printing: February 1988

AVON TRADEMARK REG. U.S. PAT. OFF. AND IN OTHER COUNTRIES, MARCA REGISTRADA, HECHO EN U.S.A.

Printed in the U.S.A.

K-R 10 9 8 7 6 5 4 3 2 .

ACKNOWLEDGMENTS

"The Jabberwock Valentine" by Talmage Powell. Copyright © 1988 by Talmage Powell. An original story used by arrangement with the author.

"Valentine from a Vampire" by Daniel Ransom. Copyright © 1988 by Daniel Ransom. An original story used by arrangement with the author.

"True" by John Maclay. Copyright © 1988 by John Maclay. An original story used by arrangement with the author.

"Two Floor Generals and the Sweetheart Dance" by J.N. Williamson. Copyright © 1988 by J.N. Williamson. An original story used by arrangement with the author.

"Be Mine" by Steve Rasnic Tem. Copyright © 1988 by Steve Rasnic Tem. An original story used by arrangement with the author.

"Die, Clown, Die!" by William F. Nolan. Copyright © 1988 by William F. Nolan. An original story used by arrangement with the author.

"From Parts Unknown" by Edward Wellen. Copyright © 1988 by Edward Wellen. An original story used by arrangement with the author.

"Recipe for a Happy Marriage" by Nedra Tyre. Copyright © 1971 by Davis Publications, Inc., from *Ellery Queen's Mystery Magazine*. Reprinted by permission of the Scott Meredith Literary Agency, 845 Third Avenue, New York, New York 10022.

"My Heart Cries for You" by Bill Crider. Copyright © 1988 by Bill Crider. An original story used by arrangement with the author.

CONTENTS

CONTENTS

INTRODUCTION: VALENTINE'S DAY

by Isaac Asimov

The Latin word *valere* means "to be strong," and from it we get such words as *valiant* and *valor*, since one expects a strong person to be brave. We also get words such as *value* and *valid*, since strength can refer not only to muscular power, but also to something that finds its strength in being worth a great deal or in being true.

In naming children, we can make use of words that imply the kind of character or virtue that we hope to find in him or instill in him. This is not so true now when we use old traditional names that had meaning in archaic terms we are no longer familiar with, but we think it fitting that a cartoon hero renowned for his strength and bravery be called "Prince Valiant."

The ancient Romans, by the same reasoning, might use the name *Valens*, which means "strength." By an irony of history, such a name became particularly popular in the later days of the Empire when Rome had grown weak. It was as though the Romans were using cheerful names to hide the dismal reality.

Thus, there was a Roman emperor named Valens, who ruled from 364 to 378, but his name turned out to be particularly inappropriate. He fought the Goths at the Battle of Adrianople on August 9, 378, and his Roman legions suffered an overwhelming defeat—a defeat from which the Empire never recovered. Valens, whose poor generalship was partly responsible, was himself killed in that battle.

Most names have diminutives, for it is almost inevitable that babies who receive a sonorous name be given a pet version of that same name; you have Dickie instead of Richard, Bobby instead of Robert, and so on. And sometimes the diminutive is retained into maturity. The Roman fashion of forming diminutives resulted in the name *Valentinianus* meaning "little Valens."

As a matter of fact, the Emperor Valens had an older brother who was named Valentinianus. (Yes, the older brother had the diminutive form of the name; these things don't go by logic.) Valentinianus reigned as co-emperor and was the more capable of the two brothers. He died first, in 375. He was succeeded by his four-year-old son, who reigned as Valentinianus II till he was assassinated in 392. There was also a Valentinianus III, who

1

reigned from 425 to 455 and was an almost complete nonentity in the days when the western portion of the Roman Empire was tottering to its fall.

The English language tends to shorten the long Roman names so that the various emperors of that name are known as "Valentinian" to us. A shorter form, even to the Romans, was "Valentinus" and this is shortened in English to "Valentine."

During the days of the Roman Empire, there were periodic persecutions of the Christians, and the Christian Church celebrated the martyrs, those who were executed in the course of these persecutions. A martyr was usually awarded sainthood and the day on which he or she was executed was held sacred to their memory. In the course of time every day in the year had one or more martyrs attached to them.

The martyrs were often of Roman descent and had Roman names. At least two of them were named Valentinus (Valentine, to us) and the day held sacred to their memory is February 14, which is therefore St. Valentine's Day.

Now it is necessary to turn to something else.

In ancient times, when infant mortality was high, and life expectancy low in any case, it was important to have many children. Consequently, people who, for any reason, had few children or none considered themselves under a curse or malevolent spell and went to some lengths to ensure fertility by some religious or mystical rite.

The ancient Romans had a holy spot where (according to legend) the wolf had suckled the twin brothers, Romulus and Remus, the former of whom eventually founded Rome. The spot was called the Lupercal from the Latin word *lupus,* meaning "wolf."

On that spot, every February 15, there was a festival called the Lupercalia, during which animals were sacrificed. Thongs were prepared from the bloody strips of animal hide, and priests ran through the crowd striking out with those thongs. Those who were struck were considered to be cured of sterility. Naturally, those who wanted children flocked to the festival. Afterwards, I imagine, they engaged in those activities that were expected to give rise to children—striking while the iron was hot, so to speak. Consequently, the Lupercalian festivities were associated with love and sex.

In 494, Pope Gelasius I forbade this pagan festival, but that sort of thing does no good. The festival simply continues under another name. Thus, for example, the celebration of the winter solstice was forbidden, but it still continues with almost all the pagan customs of the ancient Romans—under the name of Christmas. The celebration of the vernal equinox was combined with the Christian feast of the resurrection, which became Easter, and so on.

The Lupercalian festival of February 15 simply became St. Valentine's Day of February 14. (The change of one day may have come about because St. Valentine was a popular saint.) Legends arose later to the effect that St. Valentine had been kindly to lovers, but that was undoubtedly just a cover for the good old fertility rites that have always been popular (and, I strongly suspect, always will be).

The day was trivialized, of course, by the greeting card industry. Because most people are inarticulate and find it difficult to compose a letter, they gladly pay a small sum to purchase a synthetic letter. The industry encourages this and while the first greeting card was a Valentine's Day card, they have instituted cards for everything imaginable, right down to celebrating the day on which one's second cousin first fell into a mud puddle.

Consequently, a "valentine" has come to mean such a card and, by extension, someone's sweetheart. The word is redolent of paper lace and pastel shades and cherubs and hearts, and it is only because we are so accustomed to all that stuff that we avoid nausea.

In any case, *valentine* has become such a pleasant word that the thought of anything unpleasant taking place in connection with Valentine's Day carries a double load of shock, and it is this double load which you are invited to experience in the stories of this collection.

THE JABBERWOCK VALENTINE

by *Talmage Powell*

1

Out of New York, the Memphis-bound jetliner slanted its nose below the horizon and knifed into the cumulus. The clouds, so pristinely white and inviting moments ago, swallowed the aircraft in a slithery gray ooze. In my present mood it was no strain on the imagination to feel that the descent was into a repulsive nether region, primeval, roiling with unknown forces.

I looked at her lovely profile hovering in the seat beside me, looked away, forced my head to rest against the seat, and drew a long, careful breath.

I was not experiencing a reaction to flying. I flew as naturally and exuberantly as I sang off-key in an invigorating morning shower.

I was ridden with this certainty: that she was going down into the presence of death.

Since the spiritualist and shrink can't explain it, I can go no further than the experts, the specialists. I can only make a statement about that which transpires.

The first transpiration in my memory was of myself as a young boy out racing about on his first bicycle. From nothingness came a sudden sensation. It burst over me with the force of a silent scream. Colors spun through my head; they froze, in an image of a boy, myself, tangled and bleeding in the ruin of the bicycle at the next intersection.

I had stopped the bike somehow, left foot extended and touching the pavement, and now I looked wildly about, as if trying to find out what I should see.

The intersection was empty, peaceful. The image slipped away, leaving an unpleasant patina on the skin and a shortness of breath in its wake.

The sound of an engine broke the quietude, rising from snarling whisper to thunder. A car careered through the intersection, a man lolling drunkenly behind the steering wheel.

And I, having stopped my bike in the place and time that I did, missed my appointment. I saw the drunken face in profile, rather than gazing straight ahead at the loose, slavering features swaying behind an onrushing windshield.

I pedaled quietly home; said nothing to anyone, and the moment slipped into the maw of the memory of an active growing boy.

I became a senior in high school, took a job as counselor at a summer camp. And I snapped awake one warm, soft night swathed in the peculiar sweat. I punched the pillow to go back to sleep, telling myself I'd dreamed, had a nightmare. I lay back, closed my eyes. And the scene flashed against my lids: boys mindless with terror, milling and screaming while tongues of hungry flames curled over them.

Muttering scorn for my own stupidity, I rose from my sweaty cot. Wearing the shorts in which I slept, I padded from the counselor's quarters across the moon-kissed quadrangle to cabin B: it was dark, serene, steeped in sleep. But having already behaved like a fool, I went on inside.

I smelled the first acrid taint of smoke, saw the fireflylike flickering in the corner. I turned on the lights, rousted eight confused, blinking boys from their bunks, and put out the small fire before it made its way out of the waste can. It had moldered and finally found life in a wadding of shoeshine rags. Some boy, experimenting with cigarettes after lights-out, had left a spark in a butt tossed in the waste can. We turned up the identity of the culprit, notified his parents, and put him on garbage detail for a week. He departed camp, thumbing his nose and lighting a cigarette.

I was eighteen, and the Vietnam War was winding down, but the draft board had no precognition that America would cut and get out within eighteen months. So I came to manhood in walks through steaming jungles, firefights, and temporary forgetfulness in Saigon whorehouses.

The patrol that day was a piece of cake—to take up station in a friendly village. But the colors burst in my head and I halted my men. I scattered them to cover, enfilading the trail. On their bellies, like bugs, vermin, they sweated in the heat, scratched insect bites, and muttered about the sergeant's guts and sanity. ComPost crackled the radio. Where the hell is Sergeant Barnard? And I made no reply, no move, except to threaten to shoot a skinny private who finally said to hell with this, ain't it a friendly?

And as the sun was sinking, Vietcong came creeping from the village to wonder why the intended victims hadn't come. The Cong were killed; the fire sweeping the trail was too deadly for it to be otherwise. One was a thin-faced boy who had no excuse to own a razor. I wept inwardly and wished the sun would not show itself over the jungle tomorrow morning.

Back in the alien world of home, I enrolled in the University of North Carolina at Chapel Hill. Lacking the sophistication of a 'Nam education, my peers seemed childish, callow, and naive, and I formed no lasting relationships.

One day during my senior year one of those fractured moments of nontime came from nowhere, and I got in the VW and drove home to Asheville. I was not empowered to alter this future moment, but I was with my father at my dying mother's bedside.

Upon graduation, I landed a junior exec post in marketing in a corporation that made mufflers for cars, trucks, tractors, lawn mowers, boats. Lucky me. Enviable start from which I could one day achieve the privilege of lunching in the penthouse dining room.

I saved some money, got miserably seasick on a freighter wallowing its way to ports in Europe, and backpacked and bummed my way through Spain and Italy.

I thought a lot about going to India, land of gurus. But I already knew the lingo: channeling, trans-spatial existence, the Akhasic Records, trance-states, astral projection. I had done my reading and research, I had sampled cult experiences. I was way ahead of most of the field, and had discovered no guru, medium, or reincarnate worth emulating. They were either charlatans—or touched reality even more tenuously than I.

I went to work in the State Department as an assistant to an assistant secretary. As the years ticked off I became an assistant secretary, liaison to the White House, director of research, ambassadorial courier. Very nice life. Good pay, expense money, movement among the powerful, consorting with intellectual equals, lots of travel first class, in and out of American embassies in Europe. Female relationships of course, but never the satisfying of the quiet hunger within me.

Then in Paris I met her. The mellifluous voice of the ambassador at a party for a bigwig from Algiers: "Cody, I want you to meet Valentina Marlowe. Val, Cody Barnard, one of the unsung who mops up spills of politicians."

Of course I had heard her name, seen her picture. What model has been more photographed than Valentina Marlowe? I turned, and our eyes met, and I don't know how long the ambassador lingered. I can't say what she was wearing or what was said in those first moments, or how we escaped the cloying boredom of the chitchat, clink of glasses, muted strains of a string quartet. By unspoken mutual agreement we sought a quiet in the lights of Paris. We had known each other always. We talked as if picking up a conversation begun and suspended perhaps a week ago.

We had four days that time. Simple pleasures. Communion. Lovers. But more—also friends.

"I'll be leaving tomorrow, Cody. I always spend Valentine's Day with the home folks. My birthday, you know. Reason my mother tagged me with the given name."

Home was Wickens, Louisiana.

"How long will you be in Wickens, Val?"

"I'll leave the day after Valentine's Day."

"To Washington," I said.

The oblique look from the expressive violet eyes in the wonderfully devised face. A toss of the mane of black, a wisp immediately returning to nuzzle her cheek. "You rat, I might have known you were behind the invitation."

"Made a suggestion in the right ears, that's all." I laughed. "Doing my duty for my country. A symposium on women's rights wouldn't be complete without the presence of the world's most beautiful model."

"Then write my speech! I need ten minutes, and it's been driving me up a wall."

Now it was another February, month of the odd day every fourth year to reset the calendar, month of the day given to St. Valentine . . . Which? There were two saints of the name, you know.

And the clouds outside the descending aircraft were as filthy as the darkness in which I'd awakened three nights ago. The colors in frozen frame . . . her face in death, partly obscured by a swirling of water . . . the sounds of bullfrogs *harrump*ing, the smell of swampy Louisiana bayou earth . . . then only the smothering darkness.

Luminous dial of the bedside clock: 3:00 A.M. I'd got dressed, gone out, and walked the quiet streets of Georgetown until the eastern sky showed gray.

From a phone booth I had called my secretary. No apology for rousting her out of bed. "I won't be in today, nor for the next several days."

Her voice cleared the cobwebs of sleep. "I don't understand, Mr. Barnard."

"It isn't necessary for you to do so."

"But your appointments, correspondence, the report—"

"Make excuses, Miss Clowerson! You're very good at that sort of thing. Parcel out my chores, take up the slack, use your Washington logic.''

''Well, I can always say that someone very close to you suddenly died.''

I slammed the phone in its hook. Damn bitch! Damn unwitting, cruel, cruddy bitch!

A shuttle flight. A taxicab. Val surprised, her face lighting happily, heartbreakingly, when she saw me standing with a packed overnight and garment bag.

A kiss. Hug. A herding into the apartment with its view of Central Park.

''You're going to Wickens this year with me!''

''Isn't it time I met your mother, and this George you're always talking about, and Keith, Lissa, and Reba who runs the house like a Captain Bligh, and the others?''

''Oh, Cody . . . I'm so glad you could arrange it. God, this will be the best Wickens year ever!''

Now her elbow nudged me. ''Hey, Cody . . . Memphis below. Then a short commuter flight and you'll experience Wickens, no less.''

My sham yawn was convincing enough. She'd turned her attention from my closed eyes to look out the window as the jet broke cloud level, and Memphis and the Mississippi River spread like a far-flung relief map.

She laughed. ''He was a great songwriter, but he was wrong on one point.''

''Who is that?''

''Ira Gershwin . . . the lyricist. Look down there at the city, the farms, fields, docks, river craft just rolling along. I ask you. Is that an Old Man River? Male chauvinism, that's what. Old Man River indeed! Any dummy from this part of the world knows the Mississippi is female.''

Our shoulders pressed as we both looked down before the plane wheeled for approach and the wing cut the river out of sight.

''Pure female,'' I agreed. ''Giver of life. Mercurial in mood from her icy beginnings in the north to her turgid joining with the Gulf. Comforter. Angry mistress, when she spews over her banks, scorning the levees trying to hem her in.''

''Don't forget her mysteries.'' Val smiled. ''Beneath the warm, peaceful invitation of her surface are snags to rip the stoutest boat to pieces.''

''Oh, her mysteries fascinate me most.''

"I'm glad you understand, Cody." She tweaked my nose. "How could I respect a man who didn't see a truth so clearly?"

"Hell, it's obvious. If the Mississippi is an old man, then the Statue of Liberty is a transvestite."

She laughed, but I had a shriveling coldness inside.

For the nth time I thought to myself: Keep her away from Wickens, Louisiana, this Valentine year. If you can't think of a logical reason, let her think you've lost your mind. Coerce, plead. Do it physically. Lock her in a room someplace and stand guard at the door until the Valentine hour is past.

But somehow I knew that this was not the alternative future that would work. Neither Wickens nor the forces would vanish at my whim. Wickens would be there all the years of her life. The issue had to be settled. There was no escape or normal safety until the issue was put to rest.

2

Val and I were among a trickle of passengers exiting the commuter plane in Wickens. We were hardly down the ramp steps when a man and woman gathered us in, beaming joy, smothering Val, pumping my hand.

"Mom, George, this is the man!"

"Wow! Toss you for this one, Val. Hi, Cody. I'm Elva."

"I know," I said, smiling. "Would have known you anywhere." And it was true. She was the gracefully aging pattern from which Val had been cut.

"And this is George," Elva said.

"Glad to know you, George."

"Likewise." His handshake was good—firm, but not bone crushing. He was a man who didn't have to display, to prove anything. Mentally I agreed with what Val had said about George Crandall. He was a presence. You either liked him immediately or shied away. I liked the little echo of gentleness in the boom of his voice. I liked the intelligence of the perceptive brown eyes in the face that might have been carved from oak with a trench knife.

This retired army officer, this Colonel George R. Crandall, was second father to Valentina. He was hardly the stereotype southern colonel. No fine-boned aristocrat, no white Vandyke, no broad-brimmed, floppy panama hat or string necktie. He was a tanned, fit light heavyweight in sandals, poplin slacks, and a knitted shirt on which the corners of the collar curled slightly. A man who sweated easily but wouldn't particularly mind heat or cold.

"Would you like a drink?" he was asking.

"You kidding?" Val said. "We won't have to wait for the luggage. I want a drink—at home."

Elva drove. Her car was a modest Chevy. The day was lovely, February cool but touched with that southern Louisiana sense of semitropic in the breath from the Gulf, the river, the bayous and swamps. George pointed out landmarks of possible interest and asked about my work. It was the usual, expected small conversation, but his interest was real, quick, lively.

My impression of Wickens was of modern hustle and a scorn for the passage of time. Taking sustenance from its busy waterfront and natural gas industry, Wickens was state-of-the-moment shopping centers, half a dozen high-rise buildings over a downtown where revitalization had preserved the more historic sites. Wickens was also previous-century on streets where time had been barred, where there was still a corner grocery, a drugstore in an ancient building . . . it surely had a marble-counter soda fountain. A statue of a Confederate soldier stood guard over a park where old men played checkers beneath hoary live oaks and aged palm trees and pines bearded with Spanish moss. A few young mothers chatted on benches, rocking baby carriages and watching older children at play near an iron-railed fountain. Tract homes and condos hadn't conquered Wickens. There were broad, tree-shaded streets of impeccable old gingerbread houses from which maidens in crinoline might burst forth at any moment to prepare for a lawn party.

George saw my interest in passing details. "Get to you, if you're not careful," he laughed. "Best damn spot on earth—except during hurricane season. Phobia of mine."

He didn't strike me as a man of any phobias, which just goes to show.

"Last year, by God, when Charlie was taking on such a load coming up through the Gulf, twisting a drilling platform like it was wet spaghetti, Elva loaded me onto a plane and we shopped and saw the sights in Montgomery, Charlie having aimed straight for Wickens. You were in 'Nam, I understand. Jesus . . . in those parts I was once in a typhoon . . . left me without a nail on a single finger. You strike me as a tolerable sportsman, Cody. Golf? Fish? Maybe one night you'd like to break out a watersled and try your hand at frog gigging? Nobody cooks fresh frog legs quite like Elva."

"I've eaten them in Paris." I grinned.

"Paris? Where the hell is that? For good food you got to go to New Orleans, or Elva's kitchen."

We had reached the eastern suburbs, not quite in the country. The houses dotted a landscape of sweeping lawns, small pastures, hedges, fences of wood, iron, chain link, split rail; lines of trees suggested boundaries between acreages of sizes to be called estates.

Elva turned onto a white-graveled driveway that wended between rows of sheltering willows. I saw a farmhouse that was comfortably old Southern, white frame, two stories, tall windows, a porch rambling across the front, a towering fieldstone chimney snugged against the eastern end.

George led me upstairs to a spacious front corner bedroom. Beneath the tall ceiling was a solid old poster bed, chest, bureau, huge oval mirror, writing desk, a Tiffany lamp on a table beside the invitation of a lounging chair.

"Your bath is right there." George nodded at a door in the rear wall. "The wardrobe filling the corner should do. No closet . . . House was built by Valentina's great grandpa, and houses were taxed by rooms in those days. Bureaucrats of course counted a closet as a room, and a hell of lot of people decided to make the wardrobe industry what it was for a while."

He paused in the doorway. "Just follow your druthers while you're with us, Cody. We don't live on ceremony. Shoot any food allergies, or preferences, up front. We'll do our best."

"Thanks, George. Not picky in the mess hall. If it's creeping, just kill it before you serve."

"Stow your gear, freshen up if you like, and come on down as it suits your mood."

Half an hour later, I heard the pleasant rise and fall of voices as I went down the oaken-banistered stairway into the spacious lower hallway.

They were in the living room, the forepart of the house off the hall, and Val saw me instantly when I appeared in the broad doorway.

She came and took my hand, ran the fingers of her other hand lightly along my temple. "Your hair is curling a little from the shower damp." She smiled. "Come let me display you. People, this is Cody. Cody, meet Lissa Aubunelli, with whom I've had some pigtail pullings, and Keith Vereen. Careful with State Department classified in Keith's presence, Cody. He's one of those monsters known as the press. Publishes the local daily newspaper and brought the first, and only, television station to Wickens, a CBS affiliate."

Lissa was plump, dark, big brown eyes, brown hair cut short and sassy, teeth that flashed almost as perfectly as Val's, round, pink-cheeked face with chronic little moisture swatches beneath her eyes.

She gave me a hug and peck on the cheek, a sigh as she stepped back, head tilted, looking me over. "Val the stinker . . . really got the pick of the litter."

Keith Vereen was smiling at her, offering his hand to me. He was tall, slender, slightly stooped, sandy-haired with quick, sharp blue eyes in a finely boned face. His movements suggested a carefully tuned conditioning and the reflexes of a cat.

"A real pleasure, Cody. But you're no stranger. Val's carryings-on about you in letters to her mother made you a friend quite awhile back."

"How about a drink, appetizer?" Keith suggested. We drifted toward a buffet burdened with the wherewithal.

"Bourbon?" Lissa said. "I'll pour; want it neat, or with branch, soda, ginger ale?"

"A splash of branch is fine."

"How about a Sunday feature, Cody?" Keith said. "Isn't every day an assistant secretary of state surfaces in Wickens. I'd even ask Lissa to write it."

"No way," Lissa said. "Hunk like him . . . I couldn't be the least bit objective."

Our hands touched as I took the proffered drink. "You're a writer?"

"The best by-hell investigative reporter in the state of Louisiana," Keith said, "perhaps the South."

"Why stop there?" Lissa asked.

She didn't look like an investigative reporter; she looked like a jolly young woman with innocent devilment behind her eyes and pasta recipes in her head.

"She started on the *Sword*, which is what my grandpappy called the paper when he bought the first linotype machine. Unfortunately, we lost her in a short time to the *New Orleans Observer*. Been there how long now, Lissa?"

"Seven years, kiddo. Don't bother to ask my age."

"She's had offers from the *Washington Post, New York Times*, a news magazine or two," Val said in pride of her lifelong friend.

"They're not in New Orleans, lamb. They're in places where there's no old French market and the yokels don't know how to listen to Dixieland music."

Elva and George came in, beginning a pleasant hour. I felt so at home, I might have been born in Wickens.

* * *

Despite the comfort of the poster bed, I didn't sleep well. Finally, about two in the morning, I gave it up. I put on a robe and socks, and slipped downstairs to the kitchen. I filched makings, cold chicken roasted in a piquant Louisiana basting, French bread, shreds of jack cheese, and a generous slap of a cajun version of slaw.

I carried the reuben out to the front porch. The night was nippy, but not cold. A breeze whispered in the pines and palm trees, the moon glinted behind scudding clouds, the faintest insinuation of primeval earth seeped from the swamps.

"You ought to have a cup of steaming coffee and chickory with that drooly goody. The chickory—it gentles everything, lulls you to sleep on a full stomach."

At the first soft murmur I'd turned. Lissa's round face, dimly seen, was smiling from a wicker chair in the darkness. Beside the chair was its wicker twin. I sat down, holding out the sandwich. "Want a hunk?"

"Sure." She reached, carefully wrestled off a modest share, sat back, taking a bite. "Very good."

"Want a whole one? You hardly got a mouthful."

"Better not." She bit into the morsel. "What's with you? Jet lag? The quiet against big-city ears?"

I shook my head. How could I tell her? *An awful premonition won't let me sleep . . . I've had them before, not often, never know when or how, but they're more real than the wailing of that night creature, which sounds like it's in bad trouble.*

"Oh, the excitement, I suppose," I said. "The day. Coming to Val's home, meeting you people, who are so very much exactly as you should be."

"So are you." She was silent a moment. She saw me looking in the direction where the night creature had screamed, one brief wail, abruptly cut off.

"It's a million years ago, not far down state road 61. But you've been in jungle even more deadly." She rustled, leaning slightly toward me. "You can keep from telling me what's on your mind, Cody. None of my business. So I won't ask."

"I won't volunteer."

"Touché. Well, I don't mind telling you why my bed was smothery, why I finally came down to look at the familiar yard and think about when we were kids, Val and I. Fact is, I need an ear . . . someone who won't sigh crossly and tell me I'm an emotional nit, acting like a stupid child."

"Give you my word. None of us sounds altogether brilliant when we need a sounding board."

"Truth is . . ." She took a breath. "Cody, I'm frightened. And if I tell you why, I'll sound like an underdone fool kid who got hold of some crack."

"Try me."

"It's this . . . the pattern."

"What pattern?"

"The appearances of the dead bodies in Mad Frenchwoman's Cove! But of course, you don't know any of it. I'm not yet making sense."

"No, you're not, Lissa. Why not try starting at the beginning?"

She eased back in her chair; she seemed small in it. It was a big barrel of a wicker, the top a little higher than her head, the arms great convolutions of wicker curved halfway around her.

"You've heard of the events of February 14, 1929, in Chicago, of course."

I thought for a second. "The St. Valentine's Day massacre?"

"Yes . . . so it's known. Seven men waited for the arrival of a hijacked truckload of bootleg booze—six gangsters and an optometrist who enjoyed the company and life-style of gangsters. A mongrel dog was also present. Bugs Moran, the prime target in the gangland sortie, should have been there, but he was running late. As he approached the Clark Street warehouse to join the gangsters inside, he saw a big Caddy, police gong on the running board, pulling up and disgorging four men. Two were in police uniform, two in civvies. A fifth man, the driver, stayed in the car. Moran turned and made tracks while his seven pals were blasted with shotguns and submachine guns. Close range. Really gory. The gunfire attracted notice, but when two men in uniform herded two in civilian clothes out, it seemed just another Chicago episode in a time when such raids were commonplace. No one was ever convicted. Al Capone, having masterminded the tactic to wipe out members of a rival gang, had taken himself off to his Florida estate, and at the hour of the massacre was chatting with the Dade County solicitor."

"A perfect alibi," I remarked. "But why dwell on violence and murder on a day given to love?"

"Because there was another St. Valentine's Day massacre, Cody. Way back in 1865."

"Close of the Civil War," I said.

"Yes. It made regional headlines, quickly forgotten, especially in the chaotic aftermath of war. But it's still in the history books, those multivolume things covering Louisiana history. Occasionally it crops up in Sunday supplement feature stories in one of the larger state newspapers.''

"Who was massacred?"

"Seven young men, Yankee soldier boys sent in to help police a riverfront town in a region already neutralized and under Union control. They were invited to a St. Valentine's Eve party by a beautiful young woman, Marie Louchard. On the way they were captured by a band of marauders, thieves, cutthroat killers posing as die-hard Rebs. They were herded onto a barge, hands bound, and dropped into the Mississippi. One by one their bodies washed ashore in Mad Frenchwoman's Cove. It's an inlet, and the river currents twist shoreward.''

Lissa was still more than a hundred years from my fears for Valentina, but I had a foreboding that the threads were going to cross. I wanted Lissa to shut up, but I had to hear on.

And she continued, "The leader of the renegades was one Alberto Batione y Ochoa. He was of two families powerful at the time when the Spanish flag flew over the Cabildo in New Orleans, once the seat of Spanish government in Louisiana. Both families were notorious for their blood lust, sadism, and cruelties, and the genes certainly came to full expression in Alberto . . .''

She paused, taking a small breath. "Seven years ago, Cody, the first body washed up in Mad Frenchwoman's Cove. Young man. Hands bound. Cause of death, drowning. It was a run-of-the-mill report in the *Sword* and hardly made the other papers. Then the next year, another body . . . and the year following . . . always the same, a satanic valentine for Wickens. Along about the sixth year, the investigative reporter in me began to take notice, frame questions.''

"And you discovered?"

"Nothing right away. Cases unsolved . . . During the course of a full year what's one more killing in a society rife with daily murders, rapes, muggings? The seven bodies in Mad Frenchwoman's Cove in life had been as unlike as peas and potatoes, one a street person, another a filling station attendant, a drug peddler, fellow who worked for an outdoor sign company . . . but my head wouldn't let go. And I came up with a link, Cody. Dear God, I went into the history of each victim, and I discovered that two were cousins, and I backtracked them, in a growing obsession with this thing. And would you know . . . every single one of the seven young men was descended from Alberto Batione y Ochoa. Cody, I swear . . . am I going nuts? The spirits of those seven Yankee soldier boys of 1865 have been about their revenge. Eye for eye, tooth for tooth . . . spirits real, or spirits imagined in an insane head . . . the result is as undeniable as men taking a trip to the moon.''

"Seven," I said. "Seven Yankee boys, seven of Ochoa blood now accounted in Mad Frenchwoman's Cove."

"You fool," she said quietly. "You're trying to tell yourself that it's over. For some reason, you want to believe it. You're afraid for Valentina, Cody. I can see it in your eyes. I can smell your fear. I don't know how or why, but thank God you're in Wickens this St. Valentine's. This year, if the pattern holds, this is the season for the pièce de résistance. The woman who betrayed the seven Union soldiers—Marie Louchard—is yet unatoned."

I pressed back away from Lissa's sweat-beaded face. "Hush!" I said thickly. "Don't say anything more."

"All right, Cody. As you say."

"No—you must." My hand caught her arm. "Valentina . . . Marie Louchard . . ."

"Five generations, Cody. Direct descent, through Valentina's paternal grandmother."

The night was a vacuum. Then Lissa shivered. "I'm cold," she said.

I was hardly aware when she rose and slipped away into the house.

3

I opened my eyes, and the world outside was deceptively pleasant: friendly sun, blue skies, a fluttering of birds outside the bedroom window.

The sun's brilliance suggested midmorning. Puffy-eyed, I stumbled into the shower. Sleep, when it came finally, had been deep, dark, a flight into temporary death.

Steady now. The little rituals: shower, shave, brush the teeth, get dressed, comb the hair.

While I made the automatic motions, I tried to cast my thought in the mold of Lissa. More than two years now since the fifth body had washed ashore in Mad Frenchwoman's Cove, quite a bit of rope for a reporter of Lissa's gifts. It wasn't difficult to comprehend what had sparked her first curiosity. Five corpses. All young males. All drowned. Same location, same time each year. Who were they, really? Did they have anything in common? And the common ancestry had hooked Lissa.

She had probably wanted to go at it full-time, but a metropolitan editor involved in the large scene wouldn't have seen it that way. What you smoking these days, Lissa? What's this poppycock? Even if you devise a spook tale out of a riverfront town, so what? Louisiana abounds in spook tales, stories of voodoo queens, ghosts in the spreading live oak where Creole aristocrats fought duels, haunted mansions. If we're to go the sleazy tabloid route, why not go out to one of the rat holes today, buy a love potion or pin-stuck doll, and tell our readers about it? You should be in Baton Rouge, Lissa, telling me who is behind the sugar quota bill; you should be in Houston finding out where the oil brokers from Louisiana are meeting with their buddies in Texas; you should be tracing the ownership of the plot on which Parks and Recreation, City of New Orleans, is going to squander another million, sure as a piss ant crawls. Now get the hell to Baton Rouge, Lissa—and I can't pass up the old compliment that you're pretty when you're angry.

So it would have gone, whetting her interest the more, returning her spare time and thoughts again and again to Wickens.

When I came out into the upper hall, I heard the whirr of a vacuum cleaner downstairs. That would be Reba. She and Clyde, middle-aged couple, were the domestic staff, having a small home adjacent to the Marlowe place. Reba arrived each day and Clyde pruned, raked, fixed leaks, and painted as need arose, doing a little truck farming and fishing.

The vacuum was racketing in the living room, a counterpoint to Reba's work rhythm as she sang an old hymn. ("Oh, Beulah Land, sweet Beulah land, as on the highest mount I stand . . .") Her tempo would get her through the living room in short order.

Seeing no one about, I went on to the secrets of the large, airy kitchen with its walk-in cooler, gas range, sinks of old-timey zinc, racked pots and pans of cast iron and copper. A work area centered the room and a sunny breakfast nook bay-windowed on the east.

Too late for breakfast, too early for lunch. I sure as hell had been out like a light once I tipped over the edge.

Hot coffee was in the urn, and I cut crusty Louisiana French bread for toast and found marmalade in the pantry.

I was munching, listening to the house, anxious to hear those little details Lissa might have left unsaid, when footsteps sounded and George appeared in the doorway.

A smile creased his hewn face. "Must have been the Louisiana air."

"Someone should have called me."

"Why? You got an appointment with the ambassador from Paraguay? How's the coffee holding out?"

"Tastes like it was just made."

He reached into the china cabinet for a big white mug that had his initial on it.

"Hate to eat and run, George." I dropped my napkin beside the marmalade-smeared saucer. "But I want to talk to Lissa."

He glanced as he turned the urn spigot. "She's not here."

"Oh?"

"She left about half an hour ago."

"Did she say where she's going?"

He shrugged. "Who asked? Whose business?"

He sat down opposite me at the breakfast nook table. "She did mention she wouldn't be here for lunch—popping down to New Orleans and back. Something about a detail in some records that had spewed up in her mind. (Her words.) Whatever it was, she seemed a little put out with herself that it had escaped notice before. 'Spewed up in her mind' . . . tendency to overwrite despite her brilliance, wouldn't you say? She told Elva she'd be back long before dinner. My guess is that she's gone off to buy a birthday-valentine gift for Valentina. Those two . . . they trinket-shop for each other as if they were buying for Saint Anne."

He was looking at me over the top of the coffee mug. "Anything wrong, Cody?"

Was anything right? I shook my head. Nothing for it now, except to wait until Lissa got back. I said, "You've known Val a long time."

"All her life. Her mother and I . . . everyone was sure we'd wind up married."

"What happened?"

His lips made an ironic smile. "Career . . . I was hell-set on the army. Dedication to the ambition, you might say, got me in West Point despite the muscularity between the ears. Elva was hell-set against it. Radical kid in those days. Flower child, Saint Joan of the armies of righteousness. The saps do run high when you're young, don't they? We had attitudinal difficulties, it's safe to say, estrangements based on noncompromise of principles, which are the worst estrangements of all, pigheaded stubbornness on the part of both, pride, and wounded hearts. I had my career and she ended up marrying Charles Marlowe. I'd like to call him a bastard, but he was a fine man, Cody. He passed on . . ."

"When Val was fifteen," I said. "She's told me about him. She was never close to him."

"It happens with kids sometimes. They were cut in different dispositions, but she respected him, and he never had a moment's trouble with her."

"Val would never give anyone trouble, George. If the relationship was like that, then excise the relationship, however painful."

"Like her mother," he said.

"You never married?"

His beefish shoulders lifted, dropped. "Mistresses. Not cheap. Lived with three women all told. The relationships were nicer than most run-of-the-mill marriages. Difference between me and a lot of officers, I didn't change mistresses at every post, with a wife back home. Very fond of all three, but the kind of love a man should have for a woman got stranded at the altar in Saint Louis Cathedral the day Elva married Charles Marlowe. I was a shavetail on duty in Panama that day."

"Did you see Elva often after that?"

He laughed, brief belly laugh. "Son, I came back here on my first leave after her marriage, spit and polish, sabers at the ready. Ah, youth . . . I was full of fire to duel old Charlie or something like that and drag Elva off by the hair. She kept us apart. And after that meeting with her, I knew she was too Catholic to divorce him. Sure, I saw her now and then during my career years, small town, old family ties. You don't move around much in Wickens without the bumping-into."

He reached across to slap my shoulder. "You can bet your last franc I see her often nowadays."

"Why don't you marry her, George?"

"Hell, I intend to. I think she keeps stalling because of Val."

My frown questioned.

He spread his hands. "It nettles me, I'll admit, but no throwing down of the gauntlet this time. I can wait. It's like she's got some kind of notion she shouldn't think solely of herself, but should wait to tie the knot until Val is safely married and the last shred of umbilical cord cut for good. What the devil's wrong with you, Cody? Val's the loveliest, most sensitive, intelligent woman on earth, and I can't believe you're a man with a stuck zipper. Heaven's sake, Cody, marry the girl and get her the hell out of our hair."

Before I responded, Reba came into the kitchen, pleasant, robust, giving me a sniff. "Had a special cut of country ham to go with the eggs and grits for you, Mr. Barnard, and you come sneaking down behind my back."

"I'm sorry, Reba."

She went to the dishwasher to remove crockery. "Now you know. No excuse."

George stood and stretched, lazily and contentedly. "Well, Cody, what's on for today? Name it, and I'll tell you if I'm amenable or any good at it."

"I really must talk to Lissa."

"Then I'll wander over to the country club and see if I can catch a foursome or try a hand at a penny-ante poker game. Come on over. You'll meet likable people."

"Thanks, George."

As he went out, I said to Reba, "The house is very quiet. Did Val and Elva go out?"

She nodded. "They went downtown to do some last-minute shopping for the valentine–birthday party. You'll have a ball! Real blowout every year, Val coming home and all, paper lanterns and people all over the lawn. Caterers are brought in so's me and Clyde and Elva ain't got a thing to do but have fun. Last year, Lissa hired a genuine Dixie band to come from New Orleans. Sakes alive, I wondered if those decrepit old blacks had played the processional for Noah to enter the ark. The old boys propped themselves up on the bandstand George had planked together on the lawn, and when that music started—day of miracles. Those fellows shed about thirty years apiece, first tune, and they got younger and stronger with every note. Lawdy, my blood is still singing from that music."

"Any Louchards at the party, Reba?"

She stiffened, then slowly slipped the last plate from the dishwasher. "Where'd you hear that name?"

"Val's part Louchard, isn't she?"

"There ain't no more Louchards, Mr. Barnard," she said thinly. "The last to bear the name was Valentina's great grandfather. He had but one daughter. The name ain't gonna be found in any Wickens phone books."

I didn't press Reba. She'd let me know I was on verboten ground. Marie Louchard's conspiracy to murder seven Yankee boys in 1865 was not a subject for conversation in a region where family trees still cast long shadows.

The respectful quality of my silence was the best ploy, though I'd used it inadvertently. Reba was thinking about it and as she stacked the dishes, she cleared her throat and said, "I reckon you'll be part of the family and have a right to know. So to save you folks trouble, I'll give you the Louchard bit—if you'll take it as the meaningless bit of scandal it is, let it go at that, and keep your mouth shut on any further question."

"Agreed, Reba." I looked at her with fresh interest. "Fire away."

"Ain't much firing, really. Marie Louchard, the ancestress you don't talk about, was a dilly in capital letters. At fifteen she was in a wealthy planter's pants long enough to rob him. She shilled for a riverboat gambler. She was come-on for a saloon keeper who rolled his passed-out patrons in a back alley. She was part of them hoodoo'ers for a while, would go to their bonfires and naked dances in swamp glens. She bedded with that cutthroat Alberto Batione y Ochoa, who was spawned by families worse than Attila and Hitler. She had a bastard boy, Rance Louchard, who was doubtless the seed of Alberto. He ended up on the gallows for cutting a trapper's throat and selling the pelts, but not before he'd sired a son, who sired a daughter, who was Valentina's grandmother. And that's the whole of it, Mr. Barnard."

"How did she end up, this dilly of an ancestress?"

"The story goes that she gave her bastard away, met a ship's captain, went to live in France, turned professional with her hoodoo dancing, making a great hit, toast of Paris. Her salon became the watering place for artists, writers, musicians, high-ranking politicians. She lived to a great age, passing peacefully in her château in the south of France."

"Some woman."

"And I guess ninety percent of it ain't fable. You want anything else?"

I shook my head, thanked her, and left the kitchen.

Once a stable, the garage was perhaps fifty yards off behind the house where the graveled driveway ended. A pickup truck was inside the sprawling frame building, keys in the ignition. Always wheels of some sort around, Val had said, so help yourself anytime you feel ambulatory.

I got in the truck, backed out, turned it, and drove off, trying to recall the street pattern between the Marlowe place and downtown.

The *Sword* occupied a three-story concrete-and-glass building in an area that had received city and private sector planning and reclamation money. Old structures had been razed to make way for a shopping arcade, off-street parking, a modern high rise, an arts center.

The state seal and motto were inlaid in the terra-cotta flooring of the spacious entry foyer. The main-floor office was a busy, sweeping array of desks devoted to advertising, bookkeeping, circulation. Wicket gates and a counter confined the public. A girl came to the counter, smiling and asking what she could do for me.

I told her who I was and asked if I could see Keith. She clicked a switch and intercommed with someone upstairs.

"I'm sorry, Mr. Barnard. Mr. Vereen is out. He's on the parks commission and an inspection of some sort was scheduled this morning. If you'd care to wait, the reception room is off the foyer, a TV, copies of the paper . . ."

"May I wait for Mr. Vereen in your library?"

"He may be out all day and just phone in. But if you like, the morgue is on the third floor. You can take the self-service elevator in the foyer. I'll tell Mr. Vereen's secretary where you are, and let Miss Kitterling know you're coming up."

"Thank you."

Miss Kitterling was a grayish, spare, pleasantly smiling woman in a long, brightly lighted warren of filing cabinets, tables strewn with clippings, packed bookshelves, and microfilm equipment.

An efficient woman, she soon had me seated at a small table whereon was a monitor screen, beside which she deposited the films I requested.

"I'll see if my computer gives me any further cross-indexing, Mr. Barnard, but I'm sure this is the batch of it."

I thanked her, and she retired to her long table and clipping shears, giving me a covert glance that expressed curiosity . . . an assistant secretary of state, personal friend of Mr. Vereen's, poring through files covering St. Valentine's Day, unsolved murders of the past ten years.

I imagined she would have a go at the files herself, once the mysterious stranger was out of sight. She wouldn't find any answers, I finally admitted to myself. She wouldn't know what she was actually looking for. I knew vaguely, and I didn't find any answers.

The stories were routinely out of police records: DEAD MAN FOUND IN MAD FRENCHWOMAN'S COVE. DEAD WOMAN FOUND IN APARTMENT. MAN SOUGHT IN SHOOTING. GIRL STRANGLED IN BACK ALLEY.

I thought of the Atlanta child murders and how many little black boys had died before the city got the drift. Sometimes you do have to hit people over the head to get their attention. The Atlanta case had two critical elements: black boys, and a compressed time frame.

The Wickens situation lacked both. No visible relationship or common link between the victims—until Lissa, only Lissa had glimpsed a shred of light. No mounting certainty that next week or the week after would yield a dead body of prescribed race and color.

Just a body fished out of Mad Frenchwoman's Cove now and then, some of them coincidentally on St. Valentine's Day. Start digging in that direction and you might find Yuletide, even Halloween victims.

Without critical elements, there was no hue and cry, no marshaling of special forces by police, not even the same detective quoted in consecutive years, except for the past two. His name was Homicide Detective Max Dufarge.

I thanked Miss Kitterling for her hospitality and asked the directions to police headquarters.

It was less than two blocks distant.

"Max is out, can I help you?"

"Out on a case?" I asked the burly desk sergeant.

He nodded. "That's his job, isn't it? Girl this time, right under our noses."

"Your noses?"

"Cruddy parking garage . . . girl strangled, body in her car . . . before this, too many muggings, senior citizens mostly, like we should patrol every level around the clock."

Phones were ringing; a lawyer was haggling bail for a client; two cops dragged in a wildly resisting drunk.

"This girl—have you identified her?"

The desk sergeant grimaced. "Max and his people just got over there and cordoned it off. She must have been killed within the hour. Max just radioed in for a make on a tag number and driver's license issued to a Lissa Aubunelli."

A captain was yelling at the sergeant from a frosted glass cubicle.

The sergeant muttered a curse under his breath. "Look, friend, the public is always curious. That's why we have TV. You can see all about it on the evening newscast."

4

Valentina reacted to the news with a frightful calm. "Lissa is dead," she said to no one outside herself. "I won't be seeing Lissa again."

She looked then, at the faces, mine the closest. "I would like to go up to my room, Cody."

"Val—"

"I'll be okay. Just give me a small moment to accept it."

She went, quietly and quickly, up the broad stairs, and, watching from the bottom level, I heard her door close. I crept up and stood uncertainly. Then I heard her weeping beyond the closed door, and I knew she would come out, steady, dry-eyed, when she was quite ready.

George and Elva still stood in the lower hallway. George was stunned, but had presence—white faced, tight lipped, in control, the unflappable career army officer. Elva was rigidly steeled, tears in her eyes.

She shook off George's supporting arm. "I'll have to tell Reba and Clyde."

"How about Lissa's family?" I asked. "Shouldn't it be one of you, rather than a policeman knocking at their door?"

"She had no family, Cody," Elva said. "None other than us. Her parents were killed in a house fire three years ago. She had no brothers, sisters, grandparents—perhaps a distant cousin or two. We'll have to find that out." She slipped quietly toward the kitchen to look for Reba and Clyde.

George started to barrage me with questions, but driveway gravel showered outside and we heard a car door slam.

As we reached the front door, Keith burst upon the porch. The aristocratic cut of his lean face was all hard, flat planes. His blue eyes had darkened almost to black.

He jerked to a halt, looking from one to the other. "You— You've heard."

"Yes," George said, "Cody just now came with the news."

Keith let go a breath. "Then I'm not the messenger. Was certain I'd have to be. The news came across the mainframe printout, from our unit interfaced in the press room at headquarters. I got Dufarge on the wire, but as yet there doesn't seem to be much in the way of follow-up detail."

His movement was taut, uncomfortable. He pressed his buttocks against the banister, half sitting, and brooded briefly. "Apparently another mugging in the gloom of the parking garage. Frigging city out to sell it. Private owners would up the rate but provide security the city can't with its stretched-out manpower. Fatal mugging this time . . ." His thin lips tightened to disappearance. "And I might have stopped this one."

George glanced from Keith to me. My eyes were on Keith. "How?"

"Lissa called from New Orleans late in the morning. The call was relayed to my car during a parks inspection. She said she wanted to see Max Dufarge and me as soon as she got back, and

she was calling from the northern end of the parish, already out of
the city proper.''

"Did she say what it was about?''

Keith scathed me with a bitter look. "What would be the first
thing a newspaperman would ask? She said I might possibly be
bidding on a Valentine story. She'd been spare-timing a thing for
a long time, and had the gist of it in place—except for the final
identity. She'd eliminated a final false lead in New Orleans and said
the answer was here in Wickens. She said it was time now to holler
for help.''

"Did she elaborate?''

"Not on the phone. She said Max and I would get it up to this
point, all she had, before the day was out. She said she had enough
to convince us it wasn't smoke and vapor, and we would move.
Sounded a bit scary. But Lissa couldn't resist center stage; it was
the trait that breathed fire into her most mundane story.'' An invol-
untary shiver went through him, delayed reaction. He looked a little
sick, but pushed himself up. "How is Val?''

"Taking it,'' I said.

"Can I do anything?''

"Can anyone?'' George asked.

"Have we got a shot of Jack Daniel's around the place?'' Keith
asked.

"We could all use a drink,'' George said, and led the way inside.
He poured at the dining room sideboard and we went aimlessly into
the living room, George carrying the bottle. We heard a door close
in the back of the house. George tossed his drink, set the glass and
bottle on the coffee table. "That will be Elva.'' He hurried out.

Keith sank into an overstuffed chair, pulled up again. "I could
use another.'' He poured a second finger. "No ticket back for
Lissa.'' He raised his eyes, saw my confused frown, and added,
"Of course the statement is meaningless to you, Cody. But there
was a ticket back in my case.''

"Excuse me?''

He threw the drink down his throat. "Car accident. Terrible
concussion . . . trauma . . . heart stopped . . . dead as last year's
rose. A great medical team and that electric gadget they use to bang
the old ticker started me up again. But for a minute or two, the
reading of my will could have proceeded legally.''

He looked at the shot glass, decided against a third, and eased
the glass onto the table.

"I've tried to remember—but I couldn't at the time and the mists
of eight years haven't helped—how it felt to die. You've heard the

stories of people who cross over and are snatched back. A lot of them report a marvelous experience, a golden light, a feeling of joy and peace, a feeling of not wanting to be brought back, but to have the golden freedom of the light.''

"How was it with you, Keith?''

"No golden light. I really have never been able to remember. I think it was dark, cold, a feeling of terrible anxiety because I was dying, dead. Maybe my linen was soiled when I got over there . . . Poor Lissa—I hope she got over there with her linen clean.''

After the local evening newscast, the telephone began to ring. It wouldn't stop. Elva kept answering, hearing the sympathetic expressions, consoling the shocked caller, answering the same questions. Finally she took the obvious measure and left the phone off the hook.

We talked to Homicide Detective Max Dufarge, who came accompanied by one of his men. We told him everything we knew.

We sat about the table. Food was on it. Perhaps we ate.

It was St. Valentine's Eve and all the plans for the party had to be cancelled, the caterer told by phone to send his bill but not himself, likewise the booking agent in New Orleans who handled Dixieland jazz groups.

Lissa Aubunelli was stretched out in a funeral home downtown, and we, finally, in our beds.

A moon milked palely in the darkness. The night was not quiet: the scratching of a night creature scurrying across the roof; the faraway striking of the grandfather clock in the lower hall; a skirl of night wind, creak of a house timber, a whisper of movement. Here in the house? Someone up, needing an aspirin? I rose to an elbow, listening. Nothing. I eased back and gradually my senses slipped into a halfway house of nonsleep.

The colors came in a single glimpse of tangled mangrove, saw grass, heat-blasted pines weeping dead, gray moss tendrils.

A narrow, rutted road with crushed-shell surface wormed painfully through the jungle. In a clearing off the road was a tumbledown clapboard shack. Beside the road were the ruins of a mailbox. Jagged holes had rusted through. The remains hung crookedly on a weather-eaten chain from a weather-eaten stanchion creatively fashioned from the iron tire of an old wagon wheel.

Zap!

The darkness was a wall.

I jerked on my pants and shoes. Across the hallway I hesitated for a beat of a second. Then I gripped the doorknob, flung the panel open, and I saw what I was afraid of seeing: an empty bed, sheet thrown back.

"Valentina!" My shout shattered through the house. I looked back and forth wildly in the hallway, ran down the stairs, two, three at a time.

"Valentina! Val!"

I was outside, seeing the vacancy of the porch, the land, the emptiness of the whole earth.

I ran back in. The house was awakening, lights flashing on, questioning voices rising.

George was charging down the stairs, in the direction of my voice.

Just inside the front door, I grabbed his arm. "Don't ask me anything! Just tell me— You've known this swamp country for years. Do you know a deserted shack with a mailbox mounted on a wagon-wheel iron rim?"

"Cody, what in the hell—"

"Damn you! Answer my question!"

"Of course I know. It's the old LeMoines place. Belonged to Keith Vereen's grandpappy. Hunters, fishermen still use it now and then, not that it's much shelter when a storm blows in. Now you answer a question for me. What's going on?"

"It's about Valentina, you long-winded bastard! She got up during the night. I know now that it wasn't my imagination or nerves. She slipped downstairs, and he was there, where he'd told her he would be, to talk to her about Lissa, a private thing, something Lissa had meant for her ears alone. What the filthy hell does it matter how he arranged it, the bait he used? He's got her. Nothing else matters. She's with him, George, the final one. The Louchard descendant. And I must get to the LeMoines place."

He was wearing pajama bottoms, barefoot. It was sufficient. "The keys are in the pickup."

He drove daredevil fast, but not recklessly, with the expertise instilled by terrains in many parts of the world.

"Tell me," he said.

I hung on to the seat, other hand braced against the instrument panel. "You won't believe me."

"Try me. I don't know how you came by this knowledge of the LeMoines place, or how I'm so certain you know that she's out there. But tell me—who did she meet?"

"Keith Vereen."

"You can't be serious."

"Very."

"Why did he do it?"

"Because he couldn't help himself."

"A man can always help himself, Cody."

"What if he's not entirely himself? What if he is traumatized in a car accident eight years ago and dies? What if seven residual life forces, psychic echoes, spirits, ghosts, whatever the hell you choose to call them, are present inside Keith, dwelling in a level just below his own sentience, when the doctors slam an electric charge and restart his heart?"

He didn't slow the pickup. Water showered, glitters in the night, as we slashed through a shallow ford.

"He was never the same after the accident, that much is for sure," George admitted.

"Call him spirit possessed, or simply mad. The result is the same. He was compelled to search out seven male descendants of the man who murdered seven Yankee soldier boys on a St. Valentine's Eve a long time ago. He had to balance the scales, even the score."

"If any of this is true, Cody . . . if I'm not suffering a nightmare . . . that old massacre, involving Marie Louchard, it happened over a hundred years ago."

"They had time, those seven—eternity. But they had no instrument—until Keith's moment of death became a latchkey."

"And Lissa?"

"Getting too uncomfortably close. She didn't suspect Keith and forewarned him with a phone call. He simply drove out to U.S. 61, the only main road from New Orleans, and watched for her car. It was simple then to follow her into the parking garage, to say hello as she was getting from her car, to put his hands around her throat. She wouldn't have been able to make a sound."

The mailbox and rust-eaten wagon-wheel arch reared in the glare of the headlights. I was out of the truck, running, before George had fully stopped it.

I saw Keith's Mercedes parked in the weed-grown ruin of the driveway leading to the shack.

Then I saw the moving shadows, human figures, in the moon-frozen darkness just beyond and to one side of the shack.

He was carrying her across his shoulder. She wasn't moving. How hard had he slugged her?

"Valentina!"

I had outdistanced George, for all his conditioning. Keith turned slowly to face me.

"Stay back, Cody. Don't come any closer."

"Put her down, Keith. Back off. Please—you've known her all her life. She's your friend. She loved and trusted you."

"She's a Louchard, Cody. It's in the records. Go look at the records, as I did."

His every word had a different inflection. Seven inflections? Seven voices speaking through his lips?

"Kill the bastard!" George had reached my side. "Take him, Cody."

I had already decided it was the only way. A jump ahead of George, I was at Keith.

He stood unmoving.

A veil came, a gossamer shimmering through which Keith's image rippled and flowed. I gasped from a force that struck me.

I saw the moon spin, and knew that I had slammed onto my back. I heard bamboo rattling a fierce tempo. Wild palms bent and reared like slashing shadows. Night creatures were screaming, and a hard, quick wind showered jungle debris across my face, against the side of the LeMoines shack.

I realized that George was sprawled beside me, frothing incoherent sound.

"Stay back," Keith said. "She has Louchard blood in her veins. She is the guiltiest of all, and this is the moment reserved for her."

He turned and was starting to carry her away.

A bellow of anguish came from George's lips. "You fool! You mad fool! She is *not* Louchard, she's *my* bastard daughter. Not a part of the Louchard line. She was born nine months after a furlough—neither Elva nor I meant for it to happen. It was only that once. Charles Marlowe proved out infertile. Maybe he guessed, before the end, why he and Elva had not had other children. She's *mine,* you son of a bitch!"

The clearing seemed to suck a breath. Keith had heard. He hesitated, staring about as if for outside guidance.

This time my contact with him was hard, satisfying: he, I, and Valentina went down in a tangle. He thrashed, slipped free. His wild kick caught me on the cheek, breaking the skin. I heard viney tearings, and Keith was gone.

George was on his knees, gathering her up, cradling her against his chest, rocking in anguish.

"Oh, my baby! My little girl! . . ."

And she moaned softly.

* * *

As the jetliner entered the traffic pattern over the familiar grid of Washington National Airport, Valentina said quietly, "We're back, Cody."

"Yes."

"It's all over."

"Yes."

"Poor Keith"—her voice echoed a gentle pain—"making the river, trying to swim to freedom—or maybe not—washing up in Mad Frenchwoman's Cove."

"We agreed to let the past bury the past," I reminded her.

"And so we will. We'll close the door for keeps and take up life as we're meant to—after you tell me one thing. Just who am I, Keith?"

"You're the daughter of two wonderful people."

I touched her cheek. I imprinted every detail of her face in my mind forever.

"To borrow from Gershwin . . . You is my woman, Val."

Her lips parted just a little; her eyes deepened. "And I got to love one man 'til I die." A tiny crinkling at the corners of her mouth. "Aside from calling the Mississippi an old man, that poet fellow did have his perceptions."

VALENTINE FROM A VAMPIRE

by Daniel Ransom

1

There was only one way to do it, twenty-six-year-old Sam McBride told himself that gray February afternoon, and that was to plain and simple do it:

Pick her up in his Checker cab as he usually did at six o'clock and then, after she'd been riding a few blocks, say casually as possible, "You know, Ms. Ames, there's something I think you should know about the man you're going out with. He's a vampire."

So all afternoon, transporting fat old ladies and skinny old men and rude businessmen and fickle suburban housewives, Sam rehearsed his lines pretty much the way he'd memorized his part in the eighth grade play nearly fourteen years earlier (he'd played a Pilgrim)—by saying them over and over again until they'd lost all meaning. He tried variations on them, of course, trying to minimize the shock they would have on her—"Say, have you noticed your boyfriend's teeth?" or "Is this the first vampire you've ever gone out with?" or "Was that catsup all over your friend's mouth last night?" —so she wouldn't hate him for saying it. (Because hating him was the exact opposite of what he wanted her to do.)

But really, when you came right down to it, there wasn't any graceful way to say it. Because when you came right down to it, calling somebody a vampire was a pretty serious accusation.

Sam sighed and kept driving, thinking over his lonely womanless life and what an odd business life was, the older you got. Sam, six foot, slender, still gangly despite a deep voice and a need to shave twice a day, had come to the city five years ago after finishing junior college with an associate degree in retail. Unfortunately, his arrival coincided with the recession and so he'd drifted into hacking, working for a man who'd had his larynx removed and who now had to talk through one of those buzzer jobbies that sounded like bad sci-fi sound effects. The hack owner spoke just clearly enough for Sam to know he was a cheapskate.

The vampire, a man handsome as a screen star of the forties (complete with hair sleek as black ice), was named Karl Richards.

31

Sam had met him four years ago while hauling a young woman named Debbie out to Richards's Dracula-like estate. He'd seen the way Debbie had gone into the place—a real live American girl given to lots of chitchat and some flirtiness—and how she'd come out. Debbie, pale, soft-spoken now, was never the same again. He took her out there several times afterward and then one day she stayed permanently, or at least she didn't call in for a ride back to the city. He had no idea what had happened to her. Not then, anyway. All he knew for sure was that on Valentine's Day of that year her personality underwent a most curious transformation.

Then came the next two Valentine's Days and two more women—one named Janice, who had eyes soft as a young animal's, and one named Stacey, who had remarkable legs—went in one way and came out the other.

But even then Sam hadn't allowed himself to use the word. He just said to himself that there were some weird doings involving drugs or hypnotism or maybe even UFOs going on inside the vast walled estate. Because even alien creatures with pop-eyes and no voice boxes were easier to believe than—

—than vampires.

Then one night, cruising past the estate late with a drunken fare, Sam had glimpsed something truly eerie at the gate of the place.

One moment Karl Richards had been standing there and the next moment . . . Karl Richards was gone.

Sam didn't know if he'd turned into a bat or a slug or an Avon lady, but he sure went somewhere and there was only one semihuman creature who could do anything like that and that was—

—a vampire.

Sam spent the next month sitting up nights recording all this material on his Sony recorder. He had vague notions of maybe going to the police but every morning that he got up with that thought on his mind, he started thinking of the cops he'd met through hacking and what hard cynical bastards they were and how they'd respond to somebody who told them there was a vampire living in the mansion on the southeastern edge of this Midwestern city.

Right.

Then this year, three weeks before Valentine's, Felicia Ames got in his cab and asked to be taken to the mansion, and just like that, Sam fell in love. She was a glowing blond model given to deep (and, he imagined, poetic) sighing and long blue gazes out the cab window at wintry trees and snow-capped waves slamming the concrete piers.

Every twenty minutes since meeting her he had mentally proposed. Every thirty minutes he thought about their having a child (he wanted a kid even if he wasn't quite sure what the hell he was going to do with the little bugger).

And every forty minutes he faced up to the terrible fact that on this Valentine's Day, tonight, sleazy Karl Richards was going to convert one more unwitting American girl into a creature of eternal darkness (or whatever they always said on those great Hammer films WTBS always ran at 2:00 A.M. every Friday night).

He was going to turn Felicia Ames into a vampire.

Or he thought he was, anyway.

But a hack driver named Sam McBride had different ideas.

2

"Hi, Sam."

"Hi, Ms. Ames."

"Gosh."

"What?"

"You think you'll ever stop?"

"Stop what?"

"Calling me 'Ms. Ames.' "

He flushed. "Oh. Right. I forgot. Felicia. I'm supposed to call you 'Felicia,' "

"Please."

So she sat back and he aimed the Checker into traffic, making the ride smooth as he could for her.

"Boy."

"What?" he asked.

"Long day. Whoever says modeling is a glamorous profession just doesn't know."

"Tired, huh?"

"Exhausted."

"Great."

"What?"

"I said, 'Late.' "

"Late?"

"I meant—after a long day, it's late. Maybe you shouldn't go to the mansion tonight. Maybe I should turn the cab around and take you to your apartment house. Maybe you're coming down with something, Felicia, and should go straight to bed." He said all this in a rush. He was hopeful she'd agree and he'd flip the cab around

and race to her apartment and then stand guard all night to make
sure that Richards didn't get in.

But now she laughed. "Oh, no. I'd never be too tired for
tonight."

"Tonight?"

"Valentine's Day. Karl has promised me a very special gift."

Sam gulped. "You have any idea what it is?"

She laughed again, more softly this time. "No, but you can bet
when Karl Richards says a gift is going to be special, it's going to
be *very* special."

He watched her in the rearview. Outside, gray night had fallen,
the only lights red and blue and green neon reflected in dirty city
snow. But in the rearview her face positively radiated. For a
moment he did a dangerous thing—closed his eyes to say a silent
prayer for courage.

The time had come.

She'd left him no choice.

He had to tell her the truth about Karl Richards.

"Gosh, Sam, look out!"

Snapping his eyes open, he saw that he was about to sideswipe
a city bus that moved through the gloom like a giant electric cater-
pillar.

"Sam, are you all right?"

"Yes," he said. "But you're not."

"What?"

"I said you're not all right."

"Well, that's not a very nice thing to say."

"Oh, I didn't mean you're not all right OK. I meant you're not
all right—you're in danger."

"Danger?"

"Felicia, would you let me buy you a cup of coffee?"

"But, Sam, I told Karl—"

He turned around and said, "Felicia, there's something you
should know about Karl."

"Oh, Sam, I know what you're going to say." She sounded
young and disappointed. "That he's a playboy. That he'll drop me
as soon as he's bored and it won't be long before that happens."
She touched him on the shoulder and a wonderful warmth spread
through his entire body. She'd never touched him this way before.
"It's just a storybook fling, the only one I've ever allowed myself.
Really. In high school I didn't have time because I was always a
cheerleader and trotting off to games. In college I didn't have time
because my parents were poor and I had to work my way through.

And during my first five years of modeling I didn't have time because I had to take every job that was offered me. Don't you see, Sam, this is my one chance at really having a good time. That's all.''

Sam pulled into the parking lot of a McDonald's. Against the gray night it looked like a big colorful toy box filled with tiny people walking around inside.

"Felicia, there's something I've got to tell you and I guess I have to do it right here, without even waiting to go inside, right in front of Ronald McDonald and everything.''

"Gosh, Sam, what's so urgent?''

"Karl.''

"Karl's urgent?''

"No," Sam said, "Karl's a vampire.''

3

They got Cokes and Sam got french fries and they took the most isolated table they could find, right on a plastic outsize Egg McMuffin who had two red eyes and kept winking at Sam.

"Vampire," Felicia said. "Gosh, Sam, that's really the most original one I've heard yet.''

"Original what?''

"Oh," she said, "line, I guess you'd call it. I mean, I'm flattered.'' She startled him by putting her hand over his and gazing blue into his eyes. "You're a very nice guy, Sam, and over the past few weeks, we've really gotten to know each other in a strange way. And if Karl wasn't in the picture—'' She withdrew her hand and shook her wonderful blond head and laughed. "But to be honest, Sam, calling him a vampire is going overboard, don't you think? How about a drug dealer? Or Communist spy? Or even a pornographer? But a vampire?'' Then the smile faded from her eyes. "Sam, you don't really believe in vampires, do you?''

"I didn't.''

"Didn't?''

"Till I took Debbie and Janice and Stacey out to his mansion on Valentine's Day and they changed.''

"Changed?''

"Yes," Sam said, "changed.''

So he told her, in detail, how they'd changed. The chalky skin. The dead eyes. The sullen silence. "Vampires," Sam said.

She took one of his french fries and nibbled at it. She'd explained to him once that she always nibbled at food. To keep her weight for the camera, that was the most pleasure she could allow herself—nibbling.

"Have you ever been heartbroken, Sam? Wanted somebody you couldn't have?"

He stared at her. "Uh, yes."

"Do you remember how you acted?"

"Acted?"

"The depression, the weight loss, the long silences? That's what you're describing here, Sam, nothing more. Karl decided it was time to get rid of these women and move on to new ones, so he dropped them and that was how they reacted."

"Then why would they keep going back to the mansion?"

"Why, to plead their cases. Beg him to reconsider." She had another french fry. "You've been heartbroken before, haven't you, Sam? You do know what I'm talking about?"

Without hesitation, he said it, "Felicia, I'm heartbroken right now."

"You are?"

"Yes. Over you."

She blushed. For all her beauty and sophistication, Sam had found Felicia to be not only modest about her looks but just as socially vulnerable as he was himself. "Oh, Sam." She put her hand back on his. "That's really sweet and I really appreciate it but—right now there's Karl."

"Please let me take you back to your apartment tonight, Felicia. Just till after Valentine's Day passes. He's got something about Valentine's Day."

"Sam, listen, please." She sat back in the seat. "As I've tried to explain, I know this is just a fling and nothing more. But I'm enjoying it. I like being in a grand house where there are servants out of the nineteenth century and where classical music is always playing and where you sit on Louis XVI furniture and where you sip French wine from huge goblets in front of a roaring fireplace and where your tall, dark, handsome lover wears a red silk dinner jacket and speaks to you in a voice that gives you goose bumps." She laughed. "For a girl whose father ran a corner grocery store, Sam, that's pretty heady stuff."

So Sam, seeing the odds he had to overcome, said it: "He disappeared."

"What?"

"Vanished. Did you ever see the original *Dracula?*"

She sighed. "Oh, Sam, please. It isn't fun anymore. This vampire thing, I mean. It really isn't."

"He did, Felicia." He raised his hand like a Boy Scout. "On my love for you, I swear it. One second, he was in my rearview and then he just disappeared. Vanished. The only people who can do that are vampires."

A certain pity had come into her eyes now. "Sam, would you take me out to the mansion—and would you do me a favor?"

"Anything. You know that."

"Just don't talk about this anymore, please. Because I am starting to get scared—but not for myself—for you. I hope you're just saying all this because you love me and want to start seeing me. I hope you're not saying it because—" And here, for the first time, she looked uncomfortable. "Because you truly believe it, because then—"

"Then what?"

"Then I'd say you needed to see a shrink or something."

4

Gates of black iron covered the entrance to the mansion. Ground fog shone silver in the light of a half-moon. Beyond the massive stone walls light from mullioned windows spread yellow across the snow.

"I guess I should go in now."

They'd been sitting in his cab for twenty minutes now—the radio tuned low to an FM station playing some soft Stanley Clarke songs—and really not talking much at all.

It was just that every time she started to put her hand on the door handle, he turned around and said, "Please, Felicia, please don't go."

He'd said it four times now and four times she had complied.

But he knew this time—hand on the door, a kind of pity in her eyes—that she would go.

"Felicia, I—"

"I really do have to go."

"He's a vampire, Felicia. Honest and truly."

"You're sweet, Sam. You really are. You care about me so much and—"

Then she startled him by leaning forward and kissing him gently on the lips.

His mind literally spun; his heart was a wild animal.

"Felicia, please—"

But then the back door opened and the dome light went on, exposing the shabby insides of the cab, the battered dash and the smudged seat covers and the big red, white, and blue thermos he carried coffee in. This was his life—the life of a shabby hack in a shabby cab. He guessed he couldn't blame her (his eyes rising to see the imposing mansion against the gray night sky) for wanting the type of life Karl Richards offered.

Except Karl Richards was a vampire.

"Felicia—"

This time she touched a finger to her lips and then touched that same finger to his lips and then she was gone, lost in fog, the gates opening automatically now that she'd inserted the access card Richards provided all his women.

Debbie.

Janice.

Stacey.

Gone.

"Felicia!" he cried but already the gates were creaking open and then creaking closed and she was lost to him forever.

5

His were the particular pleasures of the lonely. He could eat what he wanted (Snickers, Fritos, Good 'N Plentys) and watch what he wanted. (Tonight, unable to sleep, thinking of what was happening to Felicia, he started watching *Twins of Evil* but switched channels as soon as the vampire theme started getting oppressive, and then tuned into the Home Shoppers Channel, a subculture even more fascinating than professional wrestling or professional religion. Who wanted to buy a George Washington clock that recited the names of the first thirteen colonies over and over again? Apparently thousands of people did, and at $48.31 apiece. He had purchased only one thing from the Shoppers Channel, a genuine longbow with quiver and arrows. Over the past six months the bow had become his sole hobby. He was reasonably good with it.) Finally, fitfully, he slept on the couch of his drab efficiency apartment.

Then it was morning, the sky a light shade of gray. He shaved, showered, ate his bran, did his sit-ups, and then said an Our Father and three Hail Marys for Felicia. This was around 7:30. Around 8:30 he called the modeling agency where she worked, and said he was her brother (did she even have a brother?) and asked if he could find out where she was working today and, after only a teensy bit of hesitation, the woman gave him the address and even the phone number where Felicia could be found so her brother (in from Egypt; what the hell—if you lie, lie big) could surprise her.

So he promptly called the photography studio where she was on location today and was surprised to learn that she was there.

She hadn't called in sick.

She hadn't just mysteriously vanished.

She was there.

Working.

Could he possibly speak to her?

"Afraid not. We're in the middle of a bitch of a production problem here and she's really tied up. If you'd care to leave your number, though, we could have her call you back."

Baffled, Sam said, "No thanks. Thank you." And hung up.

The rest of the morning, before he had to start hacking (you had to average seventy hours a week behind the wheel if you wanted to reach even the official poverty level of income), he went to the laundromat and to the supermarket and to the video rental store and then to the submarine place where he got this salami hogie that could have fed a Third World nation.

Somewhere in the middle of all this, he had started to whistle and the rest of the day he whistled his ass off because she'd proved him wrong and there was nothing he'd wanted more than to be proved wrong.

Karl Richards might be a jerk-off but he wasn't a vampire.

And eventually he'd dump her and then she'd go through a period of heartbreak and then she'd entrust the rest of her life to Sam.

At least, that was the notion that got Sam to whistling and kept him whistling all day.

Around two he went down to the cab company, to the underground garage that always stank of wet concrete, and said a few words to the man without a voice box and then got in his cab and started his workday.

The first two hours went slowly. There was a chatty plump woman going to the hospital to see her herniated husband. There was a somber priest who made a magnificent sign of the cross whenever they passed a Catholic church. And there was a very tiny woman who smoked those 100 mm. cigarettes and coughed so hard she jumped around on the backseat.

Then came February dusk, lights up in stores, people slanting into the bitter wind running to garages and bus stops, and then he thought of a wonderful idea.

He knew just where Felicia was.

Knew roughly what time she'd get off.

Why not go wait for her there?

Which is what he did, still whistling all the time, shaping the words of his apology, getting ready to laugh a lot about his stupid notion that Karl Richards was a vampire.

The studio was on the northwest part of town, in a forlorn section of the city. He was parked at the curb for nearly an hour before he began to think that maybe the session had ended early and she'd gone home.

Ten minutes later he sat up and was all ready to go when he saw her in the rearview coming out of the door.

Behind him, suddenly a yellow cab pulled up.

She'd phoned for somebody else.

He jumped from the car and over the roof and yelled, "Felicia! Tell him to go on and let me give you a ride!"

She saw him, of course, and recognized him. But she started to get into the yellow cab anyway.

He ran over to her, grabbed her slender wrist before she could close the door.

"I'll take her," Sam said to the angry-looking cabbie. Sam flung a ten-dollar bill at the man. Then he tugged on Felicia's arm and said, "Come on. Please. All right?"

She sighed, looked embarrassed that the cabman was watching them, and then said softly, "All right."

So she got out of one cab and got in another, and then Sam ran around and got behind the wheel and had them in traffic in moments.

"You going home or to the mansion tonight?"

"The mansion."

He shook his head and said, laughing at himself, "I don't want you to hold it against me."

"Hold what against you?"

"Come on, Felicia. You know—my theory about Karl Richards being a vampire."

"That's the trouble," Felicia said and began suddenly and madly to sob. "You were right. He *is* a vampire."

6

For the next two hours they drove through every part of the city imaginable. Past glum slums and palaces; through shopping districts and industrial zones; and along the river where ice shone like glass in moonlight.

Sometimes she talked, though little of it made sense, but mostly she alternated between sniffling and sobbing and staring out the window.

Then she slept.

The radio off, the cab gliding along two-lane asphalt, the only man-made object in sight a radio tower with a single red warning line at its top—in this silence her snoring was reassuring because he thought, She can't be a vampire: vampires don't sleep at night.

Karl Richards might have hypnotized her, or voodoo'd her, or drugged her, but he hadn't turned her into a vampire.

He drove and was hungry suddenly and thought of how good a big slice of double cheese pizza would taste along with a cold mug of beer.

"Have you looked in your rearview mirror yet?" she asked, sounding muzzy with sleep.

"Huh?"

"Your mirror. You still don't believe me, do you, Sam? So look back at me and then look in your mirror."

So he did. Turned around and saw her looking beautiful if slightly mussed in the backseat. Then turned around and looked for her image in the rearview.

And saw nothing.

"My God."

"Pretty crazy, huh?"

"My God," he said again.

"Imagine how I feel," she said, and started sniffling again.

"Then he really did bite you on the—"

"On the arm."

"The arm?"

"It's harder to see the puncture wound on the arm. He laughed about it afterwards. He said the whole world would know there were vampires if all these women walked around with big blue holes in their necks. Here."

She pushed her lovely right arm over the front seat and then pulled up her sleeve and, after pulling up a Band-Aid, showed it to him. By now the teeth marks had scabbed over into what appeared to be a very bad infection of some kind.

"So that," she said, "was my special Valentine's gift."

"Why does he do it on Valentine's Day?"

"Because that's when he became a vampire. Four hundred years ago. In London. He's sentimental about the day." She sighed. "I have to admit that part was fascinating."

"What part?"

"Hearing about London four hundred years ago."

"He talked to you?"

"Oh, sure. I mean, after I woke up from the bite—it put me out an hour or so—and after he got me calmed down, we had a pretty regular night. He made dinner—we had shrimp with black bean sauce; he's a great cook—and then we listened to his big band records and then we talked. Except now he was free to tell the truth about himself, including what London was like in those days." Then suddenly she broke into sobs again.

"Why are you crying? Except for getting turned into a vampire, it sounds like a pretty wonderful night." He heard jealousy in his voice.

"Because I haven't told you everything."

"What's everything?"

"That I'm part of his entourage now. Forever."

"His entourage?"

She had to stop crying to tell him. He took a small box of Kleenex from the front seat and handed it back to her. He looked in the rearview again just in case the first time had been a fluke.

It hadn't been.

"He has more than thirty women living there at the mansion. They're pretty regular women, for the most part—everything considered, I mean. He keeps them healthy and beautiful and he uses them for sustenance and he uses them for sex and everything's fine as long as he gradually replenishes the supply by adding a new one every Valentine's Day. It's really not a bad life if you like total security—but I hate it, Sam. Already I hate it."

"He has a harem."

"Yes," she said, "that's exactly what it is, Sam, a harem. He's the ultimate male chauvinist. He calls us vampirettes."

"But I thought vampires—"

"Skulked around alleys? Preyed on young women in the fog? Perched on window ledges disguised as bats?"

"But the night I saw him disappear—"

"It's because you looked in your rearview mirror. The thing about turning yourself into a bat is strictly comic-book stuff. Anyway, he's very squeamish about bugs and rodents and such. Unnaturally so." She paused and stared out the window at the silver hills again.

"I'm going to help you," he said.

"Sam, that's sweet, it really is. But you can't help me."

"There's got to be something—"

"What? Go to the authorities? Even if you did prove to their satisfaction he was a vampire, you'd be dooming me the rest of my life—and it's going to be a long one, Sam, it really is—to being kept in a prison somewhere by the authorities. No, Sam." She leaned up and touched his shoulder. "Please don't do anything. You'd probably only make it worse." She paused. "Do you know what time it is?"

"Eight thirty-five."

"Gosh, you'd better get me back to the mansion."

"I thought maybe we could have something to eat. A pizza or something."

"I'd like to but he's very strict about hours."

"Hours?"

"He runs the place like a dorm. We all keep our jobs—sleeping all day is another myth—but we have to be back at the mansion by nine or we get demerits."

"You're kidding."

"No, he's got this big chart in his den. He puts stars by your name—gold if you've been great, blue if you've been good, black if you've been bad."

"What happens if you get black?"

"I don't know and I'm afraid to find out."

So, not wanting her to get a black star, he broke speed limits getting back to the mansion.

It was 8:57 when he pulled up in front of the iron gates.

He said, "God, Felicia, I've got to see you again. I do."

"Even though I'm a vampire?"

"Felicia, you could be a werewolf and I wouldn't care. I really wouldn't."

"Oh, Sam," she said, and brought her face to his and kissed him tenderly on the cheek. She felt a few degrees cooler than most human beings, but that was about the only difference.

She looked up at the mansion's spires against the gold disc of moon. "Gosh," she said, "I wish we could go back to my apartment. We could order in a pizza and snuggle up on the couch and—" She started crying again. "If only I'd listened to you, Sam."

"You'd better hurry, Felicia," he said. "I don't want you to get a black star."

Miserably, she nodded. "You're right."

As she got out of the car and the dome light came on, he took her arm and said, "I love you, Felicia."

And she said what he'd waited so long to hear in return. "The weird thing is, as soon as I came to last night, the first person I thought about was you, Sam. Even before I thought about my parents or my cats or my lovebirds.'' She smiled sadly. ''I guess that must mean I love you, too.''

Then she was gone.

7

The next day he called the modeling agency to find out where she was working this time, but the woman on the other end said, ''Is this her brother again?''

''Uh, yes.''

''I checked her files. She doesn't have a brother.''

''Oh.''

She hung up.

He spent the two hours before work at the library riffling through books on vampires—they had a surprising number of such volumes—but soon discovered that most of them did little more than promote myths. In books, vampires skulked in alleys, preyed on fog-enshrouded young women, turned themselves into bats. They didn't—unlike the only vampire Sam knew—cook gourmet meals, play Tommy Dorsey records and give his thirty girl friends black stars for bad behavior.

He left the library and raced to a pay phone. He got the modeling agency on the phone again—the same woman. As she answered, he slid a handkerchief across the receiver and said, ''This is Lieutenant Carstairs from the Fourth Precinct. We need to get in touch with one of your models. A Miss—'' He paused, pretending to be looking on a notepad. ''A Miss—''

''It's you again, isn't it?''

''Huh?''

''You. The so-called brother. The pest. We've got enough creeps bothering our girls. We don't need any more.''

She slammed down the receiver.

8

That night he sat in front of the mansion, watching the ground fog wrap itself around the turrets and spires of the great stone house, hoping she'd try to make some kind of escape and would come rushing out to the gate.

She didn't and Sam just sat there drinking Diet Pepsis, and then getting out of the cab and taking a pee in thick mulberry bushes where the occupants of passing cars couldn't see him, and then getting back inside the cab for more of his lonely vigil.

Two hours later he ended up on his couch eating Ding-Dongs with skim milk and watching *The Tall T* with Randolph Scott. He fell asleep with a box of Cracker Jacks on his stomach.

In the morning, exhausted, he put on the only tie he owned and went up to the modeling agency where Felicia worked. He also brought a small spiral tablet. A 35 mm. camera was slung over his tan corduroy jacket.

The woman was about what he'd expected—short, overly made-up, with a dark-eyed gaze that could melt diamonds. "Yes?" she snapped when he went to take his place at the reception counter.

"I'm Bryant from the *Times*. I'm supposed to interview one of your models: Felicia Ames."

"The *Times?* The *New York Times?*"

He smiled. "I wish my paper was that important. No, I'm afraid I'm with *Modeling Times.*" He hoped that his self-effacing smile would convince her he was telling the truth.

"Never heard of it."

"That's because we haven't published our first issue yet."

Then the woman did something odd. She sat back in her chair, closed her eyes, and put her fingertips to her temples. "Say something."

"What?"

"Say something."

"What do you want me to—"

"It's you!" she said. "The fake brother. The phoney cop. Now, you get out of here!"

She stood up and pointed to the door, and he had no choice but to comply.

The rest of the day he drove his cab, taking every chance to cruise by the three studios where she normally worked, but finding no sign of her.

That night he took up his vigil at the mansion again. Around midnight he thought he heard a scream, faint behind the fog, but he couldn't be sure if it was only his imagination and his exhaustion.

On the couch he watched *This Island Earth* with Jeff Morrow and a woman who'd been a real babe named Faith Domergue, and fell asleep with a box of Screaming Yellow Zonkers on his chest.

He didn't wake till nearly noon and was therefore in a hurry, shaving while he peed, ironing a shirt while he ate his bran.

He was fifteen minutes late starting his shift. The man without the voice box laid some very angry sci-fi effects on him.

There were skinny people, black people, white people, pudgy

people, straight people, gay people, nice-looking people, repellent people, pleasant people, surly people—it was one of those inexplicably busy days. He didn't really get an opportunity to buzz past the studios where she generally worked and it was nearly eleven o'clock before he got to the mansion where he sat for twenty minutes and dozed off.

The stress of the past three days, plus the late hours, had drained him.

He went home and lay on the couch again, the movie tonight being one of his favorites, *D.O.A.* with Edmond O'Brien, who'd been the chunkiest leading man Sam had ever seen, but he was asleep even before the doomed Edmond realized he'd been fatally poisoned. A sack of chip-dip-flavored Lay's potato chips next to his head.

The pounding started around 4:00 A.M. At first he thought it was part of a nightmare he couldn't wake up from.

Pounding.

Finally, still thinking he was acting out a role in a nightmare, he got up and stumbled to the door, clumsily taking off the three security locks, and at last seeing who stood there.

Felicia.

Tears streaming down her face.

A small overnight bag in her left hand.

"Sam," she sobbed. "Sam, may I move in with you?"

9

Two hours later, over a pepperoni pizza delivered steaming hot, she said, "I don't blame you if you're scared of me."

"Why would I be scared of you?"

"Well . . ." she said, and stopped eating.

"Felicia—" he began, and put his hand out to her.

But she stopped him. "There's a very good possibility I'm a vampire."

"But you look fine. You look wonderful, in fact."

"I'm pale."

"Sure you're pale. But you've also been under a great strain."

"And this pizza is the first thing I've eaten in two days."

"It's just the stress really. I read a magazine article on stress and—"

"I don't want to—"

He stared at her. "To what?"

"To get you involved in this any more than you are already."

"But, Felicia, I love you and you love me."

She started sniffling again. "But maybe it's not enough."

He sprang to the couch and sat next to her. "I know this isn't much." His hand swept the drab apartment, the dated posters from the seventies, the collection of sci-fi and horror paperbacks in orange crates, and the longbow and its attendant paraphernalia. "But we'll move. Arizona. New Mexico. Oregon. Someplace, Felicia—someplace where we can get started on a new life. And—"

She put her head on his shoulder and drew him into her. "But I'm a vampire."

"Everybody's got things wrong with them, Felicia. Everybody."

"But being a vampire is more than just something wrong."

So he kissed her because it was the only way to keep her quiet. In the course of the kiss, he realized how much he loved her. It was frightening—far more than vampires could ever be.

"I'll go to the bank tomorrow and draw out my savings and then we'll go to the bus depot and we'll leave for New Mexico. He'll never find us there."

She sighed. "That's what scares me."

"What?"

"I don't think he'll give up so easily."

"Felicia, I promise. He won't even remember you."

"Oh, Sam," she said, drawing closer to him for another kiss, "I sure hope you're right."

"I am right, Felicia, I promise." Then he paused and gulped and said, "Felicia, I—"

She smiled at him. "I know. Me too." Then she said, "Do you really think we're going to be together, Sam?"

"Always."

"You're not just saying that?"

"I promise you, Felicia. I promise you."

For purposes of lovemaking and sleep, Sam decided to give her the royal treatment. He turned the sofa into a bed and dug out his only set of clean sheets from a cardboard box filled with a reasonably complete collection of Jonah Hex comic books.

The lovemaking was tender, and immediately afterward, she fell asleep in his embrace, there in the long shadows of the tiny apartment, the nimbus of streetlight like faded gold against the cracked west window, traffic sounds faint in the night.

Sam wondered: Could it really end this happily? This easily? Karl Richards just handing her over to him?

But eventually, no matter how compelling his doubts, he fell asleep, too, as crazy in love as he'd ever been, the woman in his arms all the things a woman was capable of being—lover, friend, sister, partner, conspirator.

His last waking thought was of how wonderful life could be.

He was asleep maybe twenty minutes before a sound woke him. Through one groggily opened eye, he saw Felicia in silhouette at the window. She was putting her clothes on.

"Felicia—what's wrong?"

Nothing. She said nothing. Just continued to dress.

"Felicia?"

He threw the covers back and went over to her. He wore nothing but jockey shorts.

He got around in front of her and put both his hands on her shoulders and started shaking her. He forced her face up so he could see her expression in the deep night shadows.

Her eyes were dark vacuums. All he could think of was some kind of hypnosis or mind control or—

Then he moved over to the window rimed with silver frost around the edges and looked down into the street. A long black limousine sat beneath the streetlight. A tall, slender man dressed in a black topcoat stood outside the limo. He stared directly up at Sam's apartment.

The man was Karl Richards.

"No, Felicia!" Sam screamed. "Don't go with him! Don't go with him!"

He dashed to the sink, soaked a towel in cold water, came back to her, and pressed the icy cloth against her face.

Dimly, he saw recognition in her eyes.

"Felicia?"

"Yes." She sounded robotic.

"If you go with him, you'll never be free again. Do you understand, Felicia?"

"Yes."

"Then fight back. Resist the thoughts he's sending out." He shook her hard. "Fight back, Felicia. You want to stay here with me. We'll leave for New Mexico in just a few hours. You'll be safe and happy and loved and—"

And then she let out an animal roar that paralyzed him.

He could not imagine such a sound coming from this beautiful woman.

Nor could he imagine a woman—or a man, for that matter—possessing the sheer physical strength she displayed: she took him by the shoulder and flung him across the room, slamming him into the wall where the longbow hung.

The back of his head cracked against the plaster hard enough that a darkness even deeper than the night began to spread before his eyes and . . .

Just before tumbling into unconsciousness, he heard the terrible animal roar she'd made earlier . . . and then he heard his apartment door flung back . . . footsteps down the creaking wooden steps and . . .

And then, despite every effort, he felt himself pulled inevitably down into the waiting gloom that was not unlike death.

When he woke, his teeth were chattering from the cold. His head hurt him worse than the worst hangover he'd ever had.

The window was purple-gold with dawn glowing through the frost.

The room, always a mess, was now a shambles, evidence of the strength she'd suddenly shown.

He needed clothes and he needed coffee and he needed to very carefully think through—

If he hadn't been right next to the fallen longbow, maybe the idea would never have come to him But as he started to push himself to his feet, his fingers touched the sleek wood, the curving bow, and right then—right there in his jockey shorts and needing very badly to pee—he got the idea.

And it was a wonderful idea, and he knew it was a wonderful idea as soon as he had it.

It was the idea that was going to win him Felicia back once and for all.

10

"Peace," Albert Carney said when Sam entered his carpentry shop three hours later. Albert, a fat and unkempt man with wild hair and beard turning gray these days, wiped pudgy fingers on his bib overalls and flashed Sam the V sign for peace, the way people used to greet others back in the sixties. He looked as if he hadn't shaved, bathed, or slept for several months.

Sam always thought of Albert as the last of the hippies, the one person he knew who would never give up the flower-power era. For instance, now the air was being stirred by the slashing sounds of Jefferson Airplane singing "White Rabbit" on the cassette deck. The shop, which was really a large, converted garage that smelled sweetly of wood shavings, was decorated with posters of people such as Ken Kesey, Allen Ginsberg, and Jerry Rubin. Nobody could ever accuse Albert Carney of giving up the faith.

Albert picked up a tiny marijuana roach, lit it, toked deep and true, then offered the clip to Sam.

Sam shook his head. "How's business?"

Albert nodded to various pieces of cabinetry in various stages of carpentering or staining. "Enough to last me a couple lifetimes." He smiled with teeth that would have required two dentists to get clean and then said, "Say—you're goin' to be haulin' me around Saturday night. Big sixties festival down at the Freak."

The Freak was a beer and wine bar near the railroad depot, where once a month they had a sixties night. Albert, who didn't want to get busted for drunk driving, always had Sam haul him back and forth in the cab. That's how they'd met.

"Be glad to, Albert."

Albert had another toke. "So what brings you here, man? Especially with that bow. That mother looks fierce!"

"It is fierce, Albert. Very fierce. And that's why I need to talk to you. I need to make it even fiercer."

"How you gonna do that?"

"With your help, I'm going to make a very special kind of arrow."

"What kind would that be, Sam?"

"It's got to be a wooden stake that I can notch in my bow and shoot."

"A wooden stake?" Albert laughed, taking the final toke. "What you gonna hunt—vampires?"

Sam laughed right along with him. "You think you can do it?"

Albert shrugged. "Probably."

"It would have to be able to pierce—armor."

"That's why the English invented the longbow. So it could do just that." He took the bow, examined it. "That shouldn't be any problem."

"How long?"

"How long?"

"Yeah, how long will it take?"

"Well, I'd have to use the lathe and then fire-harden it and—"

"Albert, I need this arrow by six o'clock tonight."

"You're kidding."

"I'm not, Albert."

"God."

"Albert, it's life and death."

Albert looked him over. "You look real strung out, man."

"I wish I could tell you."

Albert looked at him and said, "OK, man. The number of times you've kept me out of the drunk tank, I guess this is the least I can do for you." He nodded to the lathe. "You come back here at six tonight and I'll have it ready for you."

Sam put his hand on Albert's shoulder. "I wish there was some way I could repay you."

"There is, man."

"What's that?"

"Tell me the truth about why you want this arrow."

Sam laughed again, though the sound was obviously strained. "Like you said, I'm going to go hunting vampires."

But this time Albert didn't laugh. "You know, man, I'm beginning to wonder if you're not serious."

11

Sam spent the afternoon taking care of passengers. It seemed important to him to stay calm. What lay before him tonight required not only skill and luck but steady nerves.

Whether talking to the rich dowager who always told him about her son-in-law the songwriter ("Kenny Rogers calls him all the time just to talk") or taking Mr. Gunderson to his doctor's appointment ("I'm eighty-two and they want to know why I don't feel so good—and that's why I don't feel so good, because I'm eighty-two that's why, the stupid bastids")—whatever he did, his mind remained on the plan, or, as his mind thought of it, The Plan.

Last night, summoned to the waiting limo by Karl Richards, Felicia had forgotten her purse in which resided the electronic access card that would let whoever possessed it inside the walled estate.

The card now rested in Sam's shirt pocket.

Four dragged by; five to six crawled: it was time to go to Albert's.

This time the cassette machine played Neil Young singing "My Old Man" and Albert had himself a much more formidable joint than the little roach he'd sported before.

This one was fat enough to last for a couple hours of watching a light show.

"Here you go," Albert said, toking up.

What he handed Sam looked like a small tree that had been shaved down to the size of a baseball bat.

"Sure hope that bow of yours can handle this," Albert said.

"No problem," Sam said, holding the huge arrow. The feathers near the end of the nock were bright yellow.

"Thought I'd kind of dress it up," Albert said. "What do you think of the point?"

Pure wood, the point pricked Sam's finger at the slightest touch. A drop of blood appeared.

"Kind of heavy duty, wouldn't you say?"

"Sam, if I was into kissing guys, I'd plant a big one on your cheek." He dug into his back pocket for his wallet. "What do I owe you?"

"I already told you."

"The cab ride?"

"Right."

"You got it."

Now so intent on his mission that he even forgot to say good-bye, Sam took the arrow and started to leave the garage.

"Hey," Albert said.

Sam turned around. "Oh, yeah. Sorry. Shoulda said good-bye."

"No, not that," Albert said.

"What then?"

"Put the tip of it up by your nose."

Sam angled the long, pointed shaft of fire-hardened wood to his nose.

Immediately, he pulled the arrow away from his nostrils. "Whew. What'd you dip it in, anyway? Sheep dung?"

Albert looked very proud of himself. "What else? Garlic."

12

There was an electronic buzz and then the black grillwork of the gates parted and Sam went inside.

In the silver fog that lay across the land so heavily all he could see of the mansion was a single spire silhouetted against the round yellow disc of moon, Sam moved cautiously to the house.

Now that the gates had been opened, Karl Richards would be expecting somebody. Probably one of the women, done with her day's work.

Sam had to move quickly, and did, his feet making sucking sounds in the damp grass, the sound of his heart huge in his ears.

After ten minutes, he reached what appeared to be a large screened-in veranda. He tried the door—locked.

From his pocket he took a switchblade, clicked it open. He tore a four-foot gash in the screening and then went inside, carrying his longbow carefully in one hand, the arrow carefully in the other.

He crossed a flagstone walkway filled with summer furniture that looked dirty and cold on this winter's night. He went up three steps to a door that would take him inside. He put his hand on the knob and then whispered a prayer before turning it. If it was only open—

Locked.

Glancing wildly around, he saw a window three feet off the veranda floor. He went over to it, pulling a deck chair with him. Standing on the tarpaulin seat, he peeked through the window. What he saw was a shadowy hallway at the far end of which appeared to be a vast living room filled with Victorian antiques.

He said the same prayer he'd said before. This time his luck was better. The window eased open and he dropped inside the mansion.

He lay in the shadows, smelling furniture polish and floor wax and the remnants of a dinner that had included some kind of spaghetti sauce. Only after ten minutes did he make his move.

The living room—vast with a vaulted ceiling and huge fireplace— proved empty, as did an adjacent room which was filled with what looked like original oils by Degas and Chagall.

Carefully, he made his way through the first floor: dining room; kitchen; sewing room; den. Nothing.

Then from upstairs he heard the scream.

Racing to the bottom of a staircase that fanned wider as it stretched in carpeted splendor to the second level, Sam gulped and prepared himself for the confrontation that had been inevitable since the first time he'd dropped Felicia off at the mansion.

He crept up the stairs, the sound of an angry male voice growing louder the higher he went.

A wide corridor with walls of flocked red wallpaper; a large flattering portrait of Karl Richards himself decked out in a black suit and high white collar (eyes glistening as blackly as his hair); a partially opened door through which the man's voice came—these were the first things Sam saw.

Hefting the wooden crossbow, he got up on tiptoe and edged to the door.

Inside he saw a large group of women, dressed in everything from baby doll pajamas to diaphanous negligees, gathered in a circle in the center of a huge room appointed, as the living room was, with Victorian furnishings.

Pacing back and forth before the women was a tall man in a red silk dinner jacket and black slacks. He was flawlessly handsome and flawlessly angry.

"I want obedience!" he snapped. "Not mere compliance!" He paused and said in a lower yet curiously more menacing tone, "None of you can escape me—so why not obey me!"

"We're people, too," a strawberry blond with wonderful breasts said. "We have rights."

"You are *not* people," Karl Richards said. "You are vampires."

"So you're not even going to listen to our petition about forming a committee to change some of the rules?"

"I am the absolute master!" Richards screamed. "Not only the master of darkness—but the master of this house."

It was then that Sam saw Felicia. She sat near the back. She wore a modest blue cotton nightgown that made her look little-girlish and all the more beautiful.

She chose that moment to look up and when she did so, she saw Sam.

He held up the bow and arrow for her to see and then touched a finger to his lips, sshhhing her.

"There will be no more talk about committees or changing the rules or anything!" Karl Richards said. "And to prove it, I want all of you girls in bed within fifteen minutes—with the lights out."

Sam gulped.

The moment was here.

He notched the arrow, gulped, said another silent prayer, kicked the door open, and pulled back on the bowstring.

Karl Richards did just what Sam had hoped he would. Startled by the door's flying open, the vampire turned around to face Sam.

And Sam let go the stake that had been shaved into an arrow.

Richards, seeing what was about to happen, grabbed a nearly naked woman who had been standing a few inches from him—and pushed her into the path of the arrow.

She twisted as the stake went deep into her heart. The noise she made was nearly intolerable to Sam.

Then Karl Richards went crazy.

Teeth the size of wolf fangs appeared in the corners of his mouth, and his lips began to drip silver saliva.

"Oh gosh, Sam, now he'll get you for sure!" he heard Felicia shout.

The idea had occurred to Sam.

As Richards moved forward, hands turning into talons now, Sam

backed up against the staircase until there was no place he could
go unless he jumped the considerable distance to the first floor.

"You have enraged me long enough!" shouted Richards, his face
distorted by rage and spittle.

Behind Richards, Sam could see the fallen woman, the arrow
sticking up out of her bloody chest like a lance.

He shouted to Felicia: "Pull the arrow out and bring it to me!"

It was then that Richards's talons shredded through Sam's cheeks.

Sam spent the next two minutes dodging the taller and more
athletic man, running down the hallway, only to be tripped—then
pinned down, only to squirm free at the last moment.

He did not notice Felicia until Richards had backed him up
against a corner.

"Here, Sam!" she called and threw him the arrow.

It fell two feet short of Sam's grasp.

Richards, cursing, bent to pick up the arrow. "I'll break it in
half and then I'll do the same to you!"

But as he stooped, Sam sprang from the corner and kicked him
hard on the side of the face, sending Richards awkwardly to his
knees.

Sam snatched up the arrow and notched it for the second time
in the bowstring. It was sticky with the woman's blood.

Then Sam let go the giant arrow. It ripped through the vampire's
heart with such force that it emerged from the beast's back,
dripping blood and entrails.

The master of darkness was dead as hell.

13

"Good-bye," said the brunet, embracing Felicia in the vestibule
downstairs.

The brunet wore a gabardine business suit and carried a large
gray piece of American Tourister luggage and had a tan London
Fog draped over her arm. She sure didn't look like a vampire.

"Where will you go?" Felicia asked.

"My uncle owns a travel agency in Cleveland. I'll probably give
that a try first."

"We should have a get-together once a year."

"Yes, a picnic or something," the brunet said. Then she put out
her hand to Sam. "I owe you a lot more than I can say."

He looked at Felicia and smiled. "I had selfish reasons."

Quite seriously, the lovely brunet said, "I'll always be a vampire
but now at least I'm my own person."

An airport limo pulled up and honked.

"Well," the brunet said, "good-bye."

Then she walked outside to the sunlight that was almost white. The grass was brilliant green. As usual in the Midwest, spring had simply shown up one morning, like a lover one had almost forgotten.

Sam said, "Well, that's the last of them."

"Yes," Felicia said, smiling. "Every one of the women packed and away from this place." She leaned over and kissed him on the cheek. "Oh, Sam. We all owe you so much."

"You know I don't want gratitude, Felicia. I did it because I love you." He nodded upstairs. "Now why don't you go upstairs and pack? Then we can get out of here, too."

She kissed him again. "It won't take long."

She went up the broad stairs. He entertained himself by walking through the room with the Chagall and Degas oils. It was warm in here. The furnace in the basement was roaring. He had put Karl Richards's corpse in it.

She was back, an overnight bag in her hand, a few minutes later.

"Ready?" he said.

"Oh, Sam, if you could only know how ready I am."

"Good. Then let's lock this place up and never think about it again."

She giggled. "Let's."

So they went outside to the brilliant day and he put the key in the lock and started to turn it and that was when a rough piece of wood scraped the knuckle of his left thumb.

And several small bubbles of blood appeared.

He laughed. "Mr. Graceful strikes again," he said.

He finished locking the door and then turned around to look at her.

The fangs didn't alter her face all that much. And she wasn't spitting all over the place. And her eyes weren't psychotic and crazed.

She was a vampire, OK, but at least she was a very pretty and feminine one.

She started sobbing instantly and fell into his arms.

An hour later they had completed their second lap around the huge estate. They had seen dogs, they had seen horses, they had seen deer; they had seen oak, they had seen maple, they had seen elm; they had seen rock and grass and lake.

And they had faced a terrible truth.

Now, sitting on a porch swing in the park pavilion: "We can't be together, Sam."

"Don't say that anymore. Please."

"It's true. The mere sight of blood—I'm a vampire. My teeth—"

"You didn't bite me. You're not some terrible beast. You're—"

"As vampires go, I'm probably pretty OK," Felicia said, watching the course of a jay as it flew up to a tree limb. "I mean, I was a decent human being, so I'll probably be a decent vampire. But that still doesn't mean we can be together."

"Oh please, Felicia. Please don't say that anymore."

She stood up, then bent down to take his hands and pull him up, too. Her eyes were wet with her tears. "I love you more than I've ever loved anybody, Sam. But it won't work and you know it and I know it."

"But it's no different from my marrying a Polynesian woman. There'll be some cultural differences at first but—"

"Yes. I don't cast a reflection, my whole body surges when I see blood, and I'm probably going to live to be a few thousand years old. But other than that I'll just be a typical suburban housewife, right, Sam?"

"Felicia, I—"

She put her lips to his. Their kiss was long and tender and halfway through, Sam recognized the kiss for what it was:

Good-bye.

She entwined her hand in his and together they walked out of the estate, the grillwork gates closing behind them.

They stood on the curb and Sam said, "What will you do?"

She tried a smile but it was mostly sad. "Right now I'm not thinking very clearly, Sam. I guess I don't have any idea at all what I'll do. Just whatever comes along, I guess."

Then she waved good-bye to him and started walking away, a beautiful, retreating figure, until she rounded a corner and was out of sight.

Gone.

Forever.

14

During the next year he saw a shrink who tried to convince him that none of it had ever happened, a priest who accused him of being a satanist, a minister who wanted him to come on his TV talk show and discuss how even vampires could become good Christians.

He also tried singles bars, dating services, and old girl friends.

But no matter what he tried, there were still the lasting memories of Felicia, and of their plans, and of how much he'd loved her and loved her still.

Spring became summer became autumn became winter. A new cable channel appeared, one that played a lot of Monogram films, including the best of the Charlie Chans and Bowery Boys, and that helped some, and scores of new types of junk food came along, and that helped a little bit, too.

But mostly there was just driving the cab and lying on the couch thinking about Felicia. Thinking uselessly about Felicia. He had tried all the agencies and all the studios, but there was no word of her. Obviously she had moved away.

He contented himself with cable and food that only a chemist could love.

He had only a vague idea of what day it was, that overcast February Tuesday.

He'd had his usual afternoon-load of people he liked and people he disliked.

Now it was dusk and the dispatcher had just sent him to an address near the downtown area.

He pulled up and waited in front of an aged brick building.

A woman in a fashionable felt hat, one whose rim obscured her face, walked gracefully from the building and got in the car. She smelled wonderfully of perfume and womanness.

He was halfway down the block before he said, "I forgot to ask, where would you like to go?"

All she said was, "Why don't you look in your mirror, Sam?"

He didn't have to look in the mirror. He knew the voice.

"My God," he said.

"It's Valentine's Day," she said.

"My God," he said.

"It's selfish of me, Sam, but I just had to see you—"

"My God," he said.

"I've missed you so much and—" She whipped off her felt hat and let her lovely blond hair tumble free.

Finally, he was able to speak coherently. "I've looked everywhere for you. For a year."

"That's so sweet—"

"To tell you something."

"Tell me what?"

"That I have a plan."

"What plan?"

"There's a park up ahead."

"All right."

"And I'm going to pull into that park."

"All right."

"And then I'm going to ask you to sit up in the front seat with me."

For the first time she sounded a bit hesitant, suspicious. "All right."

He pulled into the park. At night the only illumination was the nimbus of electric light off dirty snow.

They parked next to a pavilion. "OK," he said. "Get up front."

"What's going to happen, Sam?"

"You'll see. Please, Felicia. Just get up front."

So she got up front.

As soon as she was in the front seat, he did it: grabbed the church key he kept on the dash and cut a deep gash on his hand.

In the shadows, he saw her entire body begin to tremble, saw the fangs begin to form in the corners of her mouth.

"I should have thought of this that day we walked around the mansion," Sam said, holding out his hand. "I can't turn you back into a human but you can turn me into a vampire."

"Sam, are you sure you want to—"

Sam laughed. "Make me your valentine, Felicia. Make me your valentine right now."

TRUE

by John Maclay

It doesn't really bother Tommy until sixth grade. Up until now it's been hurtful, yes, but he's always had his parents' shelter to rely on. But now, with boys becoming teenagers and girls becoming women, it's taken on a new meaning, and so has the hurt.

School ends early, and they all sit at their desks with cups of punch and napkins full of cookies. A teacher's pet opens the wooden mailbox at the front of the room, and messengers come up the rows with handfuls of little envelopes. It doesn't take long to see who's going to get the most.

Or the least. Because it's Valentine's Day, and Tommy leaves as soon as he can with the six envelopes hidden in his pocket. There are thirty kids in the class; he can do math. But what hurts most, this year, is what Cathy said when she handed him the first:

"Oh, Tommy. Here's one . . . for *you*."

But it doesn't really bother Tommy until tenth grade. He's become the guy who keeps to himself, who has "other interests" he shares with one or two like types. First it was model airplanes, but now it's auto mechanics, with that all-important license around the corner.

He's in the shop after school this February, working with his buddy Rick on a V-8. But something in Rick's attitude bothers him; something that tells him he'll soon be more alone.

"What's the matter?" Tommy asks.

"Oh, nothin'," Rick answers. "Just that . . . you know, it's Valentine's Day. No more silly cards and stuff, but I been thinkin' . . ."

Tommy watches as his friend lays down the wrench, grabs a touch-up brush and a can of red paint. Then it's there, on the concrete-block wall.

A heart, with an arrow through it:

RICK AND SUSIE

TRUE

* * *

But it doesn't really bother Tommy until the senior prom. Though he's remained outside while others have had dates, even sex, he knows that his time will come. Because he knows, and the class accepts, that he's a normal guy for all of his shyness. And besides, he dreams about girls all the time.

About Cathy. And, lump in his throat, he asks her to the prom.

She stands there in the corridor, eyes blank, newly developed chest heaving, mouth struggling to speak.

"But . . . but, Tommy. You're a nice boy, but . . . everybody knows I'm going with Rick!"

He watches her retreat to her friends. And then he hears the giggles.

Rick . . . who never had a dream in his life.

On prom night Tommy sits in his rebuilt Camaro in front of the gym, looking in, alone.

But it doesn't really bother Tommy until three years later.

Some of the guys have gone off to college, and others have married. But Tommy's all right; he's been to school in Detroit, has a good job at the Chevy garage, a decent apartment. He's had sex, yes; one time, for a fifty, when he went along with the guys from the garage. And despite the partner, it was everything he'd dreamed it would be. He's asked regular women often enough. But there's something about him, perhaps because of the dreaming, that's always made them say no.

He's lied to the guys, told them of imaginary nights with bodies described from magazines. But he's a man now, and men know. And this Valentine's Day, things finally fall.

"Hey, Tommy," says the foreman, toward closing time, brandishing a flat paper bag. "Gotta box of candy for your valentine?"

His ears burn. Then:

"Naw, Tommy's not like that," says a guy he's thought is like the old Rick, but who now suddenly isn't. "He don't like the ladies."

Tommy leaves as soon as he can. It's sixth grade again.

But it isn't sixth grade. He's a man now, and it's worse than he ever thought it could be.

Back in his apartment, Tommy thinks of Rick. And that brings Cathy. And that, in desperation, brings the telephone.

"Hello?"

"Uh . . . this is Tommy."

"Oh, hi there. Haven't thought of you in years. I mean . . ."

"Yeah. Well, what I was wondering, was if . . ."

"Well, sure, Tommy. I wouldn't mind going out with you, to a movie, or . . ."

"I mean, I thought you and Rick, but—"

"No, that's over a long time ago . . . Pick me up at eight, huh?"

After the movie Tommy drives the Camaro past the old high school, out of town to a dirt road in the woods. Stops. Turns off the engine and the lights.

"What are you doing, Tommy?"

He moves close to Cathy, puts his arm around her. His other hand on her chest. His mouth on hers, and—

"Oh *no*, Tommy. I thought we were just friends. Not *that*."

He tries again. But her body is stiff, her teeth clenched, her lips dead and cold.

"Please *stop!*"

And now she's out of the car, in the dark, running down the road.

And it finally bothers Tommy—a lot.

He's reaching in the glove compartment, for something he once made, after school, in shop. That he carries around for emergencies . . . like this.

Something steely and sharp.

Then he's outside, too, in the cold night. Outside himself; almost watching himself as he runs down the road after her, gaining with every stride.

"Tommeee!"

It's over quickly. Both the fulfillment, and the loss.

But it doesn't stop there. Because quick as it's been, it's just been too long.

The grade-school valentines . . . the heart on the shop wall . . . the senior prom . . . the guys at the garage . . .

But most of all, the heart . . .

It's found there, the next morning, by a passerby.

Fixed to a tree, the knife through it.

And underneath, in blood:

TOMMY AND CATHY
TRUE

And when the police come and take him away, it doesn't bother Tommy anymore.

TWO FLOOR GENERALS
AND THE SWEETHEART DANCE

by J. N. Williamson

Last week when I was in New York, a bag lady was pushing a
beat-up old cart along Second Avenue just when the cab Alan and
I were taking to an Indian restaurant turned onto Sixth Street. Tall,
gaunt, she looked instantly familiar but I couldn't place her until
after we'd ordered—I remember trying bhuna beef with piaza, and
a great drink my editor had told me about, called lillet—and then
I assured myself I had to be wrong.

What the hell was Alma Litchfield, who ate human hearts, doing
in Manhattan after so many years?

My next thought was that Alma was my age, not old enough, at
forty-four, to be a bag lady. But then I saw that they probably
didn't set any sort of minimum age requirement for jobs like that,
remembered that the whole Litchfield family had left Ripley County
right after she did it, and finally accepted the fact that I was largely
responsible for every miserable thing that had happened to lonely,
ugly Alma these past twenty-six years.

All because Valentine's Day was right before the draw for the
sectionals in my senior year and I was the spark plug for the
Piercetown High School basketball team.

Everett Schroeder and I were both stars, actually. This was
before Larry Bird over in Springs Valley and Steve Alford in New
Castle and after Bobby Plump led little Milan to the state
championship, and a couple of floor generals—that's what the
Piercetown Reporter called Everett and me—could still get press
without being six feet high or scoring thirty points a game. They
said we "had savvy," and "kept our heads about us," and it was
a pretty accurate compliment.

But only on the old hardwood, I saw now, remembering what
Everett and I did to poor Alma.

To understand and be fair to myself, you have to understand that
high school basketball had been the boiler that kept all
Hoosierdom—Indiana folks—warm in the winter since 1911. That's
when the first state championship tourney was held; and a million
people go to watch the month-long action yearly. Eighteen of the
country's biggest high school gyms are scattered all over the state,
almost everyone is proud of the fact that Bird and Alford and Oscar

Robertson grew up there, and I was nervous as a coach who had to play I.U.'s Bob Knight about Piercetown High's first opponent in the sectionals. That's what you had to win first, followed by the regionals, the semistate and, if you were really lucky, the state finals in a terrifying metropolis named Indianapolis. Terrifying, that is, to small-town boys.

And I hadn't gotten a date for the Valentine's Day Sweetheart Dance when that joker Everett Schroeder got it in his head that I should ask ugly Alma Litchfield.

At first, I told redheaded, skinny ol' Everett he had a box of fine gravel where his brain was supposed to be—and that I'd never get a real date with a *real* girl if I asked Alma and she said yes. To tell the truth, I'd been trying to work up the nerve all semester to see if Cindy Vandermark would go out with me but Coach Steiner had discouraged me. "Only reason a girl'd date you is because you're a Blue Devil," he'd assured me. "Time enough when you start college. Don't forget what happened to Cabby Grinsted."

I hadn't, but the memory'd blurred a bit with the passage of two terrific basketball seasons. Cabby was first string, a year ahead of me at Piercetown, and he'd begun dating when he was a junior. Sure enough, he'd got Wanda Lozier in a family way. Coach Steiner'd put Grinsted off the team and reminded us forthrightly that "the only decent outlet for all that pent-up energy is basketball."

Getting Alma Litchfield P-G, however, was the most improbable notion that had ever occurred to me. Besides, that clown Everett had said I didn't actually have to *take* her to the dance. "All you gotta do is ask. I'll be hanging around, just to tell the other guys how ugly Alma looked when a floor general like you asked her."

That was how young, how unthinking, both Everett and I were back then, and how unaccustomed we were to the sight of ugly women. Actually, I've seen a lot since then who were just as ugly as big, rawboned Alma, maybe one or two who were even harder on the eyes. But there was nothing much going on in Piercetown until the sectional draw except for practice and, of course, classes, and I figured that I had ol' Everett as a witness to the fact that it was all a big joke. In a way, I suppose, it was a test of our friendship; once Everett had promised to back me up, refusing to ask Alma might've looked as if I didn't trust him.

And teammates who couldn't go down the line with one another—in Piercetown, Indiana—didn't even get out of the sectionals.

But I waited as long as possible before going over to Alma's house on the westside. Until Valentine's Day itself, as a matter of fact, and before class—around 7:15 in the morning, if memory serves me. Might have been 7:30. I know it was early because, in a town with nothing much except a drugstore, general store, hardware store, a bank, and the Plump and Volz Wire Factory to occupy your time—apart from basketball, of course—everything started early. I'd been up since at least 5:30.

These were the three things I *didn't* know: First, Everett Schroeder had telephoned ol' Alma the night before to notify her I was coming. Second, I guess Alma Litchfield spent a tense, sleepless night waiting for the moment when the two floor generals of the fabled Piercetown High School Blue Devils knocked on her front door.

The third was what my best friend Everett put into my hands when he met me next to the vacant field just south of Alma's place: a big, bright red, heart-shaped candy box from Haag's Drugstore.

"Lord A'mighty, Everett." I frowned, tugging my windbreaker with the huge letter P tighter around my neck. It was colder than a basketball center on the free throw line with the February wind yowling through the deserted lot, and the chance that Alma Litchfield might be so overcome with excitement that she'd kiss me sent a few more shivers skittering up the nape of my neck. "Holy cow, I don't want her t'think I *love* her or somethin'!"

Which was when the red-haired little son-of-a-sea-cook said he'd phoned her last night. "And I told her you'd got her somethin' special, just for her," Everett added, wide-eyed and full of mischief. "For St. Valentine's Day!"

I almost backed out right then. I wish to Jesus I had. I shook my head a lot instead and wondered what to do with the basketball I'd dribbled all the way from my place. Everett just took it and pressed the gift for Alma into my hands.

"Don't let it come open and spoil everything," he cautioned as I accepted it.

I whirled away from him, disgusted, almost slipping in yesterday's snow. "Of course I won't," I snapped, stomping resolutely toward the Litchfields'. "Coach Steiner don't want none of the team havin' candy till after we won the state championship. You know that."

"Wait up," he called, following after me. I glanced back and saw the way he was trying to keep a grin out of sight and thought about friendship, and how fortunate I was to have a pal like that little joker for life.

Then I really saw the old Litchfield house and I remember it now, plain as day, just the way it seemed that February the

fourteenth morning. It appeared partly lived-in, at best—as if it was
a case either of an insufficient number of family members dwelling
there or that those folks who did occupied only a portion of it. Not
that it was a big place, the way some of those old, frame houses
were in Piercetown back when I starred for Piercetown High with
Everett Schroeder. Rumor even had it that half the Litchfield house
had blown away on the scoop end of a Hoosier tornado, and
whoever had dwelled in it after that had merely boarded up one
wide wall.

And with the sun still struggling to rise as halfheartedly high as
it generally did in the winter, in Ripley County, half the place
looked like it had been eaten by shadowy weeds and the other half
was lit like a jack-o'-lantern. By the time I'd clambered up the
rickety wooden steps to the porch, that redheaded fool of a best
friend practically squashing the heels of my tennis shoes, peering
through the windows on either side of the front door was exactly
like lifting a Halloween pumpkin and squinting inside.

It wasn't that the old house looked haunted. It was that I had
the impression that it was going to be, someday.

"I don't wanna do this, Ev," I said in a hoarse whisper.

"You gotta," Everett assured me. "I told everybody on the team
and they'll wanta know how she looks."

Which settled the matter then and there.

Alma Litchfield opened the door just as my knuckles were set to
rap, but she did it in two, queer motions, the first real quick, the
second as if she was attempting to seem more casual. I gawked at
her for a moment as if I'd been the one who was destined to haunt
that old place, years from then.

And what got me wasn't the fact that Alma Litchfield was taller
than ol' Gene Butte, who jumped center for the Blue Devils.
Shee-it, I'd always known she was a good inch higher than six foot
off the ground. It was how Alma Litchfield had tried to pretty
herself up that froze me on the other side of the storm door Alma'd
cranked open half a foot.

Now, that may sound funny, but Coach Steiner always said I had
the "best look" of the floor of anybody he'd had. I recall one time,
over at the Oddfellows Hall, when Coach even said I could grow
up to "be another Van Arsdale." I'd have been truly set up by that
except Coach Steiner was a mighty beer drinker in the offseason.

No, what got stuck in my head so long that a fast glimpse of a
bag lady in New York made me think about her was the way that
prettying up Alma Litchfield was kin to tying a blue ribbon round
a sow's neck. Not that Alma was fat; fact, she was the thinnest

one woman I ever did see. And she'd piled her hair atop her big head the way it was the fashion to do perhaps ten years earlier, and it caused Alma's Litchfield's neck to sprout another foot or two and take on the color of Everett Schroeder's hair when she saw me on her stoop.

Why, she'd even spread a slash of lipstick over her thin lips, and I wondered if her mom knew and if maybe they didn't have electricity inside that place. Not every house in Piercetown did; not every one does now, I imagine. And the close-set drab eyes of Alma Litchfield stared down a mile until they could look into mine, and since I was gaping at her pointy breasts and could not think of anything except what Everett wanted me to do for the team, I said: "Will you go to the Sweetheart Dance with me tonight?"

" 'Course she will," Everett scoffed, behind me, nudging my ribs hard. "Give her your gift."

"Please pardon ol' Everett," I said to Alma, suddenly aware of the look in those tiny eyes. If they hadn't had any electricity in the place before, for a second or two they did; because it was shining like crazy out of the eyes of the ugliest female in Ripley County. "The little blowhole has the manners of a warthog."

"Give her the present!" Everett hissed, shouldering my right elbow.

"Why, I'd deeply enjoy attending the Sweetheart Dance with *you*," Alma Litchfield breathed.

Well, the way she said "Sweetheart" turned my heart and my belly to pure stone. Which was when it should have occurred to me that Alma Litchfield *would* say yes, and when I ought to have been smart enough to perceive that my teammate Everett Schroeder also would've known she'd acquiesce. And when I actually should've expected the ol' red-haired fellow floor general Everett Schroeder to have arranged some means for getting his best buddy on this earth to get out of the commitment.

Nothing whatsoever occurred to me except following through with the shove Everett had given me and handing the bright red box to bony and suddenly bright-eyed Alma Litchfield.

I remember—even better than I do how that house looked outside at dawn in the middle of a Hoosier hoop season—even more clearly than I recall how joke-loving Everett Schroeder got kicked off the team just like Cabby Grinsted, and just as clearly as I recall squatting on a pinewood bench with my face buried in my big hands while the Piercetown Blue Devils lost the opening game of that year's sectionals—the expression of adoring appreciation on that poor, homely girl's face.

And how fast she moved to open the candy box with one hand and reach those long, pale fingers inside with her second hand even while Everett—horrified—was shouting, "No, don't *eat* it!"

Because her small, melting eyes never budged an iota of one inch from mine after she had plucked the human heart out of the Valentine's Day Whitman's box and taken a large, heartfelt bite right out of the pulpy center of the damned red thing.

At least Everett *said* it was a human heart right up to the instant when Coach Steiner demanded to know which one of his floor generals was responsible for a prank that had hideously misfired, and the best friend I had on earth told Coach the truth. Just where he'd gotten that heart I never did find out. Because the Litchfield family wasn't the only one that left town soon after. So did the Schroeders.

But it took the ugly girl with the awful, scarlet smear of blood all over her mouth and narrow chin enough time to grasp the terrible truth that somebody she had wanted to like her—to care enough for her to be willing to be seen in public with her—had caused her to do something unimaginably disgusting. It took time for the stink, and the metallic taste, to wise her up and for her to break the gaze she had shared with me, and peer down at what she held in her hand, and what was seeping through those long, white fingers to the single throw rug that strove to conceal the bare, scarred, hardwood floor of her half of the house.

She called me a name, worse than any I've been called before or since. And while I could put it right here on the page for anybody at all to read, I don't think I will. Because it was even worse, in some respects, than what her mom told Coach to tell me. That ol' Everett and I had done her daughter, Alma Litchfield, the supreme service of teaching her at an early age what masculine society thought about and did to women who lacked charm, and beauty, and an alertness to the unplumbable depths of human cruelty.

Maybe, had I excused myself to Alan and left the Indian restaurant, gone back out on Sixth Street and then Second Avenue, I might have caught up with the tall, gaunt, ugly bag lady. But I'd thought that it couldn't *actually* be Alma Litchfield eight hundred miles from the Blue Devils and a sectionals in which I did not compete and never would again. New York was a city of millions; all the population of Ripley County could be tucked away in a high rise or two, and no one would even know those people were there.

Exactly as Manhattan, and Piercetown, did not know I'd settled in Indianapolis, the place that had once seemed a great metropolis to Everett Schroeder and me. Writers, former high-school floor generals, and ugly women were a dime a dozen.

Still, this is the anniversary—today—of the joke we pulled. It's St. Valentine's Day. Perhaps it's time to mend the fences one can, and I have not so much as spoken to Everett since young Alma Litchfield opened a heart-shaped red box and drew from it, forever, her capacity for trust and affection. Her innate right to believe in the depths of human kindliness as long as possible. So maybe I'll phone Everett, over in Plymouth, where somebody said he's been a deputy sheriff for more than twenty years. It's an anniversary, today. A holiday.

But maybe I won't.

BE MINE

by Steve Rasnic Tem

Jan's mother had been hovering over her all day. "You got another valentine," she said.

Jan turned away from the television. She'd been watching this wildlife program about crocodiles. They had these tiny little birds that hopped around inside their mouths, and cleaned their long, sharp teeth. Jan's own mouth felt sour and gritty, and no amount of saliva seemed able to wash all that away.

"Several valentines, actually." Her mother stared at her impatiently. "Well? I said you got a whole bunch of valentines in the mail."

"You said 'several,' not 'a whole bunch,'" Jan said. She thought she could hear jealousy in her mother's voice.

"Suit yourself." Jan heard the door slam. She got up out of her chair hastily, angry with her mother, angry with herself. She knew she was being touchy; she just didn't know why. There were several small envelopes on the hall table. She opened the top one.

I can't BEAR to be without you, it said. A kid's valentine, it had a picture of a small bear on the front, a teddy bear, squeezing a heart so hard it had swollen, looked ready to explode. "Jeezus . . ." She was twenty-two. Who'd send her a kid's valentine?

But there was no name inside.

The next valentine said, *You're in my heart!* With a heart-shaped cage, its bars bloodred strings of heart muscle. An emaciated cartoon squirrel was trapped inside, its eyes swollen, lips pursed almost grotesquely. And again, no name inside.

The last one had a demented-looking duck on the front, pulling its own feathers out by the masses. *I'M CRAZY OVER YOU!* it screamed, in puke green color. On the back, in hasty, penciled scrawl, was the simple *for jan,* a jagged line drawn underneath for emphasis.

Who'd be sending her valentines like this?

In fact, who'd be sending her valentines at all? She hadn't had a date in weeks, hadn't had a steady boyfriend in over a year. She didn't know why. She knew she was nice enough looking, that— usually—her personality was pleasant enough. But no one had asked. No one had bothered with her in some time. Her mother said it was because she was needy, that needy women scared men

71

away. Well, everybody needed. And everybody was alone. Saying anything else was just playing the game.

Some practical joker—that was all. Somebody out to make her feel bad. An old boyfriend. A jealous girl (though what such a girl might have to be jealous about Jan had no idea). In any case, somebody that didn't matter.

Certainly not somebody who wanted her.

Jan got ready to go to the park. Lord knows, she wasn't going to sit around, mope around the house all Valentine's Day. Not when everybody else was going to parties they'd been invited to. Seeing boyfriends and girl friends. Dancing the night away under red hearts, blood-colored balloons, and streamers.

It had been an unseasonably warm week for a February. She'd go to the park and read a juicy romance, or maybe a historical. She'd soon forget it was Valentine's Day.

As she was leaving she found another valentine taped to their front door. *Be Mine!* it said, in bold, crimson letters. The cat on the valentine looked drowned, wasted. Its eyes desperate. Claws just peeking beyond the soft foot pads. Jan crumpled up the valentine and threw it on the ground.

She'd been on a diet. Had been doing pretty well, in fact. Almost as if the lack of boyfriends had resulted in a lack of appetite as well. But now, the image of the starved *Be Mine!* cat an irritant in her thoughts, she found herself stopping at the grocery store, loading a bag with sugary cupcakes and soft drinks and chips and pale meat sandwiches, packing her front seat for her Valentine's picnic. The cupcakes had been colored a bright red, with cartoons of cupids on their crisp, cellophane wrappers.

Her mother would be furious with her if she found out Jan had broken her diet that way. Usually she could forgive her mother for that particular display of neediness. After all, everybody wanted something more, everybody fed off one another in some way. Parents and kids, kids and other kids. Everybody. But right at the moment Jan hated being everybody else's dinner.

A thin flapping sound made her look at the bottom edge of the windshield. There, trapped beneath one of the wipers, was another valentine. She slowed the car so that the flapping also slowed, until finally the valentine rested flat against the glass. She found herself crouching a little, one eye on the road as she tried to read the thing.

Valentine! Hope I catch you! it said, in heavy black lettering. A sweet yellow chick with vampire fangs and heavy-veined wings was spread across a pale pink, near bloodless heart.

Jan reached out the driver's window, hooking her arm around, and tried to grab the valentine while she was driving. She swerved in front of a brown station wagon and, jolted alert by the mad squeals of tires and horns, forced her car back into her own lane. In the meantime the valentine blew off her windshield.

"This is *crazy*," she muttered. The colors of the passing cars, the houses, even the trees, suddenly seemed too bright, almost garish. Like the cartoon colors of kids' valentines.

Jan craved something sweet. This time carefully keeping her eyes on the road, she reached into the grocery sack, tore at the cellophane. Her fingertips went into something soft. She pinched them together quickly and pulled a lump of cupcake up toward her mouth. A piece of paper was stuck to the gooey cake: a valentine. *We go together!* it said. Two mangy-looking kangaroos were hugging—or fighting, she couldn't tell which. One kangaroo clutched the other so tightly the other's eyes had popped out. Both kangaroos looked half-dead. Jan vigorously shook the cake and card from her hand.

The park was a popular place that day; it took her half an hour to find a parking place. She checked the grocery sack determinedly before removing it from the car. No more valentines. No more surprises. Somebody was trying to make a fool out of her. Somebody was trying to make her feel bad, make her feel alone. That's what all that false sentiment did, just made you feel more alone. But she could see through the pictures. She could see what was really happening, what all those valentine messages really meant. Somebody wanted to get to her, take her attention away. It wasn't love and romance. It was owning.

She almost fell over a couple of teenagers lying in the grass, holding hands, making little kisses on each other's faces. She almost spilled the contents of the sack all over them. Would have served them right. They both looked up at her, startled. Then the boy frowned, looked angry. When Jan looked away to escape his gaze, suddenly embarrassed, she saw the enormous valentine lying on the grass beside them. *I'D DIE FOR YOU VALENTINE!* it shouted. In the illustration a dog lay on its back, a smoking gun clutched in one, humanlike paw. The blood leaking from its head had formed a heart-shaped pool by the gun.

Looking away, Jan clutched the sack to her chest and hurried deeper into the park.

It took some time, but finally she was able to find a spot away from people. There were so *many* couples out in the park today. More than she would have thought possible. She found herself ripping the wrapper off another cupcake with something akin to ferocity. Her own neediness enraged her.

Her last boyfriend, Michael, hadn't been enough for her. Her mother had always said she couldn't be pleased, and she was probably right. But at the time Jan hadn't been able to understand how anybody could *ever* be pleased. How *anything* could be enough, for *anybody*. The thirst seemed unquenchable.

You're Number 1! the valentine attached to a tree taunted her.

She stood up and tore the valentine from the trunk, crumpled it, stomped it into the ground.

The low-hanging branches brushed at her hair. She swatted at them. Leaves fell, caught in her hair. Leaves bounced off her shoulders, spun, and littered the ground around her. But it was February. There shouldn't be any leaves.

But they weren't leaves at all. They were valentines.

You're a real pal!—a huge raccoon menaced a small bird. *I'm stuck on you . . .*—a terrified butterfly glued fast to the web of a hideous spider. *My heart melts for you*—a squirrel carrying an enormous cigarette lighter, setting a pig on fire. *I'm lucky I have you*—a buzzard sitting on the back of a terrified lamb. *Don't break my heart!*—a fierce-looking dog plunging a knife into the chest of a deer.

Jan ran away from the park, bumping into a series of couples in her flight. She forgot all about her grocery sack. She forgot all about her car.

She ran down the street that led away from the park. Darkness stood at the end of that street. Tall and handsome.

"Love ya," the darkness said, in a voice that was almost sweet.

"You?" Jan said, drawn nearer despite herself.

"My heart belongs to you," the darkness said in a soft, sweet voice. Kids' valentines floated down out of an overcast sky, their tiny cartoon characters struggling, moaning. "You're a real pal," the darkness said.

Jan drew closer, trying to see her admirer's face. In the shadows that surrounded his voice, she could just make out the pale luminescence of her own eyes, high cheekbones, trembling chin, her own heart-shaped mouth pursed as if to kiss. "You can't love," she said to him. "I'm not sure anybody can."

"Valentine," the darkness said.

"You can only yearn," Jan said.

"Valentine, be mine!" the darkness, her valentine, screamed.

"And consume," Jan said.

Then her valentine kissed her.

DIE, CLOWN, DIE!

by William F. Nolan

I've never been much for holidays. Mostly, they just depress me. Christmas hasn't been any good since I was a kid. And even then it wasn't so great. Now it's just a day to get through. Easter was always a drag. Who the hell cared about looking for colored eggs? My parents used to get very drunk—and very loud—on New Year's Eve, so I've got some bad memories there. Fourth of July is okay. I've always liked fireworks. But the one holiday I really *hate* is St. Valentine's Day. And I have a damn good reason.

My brother was murdered on St. Valentine's Day.

I've never been married, so I've got no kids of my own. And no other brothers or sisters. Maybe my parents loved me, but they never took the trouble to show it. I never cared much for either of them. My fault maybe, the fact that we just didn't communicate. Danny was the only person I ever really loved. My "big brother," Danny Gregson. He was only two years older, but he was a kind of god to me—a brother to idolize. Never had any school friends.

It was just the two of us, in Oakland, California, growing up together in the 1930s—him born in '26 and me in '28. Mom told us she and Pop couldn't afford any more kids. "You take care of Bobby," Mom would say to my brother. "He's small. He gets picked on."

And I was—and did. I was a pimply runt of a boy, short for my age, while Danny was strong and tall and good-looking from the start. He could do everything I couldn't: climb the highest trees, leap across roofs, outrun any kid in the neighborhood, do cartwheels, box and arm-wrestle. And he was great at school sports. You name it, he was great at it. Not me, though. I wore glasses and always had a cold and was plain lousy at all sports. It was a world I didn't fit into. I couldn't hit a baseball or sink a basket and I was way too small for football. (Naturally, Danny was team captain.)

The bigger kids were all afraid of him. They'd be ragging me, making fun of my jug ears or my big feet and Danny would come along and light into them like a whirlwind. Got so they left me alone because if they didn't, they ended up with a black eye and some loose teeth. Courtesy of Danny Gregson.

It's like I've said, he was a god to me, the only god I ever knew personally. That's why his death hit me so hard. Almost half a century ago and sometimes I still wake up at night crying out his name. We'd still be close as ever if he'd lived. I know it. And things would have been different. My whole existence would have been different if Danny had lived. I wouldn't be alone now with nothing but books for company and I would never have become a writer, that's for damn sure. Writers are offbeat, isolated people. You turn *inside* yourself when you write. You don't live in the real world, only the world inside your head. It's kind of spooky, being a writer.

Danny would have done great things as a man, and he would have taken me right along with him. I'd be rich by now. Own a big white two-story house on Nob Hill instead of a dark, sleazy apartment here in Hollywood. Christ! Hollywood's become Freak City—and I guess I'm one of the freaks.

So I write. Mostly I do magazine work on assignment. I come up with an idea for a special feature piece, get an okay on my idea from an editor, then go out and write it.

That's how I set up the interview with old man Wainwright. I told T.J. Shaw, the author of *Legends,* that I wanted to do a feature profile on Wainwright. Shaw was skeptical; he was convinced that it was impossible to reach the old man. I told him not to worry, that I had a way.

No doubt about it, the old boy *was* a legendary character. Back in the 1930s he'd been the real-life model for Nightman, the world-famous comic-book hero. The Crime Crusher. But Wainwright's full story had never been told. Patchwork pieces had been written on him, but no one had ever been able to reach him for an interview. Not for decades, that is. He was a rich recluse, sealed off from the world behind the walls of his big estate upcoast near San Francisco. He'd been there all those years, and no one had ever seen him leave the place—not once since 1943. (That was a very fateful year in my life. Danny had been murdered on St. Valentine's Day, 1943.)

So how did *I* get to the old man? Why did the legendary Benjamin Clarke Wainwright agree to grant me a personal interview? It was the letter I wrote to him (he didn't have a phone, had never allowed one to be installed in his mansion). I wrote something in the letter that made him *want* to see me. I was about to reach him when no one else could. For the first exclusive interview in forty-five years.

It was going to be memorable.

* * *

The handwritten letter I got from him—the one I showed T.J. Shaw to notch the assignment—told me exactly how to reach his place (over a private road), how many times to honk my horn at the gate, and how many times to blink my lights. I was instructed to arrive there at midnight sharp, and he told me precisely where to find a hidden key to the mansion's front door. I was to let myself in, verbally identify myself, and then wait for him to appear. And, of course, I was to come alone. No other writers. No photographers. Just me. Alone. At midnight.

"Sounds like a visit to Dracula's castle," Shaw had declared after reading the letter. "Maybe you should take along some garlic." He chuckled. "And a sharp wooden stake!"

"So he's eccentric. All I care about is the fact that he's agreed to see me."

Shaw grunted. "Whatever you told him, it sure did the trick. This ought to make one hell of a story. Come back here with an in-depth interview and I'll tack a bonus onto your check."

Shaw didn't know what I'd put in my letter to the old man, and I'd refused to tell him. It was strictly my business. The words I'd written had earned me a ticket inside Benjamin C. Wainwright's private world.

The drive upcoast from Los Angeles took me almost eight hours. I didn't hurry because I had a lot to think about.

By the time I'd located Wainwright's private road—two miles inland from the ocean town of Bodega Bay—it was already close to midnight. A swirling fog reduced vision, and the road was giving me a bumpy ride. Its packed-gravel surface hadn't been maintained and my little Toyota jolted through deep potholes and bounced over rock-strewn sections, ridged by wild tree roots. Obviously the old boy didn't care about the condition of the road because *he* never used it. But at least I was making progress, slow but sure.

The fog's damp chill was beginning to penetrate the car's interior. It smelled of brine from the sea—a sharp, rusty odor. I switched on the dash heater, which helped.

The road seemed endless and I began to worry about being late. The old man's letter had specified that I reach the gate at "exactly twelve."

Maybe the damn gate wouldn't open after midnight. When you're dealing with a bizarre eccentric like Wainwright, you can't count on anything. So, despite the lousy road conditions and the lack of visibility, I speeded up. It was a risk I had to take.

Five minutes later the rising shape of a tall iron gate loomed in the path of my probing headlights. I stopped, sounded my horn three times, then blinked the lights twice.

Slowly, with a shriek of tortured metal, the gate swung open.

I drove inside, along a shorter (and smoother) access road, until I was able to make out the high Gothic towers of Wainwright House through a swirling gap in the fog.

I braked to a stop in front of the entrance, cut my engine and lights, and sat there thinking that Shaw had been right; this *was* a hell of a lot like visiting Castle Dracula.

I got out of the Toyota; the slammed door rang like a pistol shot in the fog-thick stillness. I looked up at the towering bulk of wood and stone. Darkness shrouded the sprawling Gothic-spired mansion. The windows were lightless. I could see no evidence of interior life.

The door key (heavy black metal, rust-pebbled) was just where Wainwright's letter said it would be—under a loose board at the edge of the wide stone entrance steps. The key was cold against the palm of my hand. I mounted the steps to the door, fitted the key into a blackened slot, twisted, and the carved wooden door swung inward with a sound like cats screaming.

I stepped into a vast, marble-floored entry hall, faintly illuminated by four sputtering, white-wax candles, set in high wall brackets. Not having a phone in the place was crazy enough—but *candles!*

Directly ahead of me a wide stairway curved upward into second-story blackness. I remembered my instructions: I was to identify myself, "in a clear voice."

I felt like a stage actor facing an empty theater. "I'm Bob Gregson," I called out. My words kicked echoes back from the somber walls.

I waited. Nothing. No sound or movement. Where was the old man? Maybe dead of a heart attack from the shock of my letter.

Then I looked upward. A light was descending the stairs, flickering against faded gold wall tapestries and gilt-framed oil paintings (of Wainwright's ancestors?).

I was about to meet a legend.

A gaunt figure slowly materialized on the stairway. He reached the last stair, moved slowly toward me across the marble floor. Limping. A thick black cane in one hand, a candle in the other. The wavering light from the candle flame threw the old man's face into sharp relief, accenting the hollows of his skull; deep wrinkles cut into his skin like wounds. He looked far older than his seventy-five years—a time-ravaged crone of a man.

"Benjamin Wainwright?" I asked.

"Who the hell *else* would live in a tomb like this?" He nodded toward a side hall. "There's brandy in the library. We can talk there."

I followed as his tapping cane reverberated along the dim hallway. Our passage was a long one, with the hall stretching forward into the depths of the house. Wainwright suddenly swayed, stumbling against me, clutching at my shoulder for support.

"Are you all right?"

"Yes, yes . . . It's just that I . . . I'm not used to walking much anymore. I must apologize for my awkwardness."

"Forget it," I said.

We moved on down the hall.

In Wainwright's cavernous library, the snapping flames from a deep stone fireplace helped warm me up a little—and a snifter of good Napoleon brandy finished the job.

I was beginning to feel human again. The oppressive dreamlike atmosphere of Wainwright House was quickly achieving a livable reality.

We were seated in two large red velour chairs, close to the fire. The old man looked up from lowered brows, fixing me with an eagle's glare. "Do you know why I have allowed you to enter my house?"

"I know."

He continued to glare at me, white hair forming a thin halo over his lowered head.

"I don't give interviews," he said. "Don't allow people to come here. You're the first outsider I've seen in more than forty years."

"How do you get food?"

"It's brought in. A servant delivers it. Then he leaves. I don't let anyone stay here at night."

"Hell of a life," I said.

His glare intensified. "It's *my* life, and you'd be no part of it except for—" He hesitated. "Except for that last sentence in your letter."

He held up the letter I'd sent, punching a withered finger at the words, repeating them aloud: " 'I'm Danny's brother.' " He tossed the letter aside. "Is it true?"

"Yes," I said. "It's true."

"Show me proof," he rasped. "I must be absolutely certain of your identity before we talk."

I reached into an inner pocket of my London Fog topcoat and

took out an 8-by-10 manila envelope. I gave it to him. "Here's your proof."

He opened the envelope with shaking fingers, drawing out the contents. Documents and photos. Leaning closer to the fire, he carefully examined each item. Sherlock Holmes couldn't have done a better job. Then he returned everything to the envelope and handed it to me.

"Well," I said, "do you believe me now?"

The old man scrubbed at his eyes; tears glittered against his cheeks. His voice was a strained whisper: "You're Danny's brother." He raised his veined hands in a helpless gesture. "God, how I loved him!"

"We both did," I said. "Danny was the most important person in my life."

Wainwright paced in front of the stone fireplace. He sighed, a racking sound of anguish. "I haven't spoken his name in all these years. To anyone." Another sigh. "But tonight . . . I *want* to talk about him . . . and about the inhuman devil who killed him."

"That's good," I said, "because I have a lot of questions to ask. No one else can give me the answers I need. Okay?"

Wainwright nodded. "I'll answer anything about Danny."

He poured more brandy into my glass. I didn't mind. Nothing better than brandy on a cold, wet night. Then he sat down next to me again, staring into the fire.

"Let's start with how you became a role model for Nightman," I said quietly. "Before you met my brother."

"You know the story, I'm sure. It was in all the papers back in '43, at the time Danny was—"

"I want to hear it from you, *your* version of what happened. Newspapers get things wrong."

I eased back in the chair with my drink, watching his eyes as he talked.

He had a lot to say.

"It began early in 1938. I'd just turned twenty-five and I was bored with life. This was in New York, and there was a lot of crime in town. All the big cities were seedbeds for crime, just as they are today. You didn't have to look to find it."

He hesitated, gathering his thoughts. I kept watching him, saying nothing. This was what I had come for.

"I was an avid reader of pulp magazines back then," the old man declared. "Four years earlier, in 1934, I'd grown fond of a character called the Black Bat—a crime-fighting hero featured in

Black Bat Detective Magazine. I don't remember who the author was."

"Murray Leinster," I said. "His real name was Will Jenkins."

Wainwright canted his head and a faint smile twisted his lips. "You *do* know the story, don't you?"

"Go ahead."

"So . . . in '38, bored out of my mind, I got this wild idea. Why not rig myself up in a costume and become a genuine crime fighter? With a mask, so nobody would know my real identity. More I thought about the idea, the more excited I got." The old man's eyes shone in the firelight. "Life suddenly took on purpose and meaning. I bought a black Halloween outfit from a costume shop in lower Manhattan, then made myself a cape out of a black silk bed sheet. Then I made a hood, with eyeholes cut into it, to fit over my head. By the time I'd added boots and black gloves and strapped a holstered .45 around my waist, I was something to see. I thought I'd laugh at myself in the mirror, wearing this kind of getup, but I looked menacing. And the gun was loaded—although I didn't plan on shooting anybody."

"And you went crook hunting in that black outfit." It was a statement, not a question.

"Sure did. The first night out I caught two punks robbing a grocery in Queens. When they left that store with the cash, I leaped from the shadows and scared the shit out of them!" A dry chuckle. "Knocked their heads together, tied them up with a length of clothesline and phoned the police. When they got there they found my note pinned to one of the punks."

"Saying what?"

"Note said, 'Courtesy of Nightman!' " Again the chuckle. "It made all the papers the next morning."

"So that started your career as a crime fighter?"

"Sure did. For about three months that year I played this role. Caught me maybe a dozen crooks. That's when the *New York Times* did their editorial on me."

"I remember seeing it," I said. "They condemned you as a vigilante, but applauded the results you were getting."

"That's when Ray Ruric got into it," Wainwright declared. "He'd seen the editorial. Ray was a young artist working in New York, drawing for *Hero Comics* . . . *Carnival Comics* . . . magazines like that. Superman had appeared in *Action Comics* in June of that year and comic-book editors were looking for more superheroes. The field was wide open for new characters. And that's when Ruric got the idea of contacting me."

"But how did he reach you? Your identity wasn't known."

"He did the only thing he *could* do—put an ad in the Personals column of every paper in New York, asking Nightman to contact him. His ad said, 'Confidential. No police.' Gave a phone number—and I answered."

"But why? You were risking arrest."

"I was curious. I wanted to find out who wanted to see me and what was behind it." The old man smiled thinly. "Hell, I was full of ginger in those days. Wasn't afraid of anything or anybody."

"So you and Ruric got together?"

"Right. He came to see me with a writer friend of his, Will Martin. Told me they wanted to use me as the model for a new comic-book character they planned to call Nightman. They wanted details on how I did what I did. Said they'd cut me in on the profits."

"And what did you say?"

"I told them to keep their money. My daddy was rich and he'd left plenty to me. I didn't want cash, I just wanted the kick of seeing a version of myself in the comic books. I said I'd cooperate all the way."

"And you did."

"Right. Showed them how I'd rigged the engine of my car, souped it up for better performance. You need a fast car when you're hunting criminals."

"The Rocket. Did you call it that?"

"No, no . . . that was Ruric's name for the car. With a space-ship on the hood or some other nonsense. I just had a Cadillac, a real fast Cadillac sedan. But it *was* black. Not as easy to spot a black car at night."

"What was next?"

"In the mail I got this copy of the June 1939 issue of *Carnival Comics,* and there he was—'Nightman by Ray Ruric'! " Cape, black hood, and all. Ruric had even used a variant of my name."

"Benjamin Wainwright became Wain Bentley."

"Right. I got a big kick out of the whole thing."

"You left New York that summer, didn't you?"

He nodded. "Moved to California, here to this house. My father willed it to me when he died."

"And where, exactly, did you meet Danny?"

"I used to go to a gym twice a week in downtown San Francisco. On Market Street. To keep myself in real good shape. I'd box and swim and jump rope, do some weights—that sort of thing. Turns out Danny was there, at this same gym. Working out. He was just a kid then.''

"He was thirteen," I said tightly.

"Right. Thirteen. But with a good, firm, muscled body for a kid. He had a copy of *Carnival Comics,* with Nightman in it, and we got to talking. I told him it was based on me, that I was a real-life crime fighter.''

"Did he believe you?''

"Not at first. Not till I showed him some clippings from New York. Kept them in my wallet. That got him real excited and he asked me if I needed any help. Could he join me in fighting criminals? Now, since I'd moved to California, I hadn't done any night fighting, but I'd seen plenty of crime flourishing, especially around the city's Barbary Coast area. So I thought, Sure, I could use some help. Two are more effective than one.''

"The deadly duo.''

He chuckled again. "Right. Well, Danny needed a costume—so we got one together, with a cape and a little domino mask and black tights and a yellow tunic. Had an M sewn onto it.''

"For Moonboy,'' I supplied.

"Exactly. That's the name Danny selected for his mystery identity. I made him swear to keep the whole thing a secret. I remember him asking, 'Can't I even tell Bobby?' And I said that he must tell *no* one. Not if he was serious about wanting to help me fight crime. He gave me his word.''

"And he *kept* it,'' I said. "I never knew about it. Not until—his death.''

"More brandy?'' asked Wainwright.

"No, I've had enough.''

"Then I hope you won't mind . . .'' And he poured another for himself, holding the glass up to allow firelight to play through the brandy's amber depths.

"What happened then . . . after Danny had his costume?''

"We formed a special game plan. Decided to go out only on holiday nights: New Year's Eve, Fourth of July, Halloween, Christmas Eve . . . that sort of thing.''

"Why just holidays?''

"There's much more crime on a holiday. People get careless. Drink too much. That's when they're ripe for criminals. Besides, in San Francisco I wanted to limit my activities somewhat. It isn't as large as New York and I had to maintain a lower profile to keep from being arrested. Our 'Holiday Plan' was the answer.''

"Was Danny good—on the street with you?''

"Absolutely. He was lithe and quick, and used a slingshot to marvelous effect. Knocked down one gunman from twenty yards away, in almost total darkness. And he could fight like a wildcat."

"When did Ray Ruric find out about Danny?"

"We kept in touch by phone. I was giving him tips on the Nightman character. When I told him I had a young associate, he got all excited again—and suddenly Moonboy evolved as a companion for Nightman. They changed his name—from Danny Gregson to Greg Dickson—and he made his debut in *Carnival Comics* in 1940."

"And how did Danny feel about it?"

"He was delighted. Said it made him feel famous in a kind of mysterious way."

Then I reached the heart of our conversation. "I want to know about the Fiend," I said, the words ominous and heavy in the firelit room.

A tense moment of silence from Wainwright. His eyes narrowed; his hands were fisted. "That murderous devil!" he said softly.

"Tell me about him."

"He wasn't real. Not at the start he wasn't," declared Wainwright. "At first he was only a face on a circus poster, a clown's smiling face. But the face was evil, with a twisted smile. Finally I took this poster and sent it to Ray Ruric with a note saying 'If Nightman needs a villain to fight, here he is!' Next thing I knew, the Nightman had an archenemy, a fellow with purple hair and a pointed chin and a satanic smile. And that's how the Fiend was born."

"When did you encounter the real-life character?"

"Not until 1942. On the Fourth of July. Danny was ill and didn't go out on our run that night."

"He had the flu," I said. "Stayed in bed at our place in Oakland. With me taking care of him."

"Well, that was the night I met the Fiend. I was checking a broken window in a large department store in the Marina district when this tall figure lunged at me from the shadows, waving a knife with a really wicked-looking blade. I was astonished to see him because he looked *exactly* like he did in the comic books. Quite fearsome, a horror of a man. I was lucky to escape with my life that night."

"You're telling me that some local crackpot had decided to imitate the comic-book character?"

"Yes. Obviously."

"Let's get to the night Danny was killed: St. Valentine's Day, 1943. I want to hear it from you . . . about how he died."

Wainwright was in his chair by the fire again; now he leaned forward, toward me, as if reaching out for an emotional contact.

"Danny and I were on a stakeout, watching a fur shop we had reason to believe was going to be hit that night. I heard a noise inside the shop. I left Danny in the car, to keep an eye on the front in case someone came out that way, while I went around back."

"And that's when you encountered the Fiend?"

"Exactly. He had a big automatic and he surprised me as I approached the shop's rear door. He jammed that gun into my stomach—and I looked into his painted face, dead white in the moonlight. His carmined lips were pulled back in that devil's smile of his."

"Why didn't he kill you?"

"Because he wanted me to watch him kill Danny. He knew that would be worse than death for me."

"Tell me exactly what happened from that point forward," I said levelly. "Every detail."

"After I'd been gone for ten minutes, Danny got worried and showed up at the rear of the shop. I tried to warn him, started to shout at him, but the Fiend slammed the barrel of the gun across my throat—and I could hardly breathe. Then he leaped past me and began firing at Danny. Three shots. The last bullet drove straight through Danny's heart."

Silence between us. Just the sound of the flames crackling in the hearth; a log fell in a thumping shower of sparks.

"What happened after that?"

"The Fiend vanished, just melted into the night shadows, leaving me alone with Danny. I felt for the pulse at his neck. But there was none. He was dead. I was numb, horrified; I didn't want to go on living without Danny. That's how much I loved him. But I wouldn't give the Fiend the satisfaction of my suicide—so I got Danny's body to the car, drove to the nearest police station and carried him inside. Told them the whole story."

"And that's when it all came out in the papers—about your being the model for Nightman . . . and Danny for Moonboy."

"Yes, I told them everything. The game was over. It ended that night—in Danny's blood."

"Why weren't you arrested?"

"I had committed no crimes."

"You acted as a vigilante. That's a crime."

"They had no direct proof of my having broken the law."

"And the cops believed you when you told them about this murderous creep made up to look like the Fiend?"

"As you know, from the news accounts of that night, there were two witnesses to back up my story. An elderly couple who happened to be passing the fur shop when the shooting took place. They saw the Fiend clearly before they fled."

"Joergans was the name," I recalled.

"Yes, that was it. Mr. and Mrs. Arthur Joergans."

"Why didn't they call the police?"

"Oh, they did. But it took them a while to locate a phone booth. By the time a patrol car got there, I'd driven away with Danny's body."

"And that ended things for you?"

"Yes. I became a recluse. Just shut myself away from the world in this house. I've been here ever since. Here with the memory of that awful night alive in my mind. I've relived that shooting a thousand times!"

"And what became of the Fiend?"

"He disappeared. Vanished utterly. I'd give my life to find him." Wainwright's closed fists were white at the knuckles; he stood facing the fire, staring into the flames, breathing heavily.

"I know where he is," I said.

The old man spun toward me. "Where? Tell me *where!*"

"He's here. Hiding in this house."

Wainwright picked up his heavy black cane. He rifled his gaze toward the doorway, brows drawn across the bright fierceness of his eyes. "By God, lead me to him! I'm an old man now, but I can still destroy the creature that murdered Danny!"

"I think we might do a better job with this," I said, removing a .38 from the pocket of my topcoat.

I walked to the far corner of the library, scanned a row of morocco-bound volumes, pulled the last one free of the shelf. As I did, the entire section swung back, to reveal an inner room.

Wainwright looked astonished. "There . . . all this time," he whispered. "And I never knew!"

"We'll need some light," I said.

He took a copper candle holder from the desk, held it high. The flame cast a hand of wavering light into the hidden room.

I stepped inside, the gun poised, Wainwright beside me.

"He's not here," the old man said.

"Oh yes he is." I moved to a dressing table with a wide mirror above it. On the table: a large leather case. I tapped a finger against it.

Wainwright stared at me.

I nodded toward a chair in front of the table. "Now," I said. "Show him to me."

He sighed, placing the candle on the table. Then he put the cane aside and sat down before the dust-clouded mirror. He opened the leather case, lowered his head, and began a series of quick movements.

When he raised his head again, he wore a garish purple wig and his skin was smeared with clown-white greasepaint, his chin pointed, his nose hooked. Then he smiled: the Fiend's smile. The effect was monstrous.

"How did you know where to find me?" he asked. Even his voice had changed. It was much smoother, deadlier, with a tone of oiled menace behind each word.

I kept the .38 steady in my hand, aimed at his head. "Last month, when I went back to visit the old neighborhood in Oakland, they were tearing up the block, clearing it for a new shopping center. Poking around through the ruins of our house, I found a notebook."

"Ah," said the clown-faced man. "And it belonged to Danny?"

"Yes. It was a kind of diary. In a section near the end of the notebook he wrote of finding a hidden room behind a bookcase in your library. And he wrote about the leather makeup case."

"Then you must understand why he had to die," said the Fiend. "He had discovered *me*. And Wainwright didn't want Danny to know about me. He didn't want anyone to know."

"*You're* Wainwright, damn you!"

"Perhaps," he said softly. "A part of me lives within the old man. But Benjamin Wainwright is a weak, sentimental fool. He still grieves for that worthless boy."

My jaw muscles tightened. "All right, let's play your sick little game. Tell me why Danny continued to come here after discovering the truth about you. Why?"

The reply was tinged with cold contempt. "Because he adored Wainwright, of course. Haven't you figured it out by now . . . about the two of them? They were lovers!"

I was stunned. The words cut at me like jagged stones. It was simply a thing I had never considered—never *allowed* myself to consider.

"You're one sick son of a bitch!" I said.

And I squeezed the trigger of the .38 three times.

It clicked emptily.

The grotesque clown smile stretched wider. "When Wainwright

stumbled against you in the hallway, he managed to pluck the gun from your topcoat pocket. When he slipped it back again, it was empty. Sometimes the old fool is helpful after all."

"I came here to kill you," I said softly. "And I will. Even if I have to do it with my bare hands."

And I went for him.

He twisted away from me, snatching at the heavy black cane. A hiss of metal, as he drew a long-bladed sword from the cane's hollow interior. It glittered, sharp and deadly, in the candlelight.

I took a quick step back from him, my eyes on the length of razored steel.

The Fiend's laugh was chilling. "You should read the comics," he declared. "I first used this sword cane against Nightman in 'Die, Clown, Die!' in 1940. I would have killed him with it, too, but that foul boy intervened." Another peal of bubbling laughter. "But he won't intervene tonight."

And he lunged at me.

I ducked under the descending sweep of steel and kicked over the dressing table. The candle toppled to the floor, igniting the bottom sheet on a mound of faded yellow newspapers. The brittle pages burst instantly into flame.

Taking advantage of the moment, I scrambled through the bookcase door back into the library—with the Fiend right behind me, brandishing his sword. The blade sliced air an inch from my neck as I bent low, closing the fingers of my right hand around an iron fire poker.

"Now, you bastard, this is for Danny!" And, as I straightened, I brought the heavy weapon up in a swift, savage arc, smashing the poker directly across the madman's head.

He screeched like a wounded bird, falling back against one of the antique chairs and dropping the sword to clutch at the bleeding bone-and-gristle ruin of his face.

Then he collapsed with a groan of expelled breath, his loose body spilling along the rug. He lay facedown, unmoving.

I stood over him as a tide of fire spilled into the library from the hidden chamber behind the bookcase.

The entire room was a mass of leaping flame when I walked away from my brother's killer, down the long corridor, across the entry hall, to pause at the outer doorway.

I listened for a long, satisfying moment to the red inferno that was rapidly devouring wood and drapes—and flesh.

"Die, Clown, Die!" I said.

Then I left Wainwright House.

FROM PARTS UNKNOWN

by Edward Wellen

He stood on high, above good and evil. Forethought empowered him to seek out in the night and strike down as with a bolt the one he would destroy. Dominion was his, and wisdom as well.

Wisdom held him from losing himself in the abstract. He balanced the concrete block on the parapet of the Edgeware Street overpass lest the weight—and the wait—cause his arms to quiver. Not luck, but his will, kept anyone from crossing to witness that he stood here. The parkway's strings of lights formed a shooting-gallery frame for the rolling ducks below.

He would know the one when he saw the glowing Mark of the Beast.

Here it came. His mastery of elemental forces told him when to lead the target.

Now.

The plummeting block crashed through the windshield. The car swerved hard right and struck the abutment and came to a crumpled halt.

The parkway policeman, a county cop, went through the driver's wallet while the ambulance attendant plugged blood plasma and oxygen into the shallowly breathing form. The cop scanned the driver's license and looked up swiftly.

"Will he make it?"

The paramedic shrugged. "We'll take him to the hospital, sure, but there's no call to rush. Poor guy's too brain-damaged to be more than broccoli if he lives."

The cop pointed to the license. "See this? Let's get him there fast anyway."

They poured on the siren and got him there fast.

He lay on a gurney. A ventilator kept him breathing, intravenous fluids maintained his blood pressure. The doctor looked at the flat reading on the scope, nodded grimly, and made a phone call. "He's legally brain dead. All activity in brain and brain stem has stopped. He's all yours now."

Day broke as the plane swung to land at LaGuardia. Dan Bowman edged forward to look past his seatmate—fellow in the aluminum-siding line. Bowman made out a toy water tower with the name LAPHAM. On the side of a nearby toy building an arrow of on–off light bulbs, probably showing the way to a shuttered tavern, seemed to aim at the name of the town Bowman headed for. Save a lot of time if he could parachute down.

Now the jet passed over Long Island Sound. First-light edged the silken pull of crosscurrents; Bowman's eyes drank in the weave of waves, swallowed the hundreds of small craft caught in the net of water. The air darkened as the day broke, and by the time they landed and deplaned, rain was falling. Bowman and his seatmate nodded on parting forever.

The siding man grimaced at the silver lines striking and streaking the terminal building's glass. "Rain."

Bowman nodded. "Beautiful, beautiful."

He stood alone in the center of the concourse, letting people swirl around him, creating his own crosscurrents. Here he was. He felt a surge of excitement. He put his carry-on bag down to let his right hand feel the pulse in his left wrist. Strong steady reading, all vital signs go. Grinning tightly, he picked up his bag. Red-eye or not, here I come.

He made for the rent-a-car counter, flashed his credit cards. He locked his carry-on bag in the trunk of the car, studied the road map of the metropolitan area, and imprinted the route numbers to the bedroom community of Lapham.

Fall foliage spread a feast for the eyes. *Smell the flowers.* The honking fools whizzing by, wasted their eyes glaring at him instead of taking in the scenery. A year ago he would have been one with the oblivious rush toward *Please omit flowers.* Now the mindlessness of it saddened him.

Lapham, the Friendly Town. So the welcoming signs said. He put on his friendliest expression and asked the first traffic cop the way to the public library. Something in Bowman's face and voice made the cop look at him hard before pointing the way. In the side mirror—lightly stenciled *Objects in the mirror are nearer than they seem*—Bowman saw the cop stare after the car. Likely couldn't make up his mind whether Bowman was an old crook or an old cop. Bowman smiled his tight smile.

The library stood in the heart of town, just past the shopping mall, as the cop had said. Bowman took note of the people streaming to and from the mall, a curious mix of the well-off and the shabby. Today's main attraction, the marquee said, was a psychic fair.

Bowman found lots of space in the library's parking lot. The library itself proved small but modern.

He stood at the information desk while the librarian gabbed with a patron about knitting. Though they had to be aware he stood there, they avoided eye contact with him and kept him waiting while they chatted. "I have an uncle who does needlepoint," the librarian said, and went on about the uncle who did needlepoint. Bowman looked around, taking in a display of schoolchildren's valentines. Flock of cupids, some cherubic, some grotesque, some a meld. But Eros is Eros is Eros.

Maybe Bowman should have got a haircut, shaved closer, worn his best suit, shined his shoes. Only a year earlier Bowman would've exploded, roaring for all the world—or at least all the library—to hear what the librarian could do with her uncle's needlepoint. Today when he tired of gazing at the valentines and the reading lists of romantic novels and love poetry, he merely cleared his throat.

The patron hurried away, the librarian gave Bowman a tentative smile. "May I help you, sir?"

"I'm looking for a news item about a local man who died in a car crash around here just about a year ago."

The librarian found him the back-copy microfilms and showed him how to use the reading machine. He had to leave his driver's license as pledge for the microfilm.

Corey Urneg's death was more than a mere item. It was a cause célèbre, the rallying point for a drive to have the county dismantle the overpass. Some ten years back, when the county constructed the parkway, which cut through right along the border between Lapham and Ranfield, the county threw a pedestrian bridge across to rejoin them—to give nearby Ranfielders access to Lapham's shopping mall and to provide Laphamites with day workers from Ranfield. Ever since, though, the Edgeware Street overpass had been a source of worry to Laphamites. Lapham was an upper-middle-class village, Ranfield a steadily deteriorating city. Laphamites fell victim to thievery, mugging, and just plain malicious mischief, with the overpass allowing fast getaway into the warrens of Ranfield. The senseless death of Urneg brought matters to a head.

A Loveday Fletcher had the original byline. She set the facts down simply and clearly.

Corey Urneg, fifty, an engineer just returned from a long stay overseas on a construction job, had died at the hands of one of the vandals from Ranfield's blighted area. Those hands had hurled a concrete block down upon Urneg's oncoming Cadillac. Since the crime seemed so motiveless and no one had witnessed it—or come forward claiming to have witnessed it—the perpetrator remained at large. A childless widower, Urneg left behind only his niece, Cora Urneg Gessler, who lived across county in Saxon Heights. Bowman jotted down the name and address and made note of the byline.

That was all the paper had to say about the Urneg case, except as it kept turning up during the mounting controversy over the overpass. Urneg lived on because those gathering names for a petition to dismantle the bridge kept citing his death.

Laphamites split on the issue. Most home owners looked upon the parkway as a moat that would keep undesirables out, most store owners feared loss of trade. But only this month two holdups had taken place, the stickup-man in each case making his getaway across the bridge. Now even the holdout shopkeepers leaned toward doing away with the bridge. An editorial in the *Lapham Courier* asked, "Are we bigots?" and answered, "We think not!" True, with the overpass gone, the long way around to Lapham's shopping center would take Ranfielders the better part of an hour as against the present ten minutes, a hardship for the elderly poor, but Lapham had itself to think of and charity began at home.

Bowman rose with a half smile and handed the microfilm in. He asked to see a map of Lapham. He photocopied the map for fifteen cents on the library's copying machine, then handed the original in and got his driver's license back.

The Edgeware Street overpass stood at the other end of town. That took him by the mall again. He parked near the overpass and stepped onto the pedestrian bridge.

At least the county learned from its mistakes. Take a catapult now to hurl a concrete block onto the highway below. A high screen of new cyclone fence stretched along either parapet, so he couldn't lean over to look straight down. But he saw enough to know how it must have happened, the concrete block balancing right about here before dropping to shatter the windshield of Corey Urneg's car. Bowman stood in perfect stillness for a solid minute, then looked across to the Ranfield side.

Blight, but in patches of raw color that made an interesting abstraction.

He looked back to the green Lapham side, to the colonial-style row of taxpayers. One of the stores was a stationer's. He retraced his steps to Lapham and went into the stationer's.

He bought a clipboard and asked for forms.

The saleswoman stared at him. "What kind of forms?"

"What kinds you got?"

She blinked, then gestured toward a section of shelves.

He pointed at random, found himself buying a sheaf of court reporter forms. "Oh, and a box of chalk."

"What color?"

"What colors you got?"

He took a rainbow assortment. Then he headed back to the overpass. He stopped at his car to drop off most of the chalk and the greater part of the forms. Make interesting notepaper to write letters on. If you had someone to write to. Then he crossed to Ranfield.

The blight was less colorful close up. He could see where landlords had walked away from their property and where they had torched for insurance. What brick buildings remained were almost visibly falling from disrepair into ruin. Graffiti helped hold them together.

He passed a young man carrying a box radio and wearing mirrored sunglasses. Boombox and shades, audiovisual aids to communicate noncommunication.

Bowman spotted loose bricks aplenty in the littered lots. Any Ranfielder out for a bit of fun could have picked up a few to chuck at Charlie from the overpass. But someone bent on malicious mischief had lugged a heavy concrete block.

Pausing every so often to jot a meaningless note on the topmost form in the clipboard and to chalk a meaningless symbol in red on a telephone pole or in blue on a lamppost, Bowman took his survey.

Surprising how many flowerpots flourished on windowsills. Smell the flowers. People with flowerpots were likeliest to have books. Lots of folks, even if they could afford better, would jerry-build bookshelves with concrete blocks and boards. Against that, those very folks were least likely to take up concrete blocks in acts of random violence. No; loose concrete blocks, if here for the taking, reposed in some backyard.

He strode, purposefully, deeper into Ranfield. He paused at each alley to draw a firm fluorescent purple X on the side of one building or the other and ran his gaze up each garbage-strewn dead end in a vain search of loose concrete blocks. He also drew hard stares, and finally a muttered "Pig." At the "Pig" he stopped dead before a building showing better upkeep than most.

A slack-bellied fortyish man enthroned on the stoop glared at

Bowman, the whites of his eyes red-streaked yellows. Two heavy women stood breast to breast just inside the open front door.

Bowman glanced at the building's number, gave a general nod, made a check mark on the form in the clipboard, and headed up the stoop. Might as well try this building. Keep putting it off, could wind up with one harder to get into and out of. Better the devil you know, his father used to say.

He smiled at the man and kept on. The man had to hump himself to one side or get stepped on. The man moved out of Bowman's way. The women stayed put.

One picked up a conversation that had frozen at Bowman's coming. "The doctor say, 'See, I can move your leg up,' and I say, '*You* moving it up ain't got nothing to do with *me* moving it up.' "

"Pardon me, ladies. Got to get in to do my job."

They took their time unblocking the doorway.

"Thank you, ladies."

He made for the stairway, looked up the stairwell into high dimness. Six stories. A year ago he would have said the hell with it.

Behind him, he heard two doors slam, then a whistle sound shrilly. He turned. The man had gone out into the middle of the street to aim his hooked-pinkies whistle up the face of the building. The women had vanished into their flats.

Bowman felt a tightness across his chest. He compressed his mouth and started climbing.

Every flight added its local color, its territorial stains and smells.

By God, he made it to the top without feeling a flutter or having to stop to get his wind.

The door to the roof stood open. He did stop to draw breath, but that was the old need of all life to swell and recharge in the face of danger. He fine-tuned his ears to the roof but heard only silence. He caught a stir of shadows, but that could have been from laundry whipping in the February breeze. He climbed the last flight and stepped out onto the roof. Three men closed in on him.

Bowman's gaze shot to a blanket spread at the base of the parapet. He nodded at the men but locked eyes with none. No sense giving them the stare direct, making this a macho thing. Still, he shifted his grip on the clipboard—held it by a bottom corner, so that if he had to swing it the metal clip would do damage. Before they could move in on him any closer he stepped briskly between two of them.

This seemed to suit them, after their initial surprise. They smiled around at one another and moved to block the doorway.

He gave no sign of alarm, he hoped. He made straight for the parapet. He leaned over and looked down. He had a good view of a half dozen backyards.

A quick scan yielded no loose concrete blocks amid the midden. The sandpaper scrape of a shoe on the rough asphalt roofing pulled him back and turned him. They had started his way.

If they meant business, he would yank the blanket and spill the first to step on it, then he would fling the blanket over the others. That and the clipboard might give him time to reach the stairs.

He gestured at the blanket. "The one who said to use the blanket is taking the other two. Blanket gives a crapshooting artist control of the roll."

All three looked startled, then two turned to the third.

That one scowled. "Honky, you unreal. You know what part of Ranfield you in? Man, you must be doing crack, flying high, to think you can come up here and give us a hard time."

The others joined in. "Yeah. Flying high. Maybe he show us how he spread his wings."

"He ain't no butterfly, neither no bee. We got to give him lift-off."

They moved in. Maybe they meant only to throw a scare into him, maybe they meant business. He gripped the clipbord tightly with one hand and got ready to snatch the blanket with the other hand the instant the man on the left set foot on the blanket.

Under the soft-shoe shuffle of their approach, he thought he caught the sound of someone wheezing up the stairs. This was their turf; whoever came would reinforce them. Likeliest candidate, the man on the stoop, the pig-baiter, the whistler. But till whoever came stepped out onto the roof, Bowman could make use of the climber.

He grinned. "Here comes my partner."

That stopped the three in their tracks. They swung their heads to listen to the labored approach.

Bowman lifted his voice. "Out here on the roof, Mike." He bulled through to the door.

A big hard belly bounced him back. A big hard man followed the belly out onto the roof.

The man mountain peeked through small eyes at Bowman and the three, took in the clipboard and the blanket.

He fixed on Bowman. "I ain't Mike. Who ain't you?"

Bowman smiled. At least he had the four of them expecting a Mike. "Just doing my job."

The man mountain became an active volcano. "Where was you when we needed you? Now we don't need you, you all over the place. We brung this building back by hard work. Fixed it up from top to bottom, inside and out. We got sweat equity in it. We don't need nobody looking for violations so he can stick out his palm for greasing."

"I'm not looking for—"

"Yeah, yeah. I know what you not looking for. What about the garbage?"

Bowman cocked his head. "What about the garbage?"

"You know what I mean. You from city hall, you damn well aware they don't make nowhere near the pickups they do in other parts of Ranfield, much less than what they do in Lapham. Taxation without representation, that's what it is. You go back to city hall and tell them Henry Tice says that. Taxation without representation."

Bowman nodded gravely. "Be glad to go back and tell them, but have to finish here first." He turned and pushed past the three men, breaking up that tableau. "Excuse me." He strode to the far side of the roof, listened behind him but caught no rasp of shoe, leaned forward to peer down into another set of backyards. No loose concrete blocks. He unclipped his pen and made a few ticks on the form, then strode back. "That does it. Now, Mr. Tice, if you'll kindly unplug the doorway . . ."

Tice stared down at him, then earthquaked a laugh. "Right, man, right." Tice backed out of the doorway.

Bowman squeezed by and headed downstairs. Behind him he heard Tice step onto the roof. He heard Tice ask the three men if they didn't remember Henry Tice telling them to use some other roof for their crapshooting. He did not wait to hear the rest.

His heartbeat slowed to normal by the time he crossed to Lapham, but he sat in his car without moving for a moment before turning the key and pressing the starter. Turned *him* on, made colors brighter and the body hum, when oxygen and adrenaline fueled the system. He savored the feeling, then shook himself and got going.

The big wall calendar, featuring a field of daisies, had seen better days, had aged fast. Only February, and the pages were curl-edged from looking ahead to deadlines or days off.

A hum came from elsewhere in the narrow building, but the *Lapham Clarion*'s office held only a young woman at the editor's desk. Nameplate said Loveday Fletcher.

She stopped reading copy and looked over her Ben Franklin glasses to eye Bowman inquiringly and take his measure.

"My name's Dan Bowman."

"What brings you to Lapham, Mr. Bowman?"

A look past him out the storefront window would have shown her his rental car.

"Remember the Urneg case?"

She shook her head, but that was not a no. "His death won't die." She tilted her chin sharply higher to get him in the lenses. "What's your interest in it?"

"Just trying to make sense of a senseless death."

Her nose wrinkled as if she smelled a story. "You a relative?"

He shook his head.

"An old friend?"

"Never knew him. Let's just say I have my reasons."

She frowned. "Let's say I'm busy right now." She glanced at her wristwatch. Her eyes widened. "Damn, it's my lunch hour already." She glared left and right out the window.

"I'll buy you lunch if I can ask you about the Urneg case between bites."

She flushed nicely. "I wasn't angling for that. Matter of fact, I'm half expecting to meet someone for lunch."

"A lunch in the hand is better than half an expect."

He saw the wheels turn behind the eyes: would there be a story here?

She gave him half a smile and kept the other half for herself. "You're on. But we'll have to wait for my relief."

He moved toward a chair over in a corner. "No problem."

The wait proved hardly worth sitting down for. A mustached youth rushed in wiping his mouth with a paper napkin. Fletcher grabbed her purse, cut the youth off at the apologies, skipped introductions, and nodded for Bowman to follow her out.

She had a shape worth watching; Bowman waited till they were on the sidewalk to catch up with her. "My car—"

"We can walk. Not that far."

And her brisk pace made it not that long. She turned in at an antique store. Bowman might have passed the place by without realizing it was also a restaurant. They knew her in there; an antique waitress found them a sheltered table for two and handed them a typed menu.

Bowman's eyes lit on the special. Rabbit stew. *Granddad . . . camp fire . . . pine needles . . . starry night.* "I'll have the rabbit stew."

Fletcher's glance condemned him. "The green salad, please, and the baked potato with sour cream substitute and chives."

The waitress nodded. "And decaf?"

"Check."

"No, I get the check."

The waitress twisted her wrist to point the eraser top of her pencil at him as she left.

Fletcher gazed at the door, on the lookout for the someone she was half expecting.

Bowman grimaced. Too much expecting. Too much waiting. Not enough use of now. "What kind of guy was Corey Urneg?"

She faced him with a small frown and looked back into her mind. "Like my story said. Childless widower. Construction engineer. Just back from a long stay on a big project."

Food interrupted.

Fletcher watched him dip his spoon in the bowl and waited till he had raised the laden spoon to his mouth. "How can you eat that?"

He eyed her over the spoonful of that. He was supposed to think of the Easter Bunny and Peter Rabbit, picture some floppy-eared cottontail with big soft eyes. "It's fair to eat anything that eats anything else."

That held her long enough for him to taste and swallow the stew. The rabbit meat was stringy and bland, but he didn't let the letdown show.

She stabbed her greens. "That's right, enjoy it."

"Thanks."

"By that reasoning, it's fair to kill anyone who kills." She tossed her hair back.

"You got it."

She twisted her fork in the green salad savagely. He caught himself smiling. A bleeding-heart do-gooder. Yet human enough to have blind spots and double standards. There was that "Are we bigots? We think not!" editorial.

Business with pleasure. "Is there anything you can tell me about Urneg that might not have got in the paper?"

She said, "I've kept my notes at home ever since cops started raiding newspaper offices. I'm pretty sure there's nothing I can add to the newspaper account, but you're welcome to stop by my place later. I knock off at four-thirty." She fished her pen out of her purse and scribbled her address on a scrap of paper. "Just give me time to shower and change."

He read the scribbling: 79 Middlebury Drive, 5C. The *i*'s had haloes. "Thanks. Maybe you can tell me the name of a nearby motel."

She peered past the foliage on her fork. "Planning to stay in these parts long?"

He shrugged. "How long depends on how soon I can clear up this Urneg thing. Overnight, at least."

The weighted fork pulled her hand down. " 'Clear up this Urneg thing'? What makes you think you can come here and do in a few days or less what the local fuzz couldn't in a year?"

"I don't know that I can. But I have to give it my best shot."

"I wish you luck. The *Courier* could use the story. About a motel: Lapham zoning forbids motels. Nearest one I know of is at the other end of Ranfield, on the Post Road—the Post Road Motor Inn."

"Thanks."

She had finished eating and was looking at her watch. Okay with him; he had eaten more than enough rabbit stew to make his point. He got the waitress's attention and the tab. He paid by credit card and left a cash tip.

He matched stride with Fletcher back as far as his car. They said their so-longs. He stood by his car watching as she went into the *Courier* office. She didn't look back.

He turned the key in the ignition but sat revving up his mind. Where to now? Urneg's niece's. Phone ahead? No. Always better to catch people off guard. Besides, setting up appointments could be as wasteful of time and effort as taking the chance of finding someone in. He unfolded the area map. Saxon Heights was *there;* Post Road Inn would be on the way. He refolded the map and got rolling.

The Post Road Motor Inn had as its sign a silhouette mailcoach-and-four, and the numbers of the individual rooms were on cutout posthorns, but that was as far as the motif went. He brought his carry-on in, stayed only long enough to take a leak, brush his teeth, and freshen his shave, then got rolling again.

He located the cloverleaf that put him on the parkway. He felt a slight twinge when he found himself passing under the Edgeware Street overpass. He drove across county to the Saxon Heights address he had jotted down in the library.

* * *

A modest house in a modest neighborhood. No curtains. A realtor's sign on the modest lawn. The house on the right had curtains and one curtain twitched.

Bowman got out of the car and shoved his hands in his pockets and studied the empty house and then strolled around to the modest backyard. Twitchy curtains followed his progress.

Vestiges of a modest garden. But what really caught his eye was a row of loosely set, unevenly spaced, frost-heaved concrete blocks that edged the property on what he took to be the Gessler side of the line. He pulled his hands out of his pockets and knelt to upend a block and look at the bottom.

A competent lab technician could get a chemical fix on the soil that clogged the block's pores, on the leachings that stained the concrete, and on the composition of the block itself. But it would be expecting too much of the police investigators to hope that they had collected and analyzed and preserved the fragments of the concrete block that had landed on Corey Urneg's car.

Bowman knew the block that had killed Urneg would match these blocks. But knowing was not proving.

He let the block fall back into place and straightened. He gave a last look around, then made for the front walk and the house next door.

The woman who answered the doorbell had a fine head of pink rollers. "Good afternoon?"

"Good afternoon, ma'am. Would you happen to know where the folks next door moved to?"

"The Gesslers?" Her face pinched. "Can't say I'm sorry they moved. Him mostly. She was nice enough, though she changed near the end and we had nothing to do with each other, but even before that on account of him I gave up going to her for my perms." She patted her curlers. "Been doing them myself."

"He gave you trouble?"

"I never trusted him because of his eyes." She shivered. "But I tried to be a good neighbor on her account. Him, though, he not only gave me trouble—when he tried to move the property line and I licked him in court he put the evil eye on my garden so all my mums wilted—he gave her trouble."

"Oh?"

"Over the daily."

Bowman frowned in puzzlement. "The newspaper?"

"No, the *daily*. The young black woman from Ranfield who came in to clean and wash. Mrs. G. thought Mr. G. got too friendly with the woman and made him fire her." Her chin thrust forward. "I couldn't help hearing the Gesslers argue about it; they got really loud." She shook her head. "Can you imagine? Him giving her cause to be jealous over one of those people from Ranfield?"

"Was the young woman pretty?"

She eyed him hostilely. "I suppose you could call her pretty. I never really noticed."

"Not that it should make a difference, of course."

The ambiguity mollified her. "Of course." She threw the weight of her rollers to one side. "Are you thinking of buying?"

"Thinking." He smiled a neighborly smile.

She glanced at his car. "Your wife's not with you?"

"Lost my wife three years ago."

"Oh. Sorry." She patted her rollers. "I know what that is; I lost my George five—no, six—years ago last December."

"Too bad."

"Yes, but life has to go on."

"True, true."

She gave him a measuring look. "You put me in mind of George. Big like him. And rough—on the outside."

"Yes, well . . ."

"You from around here?"

"No, from out of state." He caught her eyeing the car's plate. She wasn't as sharp as Fletcher and didn't spot the rental ID. "Rented car. Staying at the Post Road Motor Inn. My name's Don Bowman."

Her face cleared. "How do you do. I'm Ann Lindsay."

"Nice meeting you, Mrs. Lindsay. About the Gesslers . . ."

"Oh, the Gesslers. They moved into her uncle's house in Lapham she inherited, so they put this one on the market. But you don't need to deal with them; there's a realtor's sign on the lawn."

He looked. "So there is. Thank you."

"Don't mention it"—she cocked her head—"neighbor."

With a nod and a smile Bowman left and headed back to Lapham.

The smile hardened. He stopped once to find a pay phone with a directory, but used the directory only to look up the Gesslers' new address. Ann Lindsay was right. It was the same Lapham address he had for the late Corey Urneg.

Bowman drove past the place slowly. So this was where Corey Urneg had lived when not abroad supervising one of his firm's big construction jobs. To Bowman it looked Moorish—Morocco rococo, he'd style it, though it had to have some other name. Anyway, the Gesslers now had a lot more room indoors and outdoors than at the Saxon Heights house. This house had bright new curtains, but no cars in the driveway or any other sign of someone at home.

He wound his way out of the serpentine drives of the residential area and into the business district and stopped again at the same traffic cop to ask the way to police headquarters. This time the cop's gaze softened slightly, but the cop still stared after the car.

Police headquarters was in city hall as the cop said. Bowman identified himself at the desk and stated an interest in the Urneg case. Tom Wilkes, the detective who had handled the case, was in and swiveled around to look at Bowman through the open doorway, but swiveled back and pecked away at a typewriter to finish a report or just to keep Bowman waiting. When he was ready, he swiveled around again and beckoned Bowman in.

He didn't offer to shake hands, but nodded Bowman to a chair. "I have to tell you I don't much care for rent-a-cops."

Bowman spoke mildly. "I'm a private investigator. One day, by regulation, fate, or choice, you'll be off the force—and you might find you're not ready for a rocking chair. Why not keep your options and your mind open?"

Wilkes flushed slightly. A slight shift in position suggested a slight change of heart. His tone softened to a finer grade of sandpaper. "The Urneg case, hey? Does the identity of your client have any bearing on the case?"

Bowman shook his head.

Wilkes narrowed his already-narrow eyes shrewdly. "Insurance company, I'd guess. Or lawyer for the, what's their name, the Gesslers." He shrugged. "It's the county that's on the hook if there's a suit for negligence. Tricky jurisdiction. County highway running along the dividing line between Lapham and Ranfield. The perp stood on the half of the overpass Lapham is supposed to patrol and dropped the block from there. That's the only reason any of it lands in our lap. Technically the case stays open for the county and for us, and I suppose for Ranfield though Ranfield was no big help, till one of us finds the perp. Pragmatically . . ." He shrugged again. "As far as I'm concerned it ends as indeterminately as it began."

"Did you or the county save the concrete block that smashed into Mr. Urneg's car?"

"You mean the pieces. What for?"

"Evidence."

An explosive laugh came out of Wilkes's unchanged face. "You ought to know better than to expect anybody to raise fingerprints off anything like that."

"Yeah, I should." But then Bowman mentioned that such things as embedded soil, acquired organic and inorganic stains, and composition of the block itself could help tag the block and maybe match it to other blocks at the Gesslers' property in Saxon Heights.

Wilkes flushed again and his eyes bored black holes into space and his mouth tightened. He swung back around to his desk and stabbed touch-tone keys.

He spoke with a county investigator openly and Bowman listened openly, so Bowman knew as soon as Wilkes that the county had not thought to save the fragments of the concrete block.

Bowman raised a finger for Wilkes to hold the line a minute. "What about the car?"

Turned out that the car, ownership of which went to Mrs. Gessler, was fit only for the wrecker's yard.

Wilkes was again ready to hang up but Bowman again raised a finger.

"What wrecker's yard?"

They went there in Wilkes's car.

They returned with Wilkes glumly triumphant. "Told you it would be stripped for parts, with nothing left to take soil particles off of or concrete fragments out of."

Bowman sat slumped. "But we had to try."

Wilkes shot a sidewise glance. "Yeah. We had to try."

He let Bowman out at police headquarters next to Bowman's car. "Best I can tell you is we'll keep the Gesslers in mind, and if we ever bust them for anything . . ." He shook Bowman's hand. "But don't set your heart on that."

Bowman smiled the tight smile. "No, I won't set my heart on that."

Bowman found a parking space near 79 Middlebury Drive. He identified himself on the intercom and Loveday Fletcher buzzed the downstairs door open.

Still toweling her hair, she let him in. She wore a robe, but it was not loose; it outlined her firmly. She raised an eyebrow and took the bottle of champagne he had stopped to buy. She did not squeal with delight but she did not gnash her teeth. " 'Candy is dandy, but liquor is quicker'? I'd better go chill this in the fridge right away." But she stood watching him look around at the macramé-hung garden that made the place an overhead obstacle course. " 'What nitwit knotted these whatnots?' " Most likely she said that to every first-time caller.

"Very nice." Most likely what every first-time caller replied.

She smiled. She left the room with the bottle and came back with a file folder. "This has my notes for the story. And shots the *Courier* bought but didn't use. A free-lance photographer took them after Urneg was out of the car and on the way to the hospital."

He found pages torn from a small spiral-bound pad; the scrawls at first skim told him no more than the news item he had read. The three Polaroids, however, made his heart leap. They were in color, front and side views of a wrecked Cadillac. The front view, through the windshield gap, was the one.

The blood spattered on the upholstery gave him a twinge but the concrete chunk on the seat showed him just what he wanted to see.

He was not jumping up and down, he felt only a glow of satisfaction, but she said, "Hey, you're excited. What is that picture telling you?" She came around to look over his shoulder.

He felt another stir at her closeness and her breath in his ear, but if she read this as an excitement too, she held her tongue.

"It's the fragment of the concrete block. See the specks of soil and the stain along this edge?"

"I see. So?"

He told her about the row of concrete blocks along the property line at the Gesslers' Saxon Heights house.

"That's great!" But then she looked at his face. "You were up, now you're down. What's wrong."

"This convinces me Gessler did it, but the picture of the chunk would never hold up in court. Need the chunk itself—and the investigators failed to save it." He stared at the shot. "Even if we got the same photographer and had him use exactly the same kind of film for shots of the concrete blocks at the Gesslers' old house, that would never be admitted as evidence. Too many variables— different lot of film, different lighting conditions, different date."

"But Gessler might not know that."

"There's that. But I have to know a lot more about Gessler before I confront him." Bowman reached for the file. "What else you got in here?"

Fletcher started to pull the folder back, then handed it over.

Bowman found scrawled notes. Once again there was closeness and breathing in his ear as Fletcher had to peer through her half-glasses to translate her scrawls.

Upon moving to her uncle's house in Lapham, Cora Urneg Gessler had given up her beauty salon in Saxon Heights and leased a shop in the Lapham mall. "She changed her emphasis and her clientele. She specializes in nails. No more hairdos. Though she does sell a wrinkle cream she says she formulated for herself. And I have to say she looks much younger than the forty-nine she admits to. I've never seen such smooth skin. Karl Gessler was strange too. His eyes." Fletcher shivered. "I can't explain, but when you meet him you'll see what I mean. People claim for him that he performs surgery—in quotes—with his bare hands."

Click.

"A psychic." Bowman eyed Fletcher. "Would he be at the psychic fair in the mall?"

"One way to find out is to find out. It's on all this week. Meet you there tomorrow at 1:00 P.M.?"

"It's a date." He handed the folder back and got up to go. "Meanwhile I have a sidebar for you."

"On what?"

"Garbage."

"What?"

"Garbage collection in Ranfield."

"This is Lapham. What has garbage collection in Ranfield to do with Lapham?"

"Everything. Wouldn't there be less friction if Ranfielders didn't see Lapham as an enclave of privilege and exclusivity? Are they bigots? We think yes!"

Fletcher looked at him over her lenses. She flushed. "You saying the *Courier* owes Ranfield another editorial?"

"You laid Mr. Urneg's death on Ranfield and urged tearing down the overpass. How about doing one on building bridges?"

Henry Tice looked up from the carbon of the editorial Fletcher had typed before Bowman left her apartment. "You say this going to be in tomorrow's *Courier*?"

Bowman nodded. "Maybe the point about taxation without representation will shame Ranfield city hall into better garbage removal."

"Maybe, maybe not. Leastways, it's a start." Tice regarded Bowman. They had the stoop to themselves. "You ain't from Ranfield city hall. You ain't from Ranfield. Where is you comin' from?"

Bowman gestured vaguely. "I'm looking into the death of Mr. Urneg."

Tice drew himself up. "Why should I help you?"

"They've been trying to pin the death on someone from this neighborhood. I think the real killer is someone in Lapham."

"You got a name?"

"Karl Gessler."

Tice shook his head. "Never heard of the gentleman."

"Mr. Urneg's nephew by marriage."

Tice smiled. "Everything always comes down to money, don't it? Even this race thing." He shook his head again. "What makes you think I could help you if I wanted to?"

"A young woman from this neighborhood worked for the Gesslers while they lived in Saxon Heights. She might have heard something or seen something."

"I'll ask around. But why should she stick her neck out?"

"There's a C-note in it for her."

"Money sings, all right." Tice grinned. "What's in it for me?"

Bowman held up a twenty.

He thought at first that Tice was giving him the finger.

But Tice was displaying the ring on the finger. "Everything rolled into one. A spade with a diamond ring on a club finger that shows a heart problem." Tice took the twenty.

Bowman got up to go. "Take it easy."

"Yeah, I'll do that next time around."

The soft pounding wakened Bowman out of a dream about a lovely woman without mercy who demanded of her suitors their living beating hearts as valentines.

The pounding was not the beating of a heart but the knocking of a soft fist on the door.

He determined the time with one eye: 7:00 A.M. Who would be getting him up at 7:00 A.M.? "One minute." Bowman threw the covers off and swung around and erect and put on his robe. He padded to the door, holding the robe closed with one hand and finger-combing his hair with the other hand.

He opened the door on a thirtyish light brown woman with cornrow hair. She wore a maid's uniform and at first he took her for a worker here at the motel, though she carried no sheets or towels or dusting cloth. Then he knew who she must be.

His robe had fallen open and the woman stared at the scar on his chest.

He broke the spell. "Henry Tice sent you?"

"I'm Yevon Bowzer. My aunt heard Henry was asking about the woman who used to work for the Gesslers. My aunt phoned me, I phoned Henry. Henry told me where you were and what you wanted to ask me about, and here I am. Henry said something about one hundred dollars.''

''That's right.'' He stepped back. ''Come on in.''

She stayed by the open door. ''I'm fine here.''

He didn't blame her. He knew if he looked in the mirror he wouldn't trust himself either. He got his wallet out of the toe of his shoe and a hundred-dollar bill out of the wallet. He handed her the bill.

She glanced at the bill and folded it into the pocket of her smock. ''Can't stay long: got to get to my job. What do you want to know?''

''I want to know how the Gesslers felt about Mrs. Gessler's uncle.''

''Mr. Urneg? The man who died when somebody chucked a rock at his car?''

''A concrete block.''

''Was that it? Why, they both felt very bad when they heard what happened.''

''No, I mean before he died. Did they ever talk about him in your hearing?''

She thought back. ''Whenever Mrs. Gessler got a letter from Mr. Urneg from one of those faraway places, Mr. Gessler asked her to save him the stamps. He said Uncle Corey was making him a nice little collection.''

''That's it? No talk about the money and property Mrs. Gessler would inherit when Mr. Urneg died?''

''Can't say I heard a word about that kind of thing.''

''Why did you leave?''

A sudden smile broke up the smooth face. ''You been talking to that Mrs. Lindsay? Well, it didn't happen any way near like what she might say.''

''What might she say?''

''That Mr. Gessler and me fooled around.''

''Then how might she have got the notion?''

''Well, it was true that Mrs. Gessler was jealous. Is jealous. But Mrs. Gessler is jealous of every woman Mr. Gessler looks at—the women who consult him, the women at the places where he shops and eats, any woman he has anything to do with. And I was right there and Mrs. Gessler just naturally took every nice thing Mr. Gessler said to me the wrong way. I guess I could've stood it a while longer, but the bus line dropped a few buses from its schedule on the Ranfield–Saxon Heights route and it got to be too much of a hassle getting there on time, so I up and found me another job and quit. Reminds me I better be going if I expect to catch *this* bus.''

"Give me a chance to dress and I'll drive you. We can finish our talk on the way."

But she was already backing out. "We done finished." And before he could say more she was gone.

He told Loveday Fletcher about Yevon Bowzer. He and Fletcher were having coffee at a restaurant in the lower level of the Lapham mall.

Fletcher looked thoughtful. "I could always get the blahs and have to change something. Make an appointment with Cora Gessler and start talking about maids while she worked on my nails."

"Claws."

She glared at him. "It wouldn't be gossip for the sake of gossip. I'd be— Why are you shaking your head?"

"Keep your eye on the ball. The crystal ball, in this case, if Karl Gessler uses one. He's the one I want."

She looked at her watch. "Okay. I guess they're set up by now. Let's go."

They rode the escalator to the mezzanine. In among the mall's manicured little jungles, the psychics had their chairs and tables unfolded and were already in consultation with clients. Or— Bowman smiled to himself—with shills. Whatever, a hover of sheepish believers waited their turn.

"He's here," Fletcher whispered.

"Don't tell me," Bowman said. He surveyed the mix of palmists, numerologists, astrologers, and just plain tarot-pack fortune-tellers. "Let me tell you. The guy on the right in the first row."

"That's the one."

Had to be. Fletcher and Lindsay had spoken of the man's eyes. As the man looked up for a moment, his gaze swept past Bowman, and Bowman could almost believe that those eyes had the ability to pick one car out of thousands streaming past in the night. Gessler's foreknowledge that Mr. Urneg would be driving under the Edgeware Street overpass at that hour seemed a less mysterious matter: the engineer would have phoned his niece to say he was coming to see her and her husband, now that he had returned from his long stay abroad. But the eyes seemed eyes that might well wilt mums.

The man had no obvious gimmick, just spoke softly in a low vibrant voice that carried past his table only as a mesmerizing hum.

By a strange coincidence, he imagined Gessler would say, Gessler just happened to sit facing the PnailPhile.

The PnailPhile, as the painted-nail pennons of the *P*'s whimsically signified, offered nail and tip sculpturing, nail extensions, nail wrapping, manicures, and whirlpool pedicures. The display window featured an array of nail polish bottles.

Bowman's gaze lit on a bottle of fluorescent polish.

That cleared up how Gessler had, without benefit of psychic perception, locked on the target. Dabs of fluorescence on the Cadillac's roof and fenders would have enabled Gessler to pick Mr. Urneg's car out of the stream of traffic. Bowman visualized Gessler stealing onto Mr. Urneg's Lapham property earlier that fatal evening and, a shadow among shadows, daubing spots of fluorescent polish on the Cadillac parked alongside the Morocco rococo house.

"I'm getting in line."

Before Bowman could snap to and take that in, Fletcher had moved too near Gessler's table for Bowman to draw her away without drawing Gessler's attention.

Shaking his head, Bowman returned his scrutiny to the PnailPhile. Someone was rearranging the window display. A woman with long blond hair and smooth white skin and huge dark glasses moved bottles of concealing cream and wrinkle lotion behind the bottles of nail polish. She had to be her own best ad for the wrinkle cream someone had told him Cora Gessler whipped up.

Some of Gessler's clients must have been among Mrs. Gessler's. Cora Gessler would have picked up gossip by and about them. She was in a position to tip her psychic mate off to bits of information about the clients. A new client sat down. Gessler's eyes went casually to the PnailPhile. Bowman's gaze shot there.

The woman put a bottle of concealing cream to the fore; she paused to light a cigarette, then, gracefully as a gesture of salaam, her hand touched her neck and descended to sweep out palm down at her waist.

That translated as: the dame got a burn on her neck when she was waist high.

As he watched her, she turned his way. Why did it seem to him that she recognized him? It could have been simple startlement. At any rate, she turned quickly away and pulled back from the window into the dim recesses of her shop.

His gaze shot to Gessler's table. The client's hand had gone to her throat. Fletcher, up to bat next, looked impressed.

Bowman looked for the blond woman in the PnailPhile to appear again when Fletcher sat down, but the woman did not show. A frown briefly darkened Gessler's brow. Then he bent his gaze on Fletcher.

Bowman felt an unaccountable chill.

Bowman let Fletcher walk around a bend before he caught up with her.

"Well?"

"He's sharp. He knew right away that I wasn't there for a reading. He even knew I'm with the *Courier*, though I wasn't the reporter who interviewed him at the time of Urneg's death."

"That's easy enough. There's the little cut of your face on the editorial page."

"Anyway, he asked me what I really wanted."

"And how did you answer?"

"I asked him if he had used his psychic abilities to help the police find his uncle-in-law's killer."

"And?"

"And when he said that he had tried on his own but could not get a clear enough picture, I told him I had a clear picture of the concrete block that killed Urneg if that would help."

Bowman's heart misbeat. "That was dumb."

She looked angrier than hurt. "Why dumb?"

"If he killed Mr. Urneg, he'd kill you to cover it up."

She waved that away airily. "Oh, is that all. Anyway, he said that was most interesting and might well be worth following up. So I told him he could see the photo at my place tonight."

"Now, that was really dumb."

"You mean you're not able to be there, close by?"

"Oh. Sure. That's different."

"I'm not *that* dumb."

"I didn't say *you* were dumb. Smart people do dumb things."

"You look like you can handle him. Or is that a dumb assumption?"

"I can handle him."

"Well, let's just hope you don't do something dumb."

Bowman grinned. "On that note of mutual confidence . . ."

Bowman got up from the couch in the sitting room and went into the bedroom at Fletcher's beck.

She stood at the window and pointed down through the gauze of the curtain.

A foreshortened Gessler got out of a car parked across the street and headed their way. He stopped short, almost as though he were aware of them, and they drew back. But the cant of his head and the twist of his trunk said that someone had called to him from the car. He turned and walked back to the car. The blond leaned out to hand him a package.

A big red beribboned cardboard heart.

Fletcher giggled. "How tacky. He comes bearing a box of chocolates for Valentine's Day."

Bowman shook his head. Fletcher would be wise to take Gessler seriously. "Better test them for poison before you eat them."

Fletcher stared at Bowman. "You really think he'd do that?"

Bowman shrugged. "If he thinks you're a threat, poisoned candy is dandy."

She shivered. "I'm glad you're here. But get out of sight." She took a key from the dresser drawer and unlocked the closet door. She swung the door out and gestured him in, but then raised a hand to halt him before he started. She kicked off her flats and stepped into a pair of spiked heels she grabbed from the closet floor. She wobbled a moment seating her feet and held on to Bowman.

It was a nice moment, too soon over.

"I don't usually wear these indoors because they dent the parquet and the linoleum, but just in case I have to stomp his instep—"

The intercom rang.

"Get in."

Bowman hesitated. His stepfather had locked him in the closet and told him not to stir or cry or the vacuum cleaner in there with him would swallow him up. Ever since, Bowman had hated confined spaces. He looked inside Fletcher's closet. No vacuum cleaner. On a shelf higher than his head stood boxes of file folders and stacks of rubber-banded reporter's notebooks. A clothes-hanger rod ran across under the shelf. Most of the hangers were in use, but he could squeeze in among the dresses and pant suits. There were a few bare wire hangers, and if he stirred he might not get swallowed but he would cause jangling. He grabbed the naked hangers off the rod and put them on the floor in a corner among paired shoes. He looked at the door lock. On the inside the door had a winged turn that worked the catch but had nothing to do with the dead bolt.

Fletcher took the key out of the lock and put it on the dresser next to the Urneg story file folder. "Don't worry, you can't get locked in."

Bowman drew breath, a long one, as though it would have to last him, then stepped into the closet and let Fletcher shut the door on him.

To peep through the keyhole he had to get down on one knee and twist his rump sideways. Could've been worse: it could've been a chimney and he could have had santaclaustrophobia.

He watched Fletcher run spikily to buzz Gessler in. Bowman and Fletcher stayed so still that Bowman could hear the elevator go down and come up.

Then he heard Fletcher let Gessler in.

"For me? How thoughtful. Come right in. Have a seat on the couch. Can I get you anything?"

"Just the photo, if you please."

"Of course. But first I'd like to know how you work with something like that. Does it give you visions? Put you in touch with the scene it depicts?"

"Get the photo and I'll show you."

"All right. No, don't get up; you needn't come with me, I'll—"

But Gessler followed her into the bedroom. Bowman saw her enter carrying the heart-box and saw Gessler hard on her spike heels.

"You know, Miss Fletcher, we've met before."

She turned to face him, holding the box to her breast almost as a shield. "You mean before this afternoon in the mall?"

"Much before."

"I'm afraid I don't—"

"I recognize you from a previous existence. You were Salome."

Fletcher let a few beats pass. "And you?"

His eyes widened. "I am always the same. I do not change from life to life." He spoke with the utter sanity of utter madness.

Fletcher sounded shaken but gamely trying for lightness. "Reincarnation. That might make an interesting piece."

"Reincarnation is merely one aspect of divine power, which is the power to take life as well as to grant life. Put yourself in God's shoes. You see an ant in your path and you know that your foot may squash the ant. What are your options? At the last instant you see that your foot will indeed come down upon the ant, but you do not change stride to miss the ant. Call that: Fate, Doom, Natural Law. At the last instant you close your eyes before you determine whether or not your foot will come down upon the ant and you do not take note of what happens. Call that: Blind Fate. At the last instant you change stride to spare the ant. Call that: Grace, Mercy. At the last instant you see that your foot will indeed miss the ant, and you change stride to squash the ant. Call that: Evil, Malice.'' He paused. ''Do you get the picture? Have you put yourself in God's shoes?'' He paused again. ''Wrong. You can't put yourself in God's shoes. You're the ant.''

While he spoke he had edged nearer the dresser, out of Bowman's line of sight. Going for the folder, Bowman guessed.

When Gessler's hand came back in view it held not the folder but the key, and the key came straight at Bowman's eye.

With the key coming at his eye, Bowman jerked back without thinking to open the door. By the time Bowman recovered, Gessler had turned the key and the dead bolt had snicked into place.

Bowman turned cold inside. Gessler knew Bowman was in the closet.

Gessler was psychic after all.

Don't be dumb. He was just good at picking up cues. He caught Fletcher's nervousness and her too-carefully-not-looking-toward-the-closet. Before that, he caught the cushions on the couch, big-body—dented and body-heated.

Gessler was not psychic but psychotic.

He had left the keyhole unobstructed on purpose. He wanted the man the blond must've told him about, the watcher in the mall, to see what he was doing and to feel helpless and afraid.

''What are you doing?'' Fletcher's voice, trying to keep the panic out of itself. It had all happened so unexpectedly and so matter-of-factly that she was only now taking it in.

''Nothing to worry about.'' Through the keyhole Bowman saw Gessler's hand move as though to pat Fletcher's shoulder. The hand shot to her neck before she could think to use her spike heels.

She slumped and fell to the floor, the red box striking the floor, too, and breaking open to spill foil-wrapped bonbons. Gessler had pressed the carotid, Bowman thought.

Bowman hurled his body at the door.

Gessler glanced impassively at the thudding, then unhurriedly took a roll of tape from his pocket and bound Fletcher's wrists together behind her, stopped her mouth, and bound her ankles together. He lifted her and stretched her on the bed across from the closet in direct line of sight.

Bowman emptied his lungs in a shout. ''Let the woman alone!''

Gessler took his time turning around. He faced the closet gravely, God deigning to notice an ant. ''Or you'll do what? You don't have a gun.'' Easy conclusion. If Bowman had a weapon he damned well would have used it. ''But even if you had one you could not stop me.'' Easy boast. But somehow chilling.

Bowman pressed his back against the closet wall and tried to kick the door. The closet was too narrow to allow him any real leverage.

Could he pick the lock? He felt for the wire hangers down in the corner. Straighten one out—and then what? He didn't know the first thing about picking locks.

He fingered the useless hanger. The shape of it stirred memory. *Granddad . . . camp fire . . . pine needles . . . starry night.* They had got the rabbit with an arrow.

Almost of themselves, his fingers twisted the hook to free it of the spiral grip of the other end. They flexed the wire at the shoulders to break off the straight length. Arrows are arrows are arrows. This was his arrow, hot to the touch at the jagged ends. He stretched out of his stiffness to reach the stacks of rubber-banded notes on the shelf. Good strong quarter-inch width. One was not so strong; it snapped apart at first pull. But he had four good rubber bands. He passed loop through loop to make a foot-long chain of them. He felt the hanging clothing for a wooden hanger and tore off whatever was on the first one he came to. He slipped the end-loops of the rubber-band chain over the ends of the hanger. A bowstring. He took hold of the hanger neck with his left hand and gripped the middle of the bowstring with the other hand and drew the bowstring toward the hook and beyond, testing the stretch, feeling the stored energy. He had his weapon. One end of the arrow was sharper by a tiny jag or two than the other. That sharper end would be the point. Even the blunter end could still pierce a rubber band and hang when it came time to shoot. He tore a strip of cloth off a dress and wrapped it around the bowstring at the center to serve as a slinglike pocket.

He put his eye to the keyhole. What had the bastard been up to meanwhile?

Gessler had fitted on what looked like steel-tipped false fingernails. He had set the two heart-shaped halves of the empty valentine box on the bed beside Fletcher. He now stretched out his talons over Fletcher in some sort of ritualistic gesture, murmured some kind of incantation, and suddenly brought the steel claws raking down Fletcher's body from neck to navel. The talons ribboned her dress.

Gessler looked around toward the closet. He cocked his head as though to catch an outcry.

Bowman did not want to give Gessler the satisfaction, but he did want Gessler to keep thinking him helpless. "You damn lunatic."

Gessler smiled and turned back to Fletcher. He brought his claws to Fletcher's breasts and made a parting gesture with both hands that sent the shreds of dress and slip to either side. This was only the preliminary, to bare the flesh. The next sweep would take the claws deep through the flesh.

Did Gessler mean to tear her heart out and carry it away in the heart-shaped box? For crazy use in his crazy reincarnation mumbo jumbo?

Bowman seated the arrow in the pocket of the bowstring, thrust the shaft through the keyhole, and took as much bowstring pull as he dared. Even all it had might not be enough, but the energy it had now felt like a lot and any more might mean the ruin of it. Now he could not see his target and would have to shoot blindly. But it had to be this way and it had to be now.

Slant it a bit more to the left. He loosed the shaft.

The keyhole served to guide the arrow. The scrape of metal against metal or the rubbery twang: something turned Gessler as the arrow flew. It got him in the throat rather than in the back.

Eye at the keyhole, Bowman watched Gessler arch away from life. The arrow tore loose of its own weight and arterial blood spouted before Gessler's hands could go to his own throat, the talons wrapping around his own neck. He staggered backward out of sight.

Bowman felt around for a spike heel. He held it by the toe and hammered at the door panel at the edge nearer the dresser. The spike heel focused the force; the wood gave.

He made holes in a circle big enough to pass his arm through, knocked out the circle, then reached out and spidered for the key. As he touched it, he heard the apartment door open and high heels walk in. Must be the blond. But how—? Use your head. Gessler must've jammed the downstairs door open and must've managed to punch the apartment door's unlock button when Loveday let him in.

"How's it coming, Karl?"

He had heard that voice before. It froze him now with the icy realization of all it implied.

"Karl?"

He stirred himself to grab the key and bring it near the keyhole, but froze again just before the woman stepped into the bedroom.

The keyhole showed him the blond. She stopped on the threshold. Her mirror shades swung from Loveday on the bed to

the floor where Gessler would be lying just out of Bowman's field
of vision.

She dropped the jerrican of gasoline she carried and ran to
Gessler's body. Bowman could just see the curve of her back as
she knelt.

Quick, before she looked around and noticed that the closet door
had grown an arm. He had trouble lining the key up with the
keyhole.

The scraping and rattling must've drawn the woman's attention.
He heard a screech, then hands grabbed his forearm. It took all his
strength to hold firm against their tug. Teeth dug into his fist as he
twisted the key. He heard the dead bolt slide and he worked the
inner winged turn and as the door gave he pulled his outside arm
in and shoved hard. The swinging door sent the woman sprawling.

He strode over to her and put his fingers in her hair and pulled.
The long blond tresses came loose. He looked down at cornrow
hair and a dark scalp that lacked the concealing cream that whitened
the skin elsewhere. The mirror shades glared at him and she made
a move to gather and spring.

"It's over," he said.

And Yevon Bowzer did not get up. She bowed her head and
wrapped her arms around her knees and sat rocking and moaning.

Even in death Gessler looked scary. You could explain anything
away, and the eerie aura, the subliminal shimmer, might prove to
be phosphorescent dye in Gessler's clothing and luminescent tint in
his skin, and droplets of atropine in the eyes would give them
their strange stare. But Bowman still shivered. Part of the shiver
was for a shameful thought that had just crossed his mind: looking
at it selfishly, he had cause to be grateful to Gessler. He felt
relieved when the M.E.'s people bagged the body and carried it
away.

He glared meaningfully at Wilkes, though, because Loveday
Fletcher, holding her dressing gown tightly about her, could not
help staring in horrified fascination at the plastic evidence bag
Wilkes was absently swinging. The bag held the blond wig, which
Bowman and Wilkes and the M.E. felt pretty sure would prove to
be the hair and scalp of Cora Urneg Gessler. The things people did
for love could be more hateful than the things they did for hate.

Wilkes caught Bowman's look and reddened and put the plastic
bag behind his back. Wilkes surveyed the bloody bedroom as
though taking a mental snapshot to back up the police photographer.

That seemed to satisfy him. But when he turned again to Bowman he frowned. "I still don't know why you came here to stir up the Urneg case. You haven't been working for the insurance company. So who the hell is your client?"

"Me."

"I thought you said you never knew the guy."

"True. I never knew Mr. Urneg and he never knew me."

"Then why . . . ?"

Loveday Fletcher too looked at Bowman and seemed to wait even more curiously than Wilkes for his answer.

Bowman smiled at her. "Mr. Urneg checked the *See Organ Donor Card* box on his driver's license and kept a uniform donor card with it. I have his heart."

RECIPE FOR A HAPPY MARRIAGE

by Nedra Tyre

Today is just not my day.

And it's not even noon.

Maybe it will take a turn for the better.

Anyway, it's foolish to be upset.

That girl from the *Bulletin* who came to interview me a little while ago was nice enough. I just wasn't expecting her. And I surely wasn't expecting Eliza McIntyre to trip into my bedroom early this morning and set her roses down on my bedside table with such an air about her as if I'd broken my foot for the one and only purpose of having her arrive at seven-thirty to bring me a bouquet. She's been coming often enough since I broke my foot, but never before eleven or twelve in the morning.

That young woman from the *Bulletin* sat right down, and before she even smoothed her skirt or crossed her legs she looked straight at me and asked if I had a recipe for a happy marriage. I think she should at least have started off by saying it was a nice day or asking how I felt, especially as it was perfectly obvious that I had a broken foot.

I told her that I certainly didn't have any recipe for a happy marriage, but I'd like to know why I was being asked, and she said it was almost St. Valentine's Day and she had been assigned to write a feature article on love, and since I must know more about love than anybody else in town she and her editor thought that my opinions should have a prominent place in the article.

Her explanation put me more out of sorts than her question. But whatever else I may or may not be, I'm a good-natured woman. I suppose it was my broken foot that made me feel irritable.

At that very moment Eliza's giggle came way up the back stairwell from the kitchen, and it was followed by my husband's laughter, and I heard dishes rattle and pans clank, and all that added fire to my irritability.

The one thing I can't abide, never have been able to stand, is to have somebody in my kitchen. Stay out of my kitchen and my pantry, that's my motto. People always seem to think they're putting things back in the right place, but they never do. How well I remember Aunt Mary Ellen saying she just wanted to make us a cup of tea and to cut some slices of lemon to go with it. I could have made that tea as well as she did, but she wouldn't let me. I couldn't tell a bit of difference between her tea and mine, yet she put my favorite paring knife some place or other and it didn't turn up until eight months later, underneath a stack of cheese graters. That was a good twenty years ago and poor Aunt Mary Ellen has been in her grave for ten, and yet I still think about that paring knife and get uneasy when someone is in my kitchen.

Well, that young woman leaned forward and had an equally dumbfounding question. She asked me just which husband I had now.

I don't look at things—at husbands—like that. So I didn't answer her. I was too aghast. And then again from the kitchen came the sound of Eliza's giggle and Lewis's whoop.

I've known Eliza Moore, now Eliza McIntyre, all my life. In school she was two grades ahead of me from the very beginning, but the way she tells it now she was three grades behind me; but those school records are somewhere, however yellowed and crumbled they may be, and there's no need for Eliza to try to pretend she's younger than I am when she's two years older. Not that it matters. I just don't want her in my kitchen.

That young woman was mistaking my silence. She leaned close as if I were either deaf or a very young child who hadn't paid attention. How many times have you been married? she asked in a very loud voice.

When she put it like that, how could I answer her? Husbands aren't like teacups. I can't count them off and gloat over them the way Cousin Lutie used to stand in front of her china cabinets, saying she had so many of this pattern and so many of that.

For goodness' sake, I had them one at a time, a husband at a time, and perfectly legally. They all just died on me. I couldn't stay the hand of fate. I was always a sod widow—there weren't any grass widows in our family. As Mama said, it runs in our family to be with our husbands till death us do part. The way that girl put her question, it sounded as if I had a whole bunch of husbands at one time like a line of chorus men in a musical show.

I didn't know how to answer her. I lay back on my pillows with not a word to say, as if the cat had run off with my tongue.

It's sheer accident that I ever married to begin with. I didn't want to. Not that I had anything against marriage or had anything else special to do. But Mama talked me into it. Baby, she said, other women look down on women who don't marry. Besides, you don't have any particular talent and Aunt Sallie Mae, for all her talk, may not leave you a penny. I don't think she ever forgave me for not naming you after her, and all her hinting about leaving you her money may just be her spiteful way of getting back at me.

Besides, Mama said, the way she's held on to her money, even if she did leave it to you, there would be so many strings attached you'd have to have a corps of Philadelphia lawyers to read the fine print before you could withdraw as much as a twenty-five-cent piece. If I were you, Baby, Mama said, I'd go and get married. If you don't marry you won't get invited anyplace except as a last resort, when they need somebody at the last minute to keep from having thirteen at table. And it's nice to have somebody to open the door for you and carry your packages. A husband can be handy.

So I married Ray.

Well, Ray and I hadn't been married six months when along came Mama with a handkerchief in her hand and dabbing at her eyes. Baby, she said, the wife is always the last one to know. I've just got to tell you what everyone is talking about. I know how good you are and how lacking in suspicion, but the whole town is buzzing. It's Ray and Marjorie Brown.

Ray was nice and I was fond of him. He called me Lucyhoney, exactly as if it were one word. Sometimes for short he called me Lucyhon. He didn't have much stamina or backbone—how could he when he was the only child and spoiled rotten by his mother and grandma and three maiden aunts?

Baby, Mama said, and her tears had dried and she was now using her handkerchief to fan herself with, don't you be gullible. I can't stand for you to be mistreated or betrayed. Should I go to the rector and tell him to talk to Ray and point out where his duty lies? Or should I ask your Uncle Jonathan to talk to Ray man-to-man?

I said, Mama, it's nobody's fault but my own. For heaven's sake let Ray do what he wants to do. He doesn't need anyone to tell him when he can come and go and what persons he can see. It's his house and he's paying the bills. Besides, his taking up with Marjorie Brown is no discredit to me—she's a lot prettier than I am. I think it's romantic and spunky of Ray. Why, Marjorie Brown is a married woman. Her husband might shoot Ray.

I don't know exactly what it was that cooled Ray down. He was back penitent and sheepeyed, begging forgiveness. I'm proud of you, Ray, I said. Why, until you married me you were so timid you wouldn't have said boo to a goose and here you've been having an illicit affair. I think it's grand. Marjorie Brown's husband might have horsewhipped you.

Ray grinned and said, I really have picked me a wife.

And he never looked at another woman again as long as he lived. Which unfortunately wasn't very long.

I got to thinking about him feeling guilty and apologizing to me, when I was the one to blame—I hadn't done enough for him, and I wanted to do something real nice for him, so I thought of that cake recipe. Except we called it a receipt. It had been in the family for years—centuries, you might say, solemnly handed down from mother to daughter, time out of mind.

And so when that girl asked me whether I had a recipe for a happy marriage I didn't give the receipt a thought. Besides, I'm sure she didn't mean an actual recipe, but some kind of formula like let the husband know he's boss, or some such foolishness.

Anyway, there I was feeling penitent about not giving Ray the attention he should have had so that he was bored enough by me to go out and risk his life at the hands of Marjorie Brown's jealous husband.

So I thought, well, it's the hardest receipt I've ever studied and has more ingredients than I've ever heard of, but it's the least I can do for Ray. So I went here and there to the grocery stores, to drug stores, to apothecaries, to people who said, Good Lord, no, we don't carry that but if you've got to have it try so-and-so, who turned out to be somebody way out in the country that looked at me as if I asked for the element that would turn base metal into gold and finally came back with a little packet and a foolish question as to what on earth I needed that for.

Then I came on back home and began grinding and pounding and mixing and baking and sitting in the kitchen waiting for the mixture to rise. When it was done it was the prettiest thing I had ever baked.

I served it for dessert that night.

Ray began to eat the cake and to savor it and to say extravagant things to me, and when he finished the first slice he said, Lucyhon, may I have another piece, a big one, please.

Why, Ray, it's all yours to eat as you like, I said.

After a while he pushed the plate away and looked at me with a wonderful expression of gratitude on his face and he said, oh, Lucyhoney, I could die happy. And as far as I know he did.

When I tapped on his door the next morning to give him his first cup of coffee and open the shutters and turn on his bathwater he was dead, and there was the sweetest smile on his face.

But that young woman was still looking at me while I had been reminiscing, and she was fluttering her notes and wetting her lips with her tongue like a speaker with lots of things to say. And she sort of bawled out at me as if I were an entire audience whose attention had strayed: Do you think that the way to a man's heart is through his stomach?

Excuse me, young lady, I wanted to say, but I never heard of Cleopatra saying to Mark Antony or any of the others she favored, here, won't you taste some of my potato salad, and I may be wrong because my reading of history is skimpy, but it sounds a little unlikely that Madame de Pompadour ever whispered into the ear of Louis XV, I've baked the nicest casserole for you.

My not answering put the girl off, and I felt that I ought to apologize, yet I couldn't bring myself around to it.

She glanced at her notes to the next question, and was almost beet-red from embarrassment when she asked: Did the financial situation of your husbands ever have anything to do with your marrying them?

I didn't even open my mouth. I was as silent as the tomb. Her questions kept getting more and more irrelevant. And I was getting more stupefied as her eyes kept running up and down her list of questions.

She tried another one: What do you think is the best way to get a husband?

Now that's a question I have never asked myself and about which I have nothing to offer anybody in a St. Valentine's Day article or elsewhere. I have never gone out to *get* a husband. I haven't ever, as that old-fashioned expression has it, set my cap for anybody.

Take Lewis who is this minute in the kitchen giggling with Eliza McIntyre. I certainly did not set out to get him. It was some months after Alton—no, Edward—had died, and people were trying to cheer me up, not that I needed any cheering up. I mean, after all the losses I've sustained, I've become philosophical. But my Cousin Wanda's grandson had an exhibition of paintings. The poor deluded boy isn't talented, not a bit. All the same I bought two of his paintings that are downstairs in the hall closet, shut off from all eyes.

Anyway, at the opening of the exhibition there was Lewis looking all forlorn. He had come because the boy was a distant cousin of his dead wife. Lewis leaped up from a bench when he got a glimpse of me and said, Why, Lucy, I haven't seen you in donkey's years, and we stood there talking while everybody was going ooh and aah over the boy's paintings, and Lewis said he was hungry and I asked him to come on home with me and have a bite to eat.

I fixed a quick supper and Lewis ate like a starving man, and then we sat in the back parlor and talked about this and that, and about midnight he said, Lucy, I don't want to leave. This is the nicest feeling I've ever had, being here with you. I don't mean to be disrespectful to the dead, but there wasn't any love lost between Ramona and me. I'd like to stay on here forever.

Well, after that—after a man's revealed his innermost thoughts to you—you can't just show him the door. Besides, I couldn't put him out because it was beginning to snow, and in a little while the snow turned to sleet. He might have fallen and broken his neck going down the front steps and I'd have had that on my conscience the rest of my life.

Lewis, I said, it seems foolish at this stage of the game for me to worry about my reputation, but thank heaven Cousin Alice came down from Washington for the exhibition and is staying with me, and she can chaperon us until we can make things perfectly legal and aboveboard.

That's how it happened.

You don't plan things like that, I wanted to tell the girl. They happen in spite of you. So it's silly of you to ask me what the best way is to get a husband.

My silence hadn't bothered her a bit. She sort of closed one eye like somebody about to take aim with a rifle and asked: Exactly how many times have you been married?

Well, she had backed up. She was repeating herself. That was practically the same question she had asked me earlier. It had been put a little differently this time, that was all.

I certainly had no intention of telling her the truth, which was that I wasn't exactly sure myself. Sometimes my husbands become a little blurred and blended. Sometimes I have to sit down with pencil and paper and figure it out.

Anyhow, that's certainly no way to look at husbands—the exact number or the exact sequence.

My husbands were an exceptional bunch of men, if I do say so. And fine-looking, too. Even Art, who had a harelip. And they were all good providers. Rich and didn't mind spending their money— not like some rich people. Not that I needed money. Because Aunt Sallie Mae, for all Mama's suspicions, left me hers, and there was nothing spiteful about her stipulations. I could have the money when, as, and how I wanted it.

Anyway, I never have cared about money or what it could buy for me.

There's nothing much I can spend it on for myself. Jewelry doesn't suit me. My fingers are short and stubby and my hands are square—no need to call attention to them by wearing rings. Besides, rings bother me. I like to cook and rings get in the way. Necklaces choke me and earrings pinch. As for fur coats, mink or chinchilla or just plain squirrel—well, I don't like the idea of anything that has lived ending up draped around me.

So money personally means little to me. But it's nice to pass along. Nothing gives me greater pleasure, and there's not a husband of mine who hasn't ended up without having a clinic or a college library or a hospital wing or a research laboratory or something of the sort founded in his honor and named after him. Sometimes I've had to rob Peter to pay Paul. I mean, some of them have left more than others and once in a while I've had to take some of what one left me to pay on the endowment for another. But it all evened itself out.

Except for Buster. There was certainly a nice surplus where Buster was concerned. He lived the shortest time and left me the most money of any of my husbands. For every month I lived with him I inherited a million dollars. Five.

My silent reminiscing like that wasn't helping the girl with her St. Valentine's Day article. If I had been in anybody's house and the hostess was as taciturn as I was, I'd have excused myself and reached for the knob of the front door.

But, if anything, that young lady became even more impertinent.

Have you had a favorite among your husbands? she asked and her tongue flicked out like a snake's.

I was silent even when my husbands asked that question. Sometimes they would show a little jealousy for their predecessors and make unkind remarks. But naturally I did everything in my power to reassure whoever made a disparaging remark about another.

All my husbands have been fine men, I would say in such a case, but I do believe you're the finest of the lot. I said it whether I really thought so or not.

But I had nothing at all to say to that girl on the subject.

Yet if I ever got to the point of being forced to rank my husbands, I guess Luther would be very nearly at the bottom of the list. He was the only teetotaler in the bunch. I hadn't noticed how he felt about drink until after we were married—that's when things you've overlooked during courtship can confront you like a slap in the face. Luther would squirm when wine was served to guests during a meal, and his eyes looked up prayerfully toward heaven when anybody took a second glass. At least he restrained himself to the extent of not saying any word of reproach to a guest, but

Mama said she always expected him to hand around some of those tracts that warn against the pitfalls that lie in wait for drunkards.

Poor man. He was run over by a beer truck.

The irony of it, Mama said. There's a lesson in it for us all. And it was broad daylight, she said, shaking her head, not even dark, so that we can't comfort ourselves that Luther didn't know what hit him.

Not long after Luther's unfortunate accident Matthew appeared—on tiptoe, you might say. He was awfully short and always stretched himself to look taller. He was terribly apologetic about his height. I'd ask you to marry me, Lucy, he said, but all your husbands have been over six feet tall. Height didn't enter into it, I told him, and it wasn't very long before Matthew and I were married.

He seemed to walk on tiptoe and I scrunched down, and still there was an awful gap between us, and he would go on about Napoleon almost conquering the world in spite of being short. I started wearing low-heeled shoes and walking hunched over, and Mama said, For God's sake, Baby, you can push tact too far. You never were beautiful but you had an air about you and no reigning queen ever had a more elegant walk, and here you are slumping. Your Aunt Francine was married to a midget, as you well know, but there wasn't any of this bending down and hunching over. She let him be his height and he let her be hers. So stop this foolishness.

But I couldn't. I still tried literally to meet Matthew more than halfway. And I had this feeling—well, why shouldn't I have it, seeing as how they had all died on me—that Matthew wasn't long for this world, and it was my duty to make him feel as important and as tall as I possibly could during the little time that was left to him.

Matthew died happy. I have every reason to believe it. But then, as Mama said, they all died happy.

Never again, Mama, I said. Never again. I feel like Typhoid Mary or somebody who brings doom on men's heads.

Never is a long time, Mama said.

And she was right. I married Hugh.

I think it was Hugh.

Two things I was proud of and am proud of. I never spoke a harsh word to any one of my husbands and I never did call one of them by another's name, and that took a lot of doing because after a while they just all sort of melted together in my mind.

After every loss, Homer was the greatest solace and comfort to me. Until he retired last year Homer was the Medical Examiner, and he was a childhood friend, though I never saw him except in his line of duty, you might say. It's the law here, and perhaps elsewhere, that if anyone dies unattended or from causes that aren't obvious, the Medical Examiner must be informed.

The first few times I had to call Homer I was chagrined. I felt apologetic, a little like calling the doctor up in the middle of the night when, however much the pain may be troubling you, you're afraid it's a false alarm and the doctor will hold it against you for disturbing his sleep.

But Homer always was jovial when I called him. I guess that's not the right word. Homer was reassuring, not jovial. Anytime, Lucy, anytime at all, he would say when I began to apologize for having to call him.

I think it was right after Sam died. Or was it Carl? It could have been George. Anyway, Homer was there reassuring me as always, and then this look of sorrow or regret clouded his features. It's a damned pity, Lucy, he said, you can't work me in somewhere or other. You weren't the prettiest little girl in the third grade, or the smartest, but damned if from the beginning there hasn't been something about you. I remember, he said, that when we were in the fourth grade I got so worked up over you that I didn't pass a single subject but arithmetic and had to take the whole term over. Of course, you were promoted, so for the rest of my life you've been just out of my reach.

Why, Homer, I said, that's the sweetest thing anybody has ever said to me.

I had it in the back of my mind once the funeral was over and everything was on an even keel again that I'd ask Homer over for supper one night. But it seemed so calculating, as if I was taking him up on that sweet remark he had made about wishing I had worked him in somewhere among my husbands. So I decided against it.

Instead, I married Beau Green.

There they go laughing again—Eliza and Lewis down in the kitchen. *My* kitchen.

It's funny that Eliza has turned up in my kitchen, acting very much at home, when she's the one and only person in this town I never have felt very friendly toward—at least, not since word got to me that she had said I snatched Beau Green right from under her nose.

That wasn't a nice thing for her to say. Besides, there wasn't a word of truth in it. I'd like to see the man that can be snatched from under anybody's nose unless he wanted to be.

Eliza was surely welcome to Beau Green if she had wanted him and if he had wanted her.

Why, I'd planned to take a trip around the world, already had my tickets and reservations, and had to put it off for good because Beau wouldn't budge any farther away from home than to go to Green River—named for his family—to fish. I really wanted to take that cruise—had my heart especially set on seeing the Taj Mahal by moonlight; but Beau kept on saying if I didn't marry him he would do something desperate, which I took to mean he'd kill himself or take to drink. So I canceled all those reservations and turned in all those tickets and married him.

Well, Eliza would certainly have been welcome to Beau.

I've already emphasized that I don't like to rank my husbands, but in many ways Beau was the least satisfactory one I ever had. It was his nature to be a killjoy—he had no sense of the joy of living and once he set his mind on something he went ahead with it, no matter if it pleased anybody else or not.

He knew good and well I didn't care for jewelry. But my preference didn't matter to Beau Green, not one bit. Here he came with this package and I opened it. I tried to muster all my politeness when I saw that it was a diamond. Darling, I said, you're sweet to give me a present, but this is a little bit big, isn't it?

It's thirty-seven carats, he said.

I felt like I ought to take it around on a sofa pillow instead of wearing it, but I did wear it twice and felt as conspicuous and as much of a show-off as if I'd been waving a peacock fan around and about.

It was and is my habit when I get upset with someone to go to my room and write my grievances down and get myself back in a good humor, just as I'm doing now because of that girl's questions; but sometimes it seemed like there wasn't enough paper in the world on which to write down my complaints against Beau.

Then I would blame myself. Beau was just being Beau. Like all God's creatures he was behaving the way he was made, and I felt so guilty that I decided I ought to do something for him to show I really loved and respected him, as deep in my heart I did.

So I decided to make him a cake by that elaborate recipe that had been in our family nobody is sure for how long. I took all one day to do the shopping for it. The next day I got up at five and stayed in the kitchen until late afternoon.

Well, Beau was a bit peckish when it came to eating the cake.
Yet he had the sweetest tooth of any of my husbands.

Listen, darling, I said when he was mulish about eating it, I
made this special for you—it's taken the best part of two days. I
smiled at him and asked wouldn't he please at least taste it to please
me. Really, I was put out when I thought of all the work that had
gone into it. For one terrible second I wished it were a custard pie
and I could throw it right in his face, like in one of those old
Keystone comedies; and then I remembered that we were sworn to
cherish each other, so I just put one arm around his shoulder and
with my free hand I pushed the cake a little closer and said, Belle
wants Beau to eat at least one small bite. Belle was a foolish pet
name he sometimes called me because he thought it was clever for
him to be Beau and for me to be Belle.

He looked sheepish and picked up his fork and I knew he was
trying to please me, the way I had tried to please him by wearing
that thirty-seven-carat diamond twice.

Goodness, Belle, he said, when he swallowed his first mouthful,
this is delicious.

Now, darling, you be careful, I said. That cake is rich.

Best thing I ever ate, he said, and groped around on the plate
for the crumbs, and I said, Darling, wouldn't you like a little coffee
to wash it down?

He didn't answer, just sat there smiling. Then after a little he
said he was feeling numb. I can't feel a thing in my feet, he said.
I ran for the rubbing alcohol and pulled off his shoes and socks and
started rubbing his feet, and there was a sort of spasm and his toes
curled under, but nothing affected that smile on his face.

Homer, I said a little later—because of course I had to telephone
him about Beau's death—what on earth is it? Could it be something
he's eaten? And Homer said, What do you mean, something he's
eaten? Of course not. You set the best table in the county. You're
famous for your cooking. It couldn't be anything he's eaten. Don't
be foolish, Lucy. He began to pat me on the shoulder and he said,
I read a book about guilt and loss and it said the bereaved often
hold themselves responsible for the deaths of their beloved ones.
But I thought you had better sense than that, Lucy.

Homer was a little bit harsh with me that time.

Julius Babb settled Beau's estate. Beau left you a tidy sum all
right, he said, and I wanted to say right back at him but didn't:
Not as tidy as most of the others left me.

Right then that young woman from the *Bulletin* repeated her last
question.

Have you had a favorite among your husbands? Her tone was that of a prosecuting attorney and had nothing to do with a reporter interested in writing about love for St. Valentine's Day.

I had had enough of her and her questions. I dragged myself up to a sitting position in the bed. Listen here, young lady, I said. It looks as if I've gotten off on the wrong foot with you—and then we both laughed at the pun I had made.

The laughter put us both in a good humor and then I tried to explain that I had an unexpected caller downstairs who needed some attention, and that I really was willing to cooperate on the St. Valentine's Day article; but all those questions at first hearing had sort of stunned me. It was like taking an examination and finding all the questions a surprise. I told her if she would leave her list with me I'd mull over it, and she could come back tomorrow and I'd be prepared with my answers and be a little more presentable than I was now, wearing a rumpled wrapper and with my hair uncombed.

Well, she was as sweet as apple pie and handed over the list of questions and said she hoped that ten o'clock tomorrow morning would be fine; and I said, yes, it would.

There goes Eliza's laugh again. It's more of a caw than a laugh. I shouldn't think that. But it's been such a strange day, with that young reporter being here and Eliza showing up so early.

Come to think of it, Eliza has done very well for herself, as far as marrying goes. That reporter should ask Eliza some of those questions.

Mama was a charitable woman all her life and she lived to be eighty-nine, but Eliza always rubbed Mama's skin the wrong way. To tell the truth, Eliza rubbed the skin of all the women in this town the wrong way. It's not right, Baby, Mama said, when other women have skimped and saved and cut corners all their lives and then when they're in their last sickness here comes Eliza getting her foot in the door just because she's a trained nurse. Then the next thing you hear, Eliza has married the widower and gets in one fell swoop what it took the dead wife a lifetime to accumulate.

That wasn't the most generous way in the world for Mama to put it, but I've heard it put much harsher by others. Mrs. Perkerson across the street, for one. Eliza is like a vulture, Mrs. Perkerson said. First she watches the wives die, then she marries, and then she watches the husbands die. Pretty soon it's widow's weeds for Eliza and a nice-sized bank account, not to mention some of the most valuable real estate in town.

Why, Mrs. Perkerson said the last time I saw her, I know that

Lois Eubanks McIntyre is turning in her grave thinking of Eliza inheriting that big estate, with gardens copied after the Villa d'Este. And they tell you nursing is hard work.

I hadn't seen Eliza in some time. We were friendly enough, but not real friends, never had been, and I was especially hurt after hearing what she said about me taking Beau Green away from her. But we would stop and chat when we bumped into each other downtown, and then back off smiling and saying we must get together. But nothing ever came of it.

And then three weeks ago Eliza telephoned and I thought for sure somebody was dead. But, no, she was as sweet as magnolia blossoms and cooing as if we saw each other every day, and she invited me to come by that afternoon for a cup of tea or a glass of sherry. I asked her if there was anything special, and she said she didn't think there had to be any special reason for old friends to meet, but, yes, there was something special. She wanted me to see her gardens—of course, they weren't her gardens, except by default, they were Lois Eubanks McIntyre's gardens—which she had opened for the Church Guild Benefit Tour and I hadn't come. So she wanted me to see them that afternoon.

It was all so sudden that she caught me off guard. I didn't want to go and there wasn't any reason for me to go, but for the life of me I couldn't think of an excuse not to go. And so I went.

The gardens really were beautiful. And I'm crazy about flowers.

Eliza gave me a personally guided tour. There were lots of paths and steep steps and unexpected turnings, and I was so delighted by the flowers that I foolishly didn't pay attention to my footing. I wasn't used to walking on so much gravel or going up and down uneven stone steps and Eliza didn't give me any warning.

Then all of a sudden, it was the strangest feeling, not as if I'd fallen but as if I'd been pushed, and there Eliza was leaning over me saying she could never forgive herself for not telling me about the broken step, and I was to lie right there and not move until the doctor could come, and what a pity it was that what she had wanted to be a treat for me had turned into a tragedy. Which was making a whole lot more out of it than need be because it was only a broken foot—not that it hasn't been inconvenient.

But Eliza has been fluttering around for three weeks saying that I should sue her as she carried liability insurance, and anyway it was lucky she was a nurse and could see that I got devoted attention. I don't need a nurse, but she has insisted on coming every day, and on some days several times; she seems to be popping in and out of the house like a cuckoo clock.

I had better get on with that reporter's questions.

Do you have a recipe for a happy marriage?

I've already told her I don't, and of course there's no such thing as a recipe for a happy marriage; but I could tell her this practice I have of working through my grievances and dissatisfactions by writing down what bothers me and then tearing up what I've written. For all I know it might work for somebody else, too.

I didn't hear Eliza coming up the stairs. It startled me when I looked up and saw her at my bedside. What if she discovered I was writing about her? What if she grabbed the notebook out of my hands and started to read it? There isn't a thing I could do to stop her.

But she just smiled and asked if I was ready for lunch and she hoped I'd worked up a good appetite. How on earth she thinks I could have worked up an appetite by lying in bed I don't know, but that's Eliza for you, and all she had fixed was canned soup and it wasn't hot.

All I wanted was just to blot everything out—that girl's questions, Eliza's presence in my home, my broken foot.

I would have thought that I couldn't have gone to sleep in a thousand years. But I was so drowsy that I couldn't even close the notebook, much less hide it under the covers.

I don't know what woke me up. It was pitch dark, but dark comes so soon these winter days you can't tell whether it's early dark or midnight.

I felt refreshed after my long nap and equal to anything. I was ready to answer any question on that girl's list.

The notebook was still open beside me and I thought that if Eliza had been in here and had seen what I had written about her it served her right.

Then from the kitchen rose a wonderful smell and there was a lot of noise downstairs. Suddenly the back stairway and hall were flooded with light, and then Eliza and Lewis were at my door and they were grinning and saying they had a surprise for me. Then Lewis turned and picked up something from a table in the hall and brought it proudly toward me. I couldn't tell what it was. It was red and heart-shaped and had something white on top. At first I thought it might be a hat, and then I groped for my distance glasses, but even with them on I still couldn't tell what Lewis was carrying.

Lewis held out the tray. It's a St. Valentine's Day cake, he said, and Eliza said, we iced it and decorated it for you; then Lewis tilted it gently and I saw L U C Y in wobbly letters spread all across the top.

I don't usually eat sweets. So their labor of love was lost on me. Then I thought how kind it was that they had gone to all that trouble, and I forgave them for messing up my kitchen and meddling with my recipes—or maybe they had just used a mix. Anyway, I felt I had to show my appreciation, and it certainly wouldn't kill me to eat some of their cake.

They watched me with such pride and delight as I ate the cake that I took a second piece. When I had finished they said it would be best for me to rest, and I asked them to take the cake and eat what they wanted, then wrap it in foil.

And now the whole house is quiet.

I never felt better in my life. I'm smiling a great big contented smile. It must look exactly like that last sweet smile on all my husbands' faces—except Luther, who was run over by a beer truck.

I feel wonderful and so relaxed.

But I can hardly hold this pencil.

Goodness, it's
        f
         a
          l
           l
            i
             n
              g

MY HEART CRIES FOR YOU

by Bill Crider

I met Ethel Ann Adams on Valentine's Day and we met cute, just like in the movies. I was in the flower department at Kroger, thinking I might buy some flowers to send to the woman who'd just ditched me two days before for a man who drove a BMW. I thought maybe she'd feel sorry for me and give me another chance. I don't know. Anyway, I was standing there looking at the roses when Ethel Ann ran into me with her grocery cart.

She didn't knock me far, not more than a foot, and I figured the bruises would go away in a week or two, so I told her not to worry about it. To forget it. I was fine.

If she'd been good-looking, it might've been a different story, but she wasn't the kind of woman I was interested in at all. She was short and chunky, about five-three and 140 pounds. Solid. She had black hair like wires—curly wires, the kind inside a sofa cushion. Those were on her head. Her mustache was black, too, but the hairs weren't curly. They were too short.

She wouldn't leave me alone, though. She acted like she'd done me irreparable harm and it was her duty to make it all right.

"Here, let me help ya," she said. She had a voice like a steve-dore. "I'll pick up ya packages."

She scuttled around like a crab with Saint Vitus's Dance and picked up the cereal box and the granola bars and the Hamburger Helper, then stuffed them back on top of my basket.

"Ya OK now?" she said.

"I'm fine," I said, always the gentleman. "I'll be just fine, thanks."

"Good, good. I'm glad. Ya buying some posies for your chick?"

She really said things like that: Posies. Chick.

"No," I said. "I was thinking of sending some to my mother." My mother had been dead for ten years, but how do you say you were thinking of sending flowers to someone who'd just dumped you?

"Ya got a chick?"

"I beg your pardon?"

"Ya got a chick? A babe? A hotsie-totsie?"

She really said that. Hotsie-totsie.

"No," I said, rather coldly I'm afraid.

133

"A nice-looking hunk like you? All alone on the most romantic day of the year? I can't believe it."

I am rather nice-looking, I have to admit. A slight natural wave in my hair, a nice smile (thanks to extensive orthodontic work in my youth), and a trim body (thanks to a three-times-a-week jog of up to three miles).

"Ya got cute buns too."

Buns. I ask you.

"I betcha wouldn't believe I don't have a fella myself."

"Uh . . ."

"Yeah, I know. Hard to believe. But true." She tried to look wistful, but instead looked only dyspeptic. She had on a horrible pair of knit stretch pants that did nothing to help the effect.

"Look," she said. "Why don't you and me get together? I mean, it's a real shame, two hot numbers like us, all alone on the most important romantic day of the year."

She stood there and looked up at me with her black eyes way back in her head under the heavy ridges of her brows. The brows were black and straight, like her mustache. I had heard of the supermarket as being one of the hot places to meet dates nowadays, but this was too much. Hot numbers. I mean, give me a break.

Still, there I was. Ditched not two days before by the light of my life, who said she thought I lacked ambition and "charisma." I had told *her* that I liked selling shoes, and that you didn't need charisma to do that. She had laughed at me and said she could tell I'd never amount to anything and that she was going to start dating somebody named Chris. "He drives a BMW," she said. "Not a tacky old Subaru." I told her that Subarus had even better repair records than BMWs, but it didn't do any good.

So call it temporary insanity. Call it irresponsible. Or call me a masochist, which is probably more like it. I was punishing myself for losing somebody who liked a car better than she liked me. Anyway, for whatever reason, I looked into Ethel Ann's pitchy black eyes and said, "Why not?"

She told me her name then, and I told her mine, which is Wayne G. (for Garfield, but I never tell anyone that, not since that cat in the comic pages) Cook, and we agreed that she would come by and pick me up later at my apartment.

"I got a nice car," she said. "You'll like it. Plus I like to drive. We'll have a few drinks, tell a few jokes, see what develops."

Then she leered at me, a truly frightening sight, and icy fingers ran up and down my spine. Not the Old Black Magic kind. The kind that you get when you're reading Stephen King on a dark and stormy night, except that she was even scarier . . .

But I'd given my word and that was that. I finished my shopping, without buying any roses, checked out, and went home to get ready.

She arrived right on time, wearing a red skirt with a white blouse that just sort of hung on her flat chest. She had a white envelope in her hand. "Here," she said, sticking the envelope at me. "I got ya a valentine."

I hadn't gotten her one, of course. The thought never even entered my mind, and if it had I would have rejected it instantly. I took the envelope.

"Aren't ya gonna ask me in?" she said.

I opened the door a little wider and she walked through. My living room is nothing to brag about, not being much larger than most people's second bedroom, but it is at least tidy.

She walked over and sat down on the couch while I tore at the envelope. When I got it open, I pulled out the card. It was in the shape of a heart (not a real one, of course, but a valentine one, which has absolutely no relationship to the human heart that I can see) with eyes and a mouth drawn on it. The mouth was turned down in a frown, and there were tiny tears in the corners of the eyes.

I opened the card. Inside it was written in red letters, *My heart cries for you.*

"Cute, huh?" Ethel Ann said.

"Very," I said. I put the card down on my coffee table.

"So where ya wanta go?" she said. "Find a nice spot, hoist a few brewskis?"

Brewskis. Of course.

"I was thinking more along the lines of a movie," I said. The idea of what Ethel Ann might be like after a couple of "brewskis" frankly terrified me.

"Aww ri-i-i-i-ght!" she said. "There's this new one out I've been wanting to see over at the Plaza Town Eight."

"Fine," I said. "What is it?"

"It's a new one for Valentine's Day. *I Eat Your Heart.* It's about these teenagers, see, who have this Valentine's party and this maniac or something—"

"I can't wait," I said.

She was right about one thing, at least. I loved her car. It was a perfectly restored 1957 Chevrolet.

"Original factory paint," she said. "It was a bitch to find the purple, too, believe me."

"I can imagine."

"The white for the top was easy, though. I wanted to go with red, but the guy who did the work wouldn't go for it. Some people got no taste at all."

"Too right," I said.

The movie was worse than I'd thought it might be. It wasn't so much the actual movie, though the sight of entrails and brains and exploding teenage skulls didn't really do much for me. No, the worst thing was the way Ethel Ann behaved.

She belched.

I suppose that could be my fault. After all, I did ask if she wanted something to drink to go with her popcorn (two large tubs, buttered), and carbonated water does that to some people.

She didn't have to do it so often, however. I think some of it must have been deliberate.

Also, she laughed raucously every time some semi-innocent victim lost one of his or her vital body parts or got skewered with a tree limb, broken boat paddle, lug wrench, or whatever.

Everyone else cringed, gagged, or simply looked away. Not Ethel Ann. She brayed like a mule. Or is it donkeys that bray? Well, you get the idea.

And then she . . . there's simply no delicate way to put this, really. She . . . broke wind.

Loudly.

At a time when the audience sat in absolute silence as the maniac crept quietly up on yet another teenage beauty who had thoughtlessly rejected him and who in fact had laughed when he sent her a valentine.

Just as he raised his arms high, prepared to bring the jagged mop handle down into her chest as she lay sleeping on a sofa, just as the quiet in the theater had grown almost unbearable, Ethel Ann broke wind.

It was like a gunshot, but more drawn out, if you understand what I mean.

Heads turned.

Giggles began.

Ethel Ann joined in the giggles, looked at me, and pointed her finger, shaking her head sadly as if to say, "He does that all the time."

The giggles turned to laughter as I tried, without much luck, to melt through the bottom of my seat.

It was, beyond any doubt, the worst evening of my life. I can't recall ever being more repelled or disgusted. People were still giving me surreptitious glances as we left the theater. Then they would look away quickly and laugh, sometimes putting their hands over their mouths as if they didn't want me to see.

Ethel Ann wasn't bothered in the least. "That was great, huh? I don't know when I've seen so much guts on the screen."

I didn't say anything. I just wanted to get home, lock my door, and get away from her. Thank God, I would never have to see her again.

Exactly three months later, Ethel Ann Adams and I were united in what is loosely referred to as holy matrimony.

It was a lovely service, and the bride wore white. She hadn't lost any weight over the intervening months, and she looked a little like a sow stuffed into a wedding gown. Her little piggy eyes watched me from under her veil as we repeated our vows.

I managed not to throw up as I kissed her. The hairs of her little mustache pricked me under my nose.

It all came about because of her brother.

The day after Valentine's, he'd come by my apartment. It was late afternoon, and I'd just gotten in from a hard day of trying to make women's feet fit into shoes that were generally ill made and about a size too small for the feet that were being forced into them.

I wasn't in a good mood, and Ethel Ann's brother didn't cheer me up.

He stood there in my doorway wearing a lavender silk shirt and a pair of jeans so tight that you could see the outlines of certain personal portions of his anatomy. The jeans were bell bottoms, so when he told me that he was Ethel Ann's brother, I wasn't surprised. He didn't mention that he had chosen what we call these days an "alternate life-style," but then, he didn't have to. I could just tell.

His name was Raymond, and I asked him to come in. I didn't know what else to do with him.

"This is such a *sweet* little place," he said, pirouetting around to get a good look at it. "Ethel Ann said that you were charming and handsome, and she certainly didn't exaggerate. She has a tendency to do that, you know." He posed there with one hand on his hip and another in the air. "Is it all right if I sit?"

"Look," I said. "I just got in from work, and I'm not feeling too well. I'm not sure what you want, but if it's about your sister, well, I'm sorry, but I don't really think I want to see her again."

I hoped that was all it was. I hoped that Ethel Ann wasn't a recruiting service for her brother. I didn't feel like fighting him off. I really didn't.

"Oh, my dear boy," he said. "It's not at all what you think, I'm sure. Not at all. Why, you wouldn't be able to guess in a million, trillion years what I want. I'm *sure* you wouldn't."

"Why don't you tell me, then," I said.

"All right, I will, if you insist on rushing me into it. I had hoped that we might discuss the matter in a civilized manner, you know. Not rushing into it like a pair of primitives."

"I'm sorry," I said. "I'm tired, and I need my rest. If you have something to say, please say it."

"Very well. It's simple, really." He waved the hand that was in the air. "I want you to marry Ethel Ann. And then to kill her."

I just looked at him for a second or two. Then I asked him to sit down.

It was all very simple, really. I hadn't realized that Ethel Ann's father was Ronald H. Adams, the richest man in town, an oil millionaire from one of the big booms of the twenties. He was quite old now, and, according to Raymond, on his last legs.

"The old dear is going to kick off any day now" is the way Raymond put it.

As far as Raymond was concerned, that was just fine, since there was no love lost between the two of them, and that was just the problem: Raymond was cut out of the will.

"Almost, dear boy. Al*most*. Should my sweet, ingenuous sister die first, predecease me as they say in the legal offices, then the money goes to me. Not that there is much of a chance of that in the natural order of things. Ethel Ann is as healthy as a horse." He sighed. "Still, there are ways."

"Why me?" I said. "I'm just a shoe salesman. There are professionals for that kind of thing." It wasn't that I had anything against the idea. If ever anyone deserved to go, it was Ethel Ann Adams.

"Oh, *please*," he said. "Are you suggesting that I get some sort of *hit* man? That is so *common*."

Common. Well, he was probably right. I wondered how he and his sister got to be so different. Ethel Ann would have gone to a hit man in a minute. Less, probably.

"Besides, dear boy, don't you read the newspapers? Every single hit man in this city is a policeman working undercover. The last three people who have hired hit men around here have wound up in prison."

"That's right," I said. "Not a nice place. You could get raped in there."

"I didn't say it didn't have its attractive side," he said. "It's just that I don't want to spend my *life* there."

"What about *my* life?"

"It would have to look like an accident, of course. There could be no question of your involvement. No hint of scandal would ever touch you."

"If that were possible, which I don't for a minute say it is, what's in it for me?"

"Why, money, of course; money, dear boy."

Of course.

It turned out that Raymond had managed to find out a good deal about me in the course of the day. As soon as he discovered that his sister had managed to find an actual *date*, he got the name and started to work. The idea had been in his head for weeks.

And I was the ideal subject, as it turned out. A man who had been recently rejected by a woman and who had a history of such rejection.

"How did you find that out?" I said.

"It was easy," he said, but he wouldn't elaborate. I didn't argue. It was true. The latest was just one of a continuing series. All of them for more or less the same reasons.

"And that's the problem we can solve," Raymond said. "You can show them that they were all wrong. You can show them that you are virtually *filled* with drive and ambition. That you can marry the richest woman in town and obtain a great deal of money in the process."

"If they can stop laughing," I said.

Raymond smiled. "People seldom laugh at rich people very long." He sounded as if he knew whereof he spoke.

"How much?" I said.

He told me. It was more than I'd ever dreamed of.

"And my share?"

"Let's say . . . half."

"Let's say sixty percent."

"Done," he said, and stuck out a soft pink hand.

"I don't suppose we could put this in writing," I said.

He tittered. I don't think I'd ever heard anyone titter before, but that was what he did. There's no other way to describe it. "I don't suppose we could," he said. "You'll just have to trust me, dear heart."

"I'll think about it," I said, and I did.

It took a lot of thought. I'd never even thought of killing anyone before, and it took some getting used to. On the other hand, I'd never had the chance to become a millionaire before. And, let's face it, there was never anyone on the face of the earth that I could more cheerfully kill than Ethel Ann Adams.

Raymond had given me his number. I called him back two days later. "I'll do it," I told him. "For sixty-five percent."

"Greedy, greedy," he simpered. "But all right. Sixty-five percent."

"I may need a little help."

"We'll talk later. After the marriage."

"I've been thinking about that part. Why do I have to marry her?"

"Opportunity, of course," he said. "You'll be close to her at all times. Who knows what might come up? She might climb a ladder. Slip in the bath. And you'll be right there."

"We'll talk later," I said.

After I hung up, I called Ethel Ann and, God help me, asked her for a date.

I won't try to tell you what the marriage was like. If you have the nasty habit of imagining the bedroom scenes played out in other people's lives, then feel free to go ahead, but such events are far beyond my own poor powers of description. Suffice it to say that those scenes were as horrible as I had anticipated they might be, and in some ways even worse. I'd prefer not to think about it.

I called Raymond after a month. He said the time was "not ripe as yet, dear boy," and that his father still had a while to live. There was no rush.

I called after another month had dragged its way past, and after that I called every week. Raymond didn't seem in a great hurry. "Remember," he said, "if anything happens too soon after the wedding, there are bound to be nasty rumors and suspicions. Caesar's wife, dear boy. Caesar's wife."

I wasn't worried about Caesar's wife. I was worried about mine. She snored like a riveter. She ate like a horse. She wallowed in the bed like a wounded rhino.

She couldn't cook, and she refused to allow me to do so, though I am fairly competent in the kitchen. "It wouldn't be right to let ya do it," she said. "I'll take care of the meals."

So we subsisted on a diet of Budget Gourmet frozen dinners, along with occasional treats such as Mrs. Paul's fish sticks and Pepperidge Farms croissant pizza.

And she was a far worse housekeeper than cook. If she used a tissue, she left it in the chair or couch. Or she tossed it aside on the rug. She never dusted, and she was too lazy even to put such dishes as we used in the dishwasher. Powder covered the washstand in the bathroom. Mildew grew rampant in the shower and in the piles of towels that began to accumulate in a corner by the shower stall.

My formerly tidy apartment into which we had moved was becoming a slum area. It was almost unrecognizable.

I tried to avoid taking her out in public. She looked far worse than when we first met. As she put it, "Now that I got ya, I can afford to let myself go."

And go she did. Up by twenty or more pounds. She quit using makeup. "Too much trouble, sweetie. Bring me another brewski."

Ah, yes, the beer. Four six-packs a day at the very least. She guzzled the stuff.

Still, her father doted on her. We visited him twice a week, every week. He was a frail old man with a pink scalp and a few strands of white hair. Hands like claws.

After every visit, I called Raymond.

"Now, now," he said. "Don't be in a rush. If you're so eager for the money, just let the old man die. Then your wife will have it all."

"I don't want her to have it. I want her out of the way. Besides, if she dies then, I'll be suspected for sure. No one knows how I can stand her anyway."

"Just smile mysteriously if they ask," he said. "And don't worry."

I did worry, though, and finally I couldn't take it anymore. It was just after Ethel Ann threw up on the carpet—"Too many brewskis, I guess, honey"—and then passed out on the couch, leaving me to clean up the mess.

I called Raymond. "This is it," I told him. "Now, tonight."

"Wait—" he said.

I hung up the phone.

Looking at Ethel Ann there on the couch, her mouth open, the snoring rattling the windows in the apartment, I knew I could do it. Oddly enough, I'd worried about that earlier. When it came right down to it, could I actually kill another person?

The answer was yes if the person was Ethel Ann.

I didn't think much about how to do it. I concocted some wild
story about rapists and killers and went to the kitchen for a knife.
I didn't have a gun, or I would have used that.

I'd slit her throat, then leave. Go to a movie. Make sure I was
noticed. Then come home and find her dead. I would be the
grieving husband. No one would ever know.

In my current state, it even sounded logical.

I got out the knife and tested the edge with the ball of my thumb,
a stupid error, since I always kept my knives sharp.

I cut a deep gash in my thumb.

Blood was running everywhere. I got a towel from under the sink
and wrapped my thumb. The bitch was going to pay for this. I
rarely use foul language, but that was the way I thought of her then.
The bitch.

Even then I might have done it if I hadn't stepped in the vomit.
I should have cleaned it up first, I know, but I forgot. In my haste,
I forgot, and I put my foot right in the middle of it.

What a vile feeling that is, knowing what you've stepped in even
though at the same time you're surprised. I brought one hand up
and the other hand down. The sharp blade of the knife just missed
the towel and sliced neatly into the palm of my hand. Neatly and
fairly deeply. I hardly felt it at first.

Later, I felt it, of course.

I managed to get the towel around my hand and stop the blood.
I knew the cut was bad. Somehow I didn't think the police would
buy my story about the movies now. I left Ethel Ann lying there
and went to the Emergency Room instead.

I said I'd been chopping lettuce, but no one really cared.

I bled a little on the seat covers of Ethel Ann's '57 Chevy. That
was the only satisfaction I got.

The next time I vowed to be much more careful. And to plan
better.

I waited until just the right moment, after she had drunk her daily
allotment of brewskis—*beers;* after her daily allotment of beers.
Then I offered to take her to the movies.

"Ya mean it? We don't hardly go out much no more."

"I mean it," I said. "*Nightmare on Elm Street V.*"

"Aww ri-i-i-i-ght!"

She got ready in mere moments, ready to see Freddy.

"Where's the car?" she said as we got to the street. "Has the
car been stole?"

"No, no," I said. "I just had to park across the street. It's right over there.'' I pointed, and sure enough the car was there, right where I'd parked it. "Just a minute, before we cross," I said. "My shoelace is untied.'' I knew it was untied because I'd never tied it. I bent down.

My plan was simple. We lived on a fairly busy street. We were standing between two parked cars. I would wait until I heard a car coming, rise up fast, and bump Ethel Ann in her gigantic rear end.

She, in turn, would stumble in front of the oncoming car and be crushed to jelly.

It should have worked, but what happened was rather different.

Apparently, she moved. So, when I made my move, she wasn't where she should have been. That, in itself, wouldn't have been so bad.

The bad thing was that, while pretending to tie my shoe, I had actually done so. But in trying to keep an eye out for the oncoming car, tie the shoe, and judge Ethel Ann's position, I had managed to tie my shoelaces together.

I raised up, took a half step, which was all the step I could take with my shoes tied to one another, and pitched forward into the street.

I have to give the driver full credit. He was much more alert than I would have thought he might be.

He almost managed to stop.

One of the doctors in the Emergency Room asked if I had been in before. He thought I looked familiar.

I didn't answer him. I just lay there and suffered.

Three cracked ribs. Numerous contusions and abrasions, most of them coming from skidding along the concrete street. Several gashes which required stitches.

Aside from that, I was just fine. Ethel Ann couldn't wait to get me home.

"Oh, he is my ittle itsy boogums," she said. "I take care wuv itsy boogums.''

Itsy boogums. Good God.

She kept me in bed and fed me Budget Gourmet, potato chips, ice cream, and brewskis—*beers*.

She kept the television set on all the time: "The Love Connection.'' "The New Hollywood Squares.'' "Divorce Court.'' "The People's Court.'' "Superior Court.'' A few more weeks of convalescing, and I might have been able to pass the bar in most states. "The New Newlywed Game'' was the worst. The only thing the announcer didn't ask the contestants—if indeed they should be dignified by that word—was whether they liked to grease their mates with salad oil before they "made whoopie." (I was beginning to learn where Ethel Ann picked up her expressions.) Of course, he might have asked them that on an earlier show.

"I wonder if any of 'em ever made whoopie in bed with broke ribs?" Ethel Ann said one day. Then she leered at me. Then . . . Frankly, I don't want to talk about it.

After more than a week, I was able to go back to work. It was a frightening experience. At odd moments I found myself wondering what Chuck Woolery was prying out of some woman about her date with the sleazoid of her choice, or whether the audience would vote for date number one, number two, or number three.

Occasionally, I would crave a brewski.

When I was getting about as scared of myself as I was of my wife, I called Raymond from work. "We've got to meet," I said.

He didn't like it, but he agreed. He was afraid of being seen with me.

We met on my lunch hour, in the third row of a movie theater, a place that showed third-run films for a dollar admission.

The theater was practically deserted, which was a good thing, since Raymond had no idea of protective coloration. He would have stood out in any crowd. It wasn't that he looked like his sister— quite the contrary. He was taller, and much thinner. Where her hair curled, his waved. Where she was coarse, he was refined. Except in the matter of proper dress.

It was too dark in the theater for me to tell what color his pants were, but his shirt was shocking pink. He was wearing an ascot of some dark color, and it was covered with tiny pink hearts.

My heart cries for you, I thought for some reason.

He sat down beside me. "I simply *adore* Paul Newman," he said. "He is just so *butch* with that little mustache."

So is Ethel Ann, I thought.

"But really, dear boy, we shouldn't meet like this. It's much too dangerous. What if someone should see us?"

My reputation would be ruined, I thought.

"I don't know why you're so *eager*," he went on. "If you could only be patient, I'm sure—"

"I can't wait," I said. "I think something's happening to me. Living with your sister is doing something to me. I . . . I can't explain it, but I don't think I like it."

He shook his head without taking his eyes off Paul Newman, who was stalking around a pool table in full color. "I know what you mean," he said. "I went out on my own early in life for much the same reason."

"Then *why*—" I stopped and started over, realizing I had raised my voice considerably. "Then why did you do this to me?"

"To be quite frank, I thought my father would have died by now. Surely you've *seen* him?"

I admitted that I had.

"Then you know what I mean. The strength of that man amazes me."

"But couldn't I kill her now and remain a grieving widower until you get the money? Why do I have to suffer like this?"

He managed to take his eyes off the screen and look at me. "I should think that would be quite evident," he said.

"It's sure as hell not—it's surely not evident to *me*."

He sighed theatrically. "Should she die too soon, too long before dear father's own crisis, then he would have time to change his will. Don't you see? Why the old fool might do something *dras*tic, like leaving his money to the Friends of the Earth or the Save the Whales Club. Not that I don't think that whales are quite *sweet* in their own way, but really I would much prefer to see the money go to a worthier cause. Such as myself." Then he gave me the old up and under. "And you, of course."

"Of course."

"So wait. Persevere." He pronounced it with the accent on the next-to-last syllable, so that it rhymed with *ever*. "You will be rewarded in the end."

"I'll try," I said.

He looked at me kindly. "Please do, dear boy. Please do. For both our sakes."

I left the movie then. Raymond said he thought he'd stay. "That Tom Cruise is just simply *gor*geous," he said as I stepped into the aisle.

I looked back, and he was leaning forward in his seat. Drooling, probably.

Months went by.

Slowly.

So slowly.

Ethel Ann and I continued to visit her father. It was after one such visit that Ethel Ann said, "The old guy's lookin' better, don't ya think, hon?"

My pace faltered. She had confirmed my own suspicions. He *did* look better. Healthier, somehow.

"He's fillin' out, did ya notice? His color's better, too. He says his arthur-itis"—as God is my witness, that's what she said—"is better, even. He can open and close his hands real good."

I must have shuddered then.

"What's 'a matter?" Ethel Ann said. "Is my sugar booger cold?"

Sugar booger. Holy shi—I mean, good grief.

It was a few weeks later that I noticed that I was eager to get home after work in time for "Wheel of Fortune."

"That Vanna's such a doll," Ethel Ann was fond of saying. "If we ever have a kid"—she leered hopefully—"a girl kid, let's name her Vanna."

"I . . . uh . . . it's a lovely name," I said.

"And that Pat Sajak? A doll. Just a doll. Lucky for you ya got me when ya did. I could really go for a guy like that."

"Be quiet," I said. "You made me miss what letter that idiot asked for."

"It was an *m*," she said. "I thought it was a pretty good guess, myself."

"Hush," I said. "I'll miss the next one, too."

And it wasn't long after that when I realized that I was getting used to the filthy apartment. I tossed my towel in the floor right by Ethel Ann's, though I still used one more often than she did.

"After all, I hardly done a thing today," she said. "Why bathe?"

Why, indeed?

The dirty dishes piled up, the Budget Gourmet containers accumulated in the trash can, and there was actual grit on the kitchen floor. I saw roaches creeping and scuttling across the cabinets.

And at work I wondered: Who will sit in the center square on "New Hollywood Squares" today? And I wondered: Why didn't that fool take door number three yesterday? Anybody would have taken door number three. And I wondered: How could that nincompoop not have written down his answer in the form of a question? Does he have a death wish?

Worst of all was the time I thought, Gee, I wish I had me a brewski. It made my palms sweat, and my hands slipped on the smooth brown leather of the shoe I was trying to force onto the foot of a woman who obviously should have asked for a much larger size.

"What's the matter with you, fella?" she said. "Trying to feel me up?"

"You wish," I said. It slipped out. Honestly.

"What did you say, buster?"

"I . . . uh . . . said this *shoe* ish sized wrong. I'm shorry."

She looked at me with a great deal of suspicion, but she let it pass. She didn't buy any shoes, though.

I knew then that it couldn't go on any longer. I didn't care if Mr. Adams left his considerable fortune to Morris the Cat or the Liberace Museum. Something terrible was happening to me, and the longer I lived with Ethel Ann, the worse it got. I was crazy to have gone along with Raymond in the first place. For my own sanity, Ethel Ann had to go. And she had to go soon.

I didn't say anything about it to Raymond. There was no need for him to know, and I was sure he would have objected. He would have had good reason. Only two days before, Mr. Adams had gotten so much better that he had asked the doctor for an exercise program.

There was no doubt in my mind that he would live to be a hundred.

This time I made sure that nothing could go wrong. I planned everything carefully, even went over it in a practice run of sorts. This time was for keeps.

I waited until the perfect night—dark, cloudy, a little drizzle. I asked Ethel Ann if she'd like to take a drive.

"Gee, I don't know, hon. On 'Lifestyles of the Rich and Famous' tonight, Robin Leach is gonna give us a tour of one of Wayne Newton's places."

"No kidding? Well— No. *No.* We really ought to get out more. All we do is watch the tube—the television set. A little drive is what we need. And you know?" I smiled at her in what I hoped was a provocative manner. "A drive in the cool night air just might give me some hot ideas."

She jumped off the couch. Well, actually, she more or less rolled off. At her size and weight, which must have been nearing 190 by then, jumping was more or less out of the question. "Why didn't ya say so the first time, sport? Lemme get some shoes on."

She did, and we left.

"Let me drive," I said. "I like to drive the Chevy."

"Fine by me, kiddo. That way I can snuggle-bunny on you."

Snuggle-bunny. Give me strength.

We drove around town for a while, nowhere in particular, listening to the radio. Ethel Ann had put a really good stereo in the old car, and a good set of speakers. Unfortunately, she usually insisted on playing her Slim Whitman tapes, but tonight she had forgotten them in her haste to get to the car and make snuggle-bunnies.

Then I headed out toward Mount Granton.

She caught on fast. "I know where y're goin', big boy," she said. "Thinkin' about makin' a little time, huh?" She wormed her way even closer to me. "Well, I'll tell ya, ya got a good chance."

I held my gorge down and kept driving. Mount Granton was a popular spot for parking and engaging in sexual activity. It had quite a good view of the city, actually, and at night the lights could look quite attractive if you were in the right mood. Of course, on such a rainy night as this, there wouldn't be many couples there. The view was terrible, it was cold, and these days most people simply preferred to stay at home and do it in the bed.

Or at least, so I hoped.

Near the top, there was a small turnout. As we neared it, I said, "Gosh, honey, I think there's something wrong with one of our tires."

There was, too. I'd let a great deal of the air out of it when I came home that afternoon. Not enough to be really bothersome, but enough to be noticeable if someone called your attention to it.

"It's in the back on my side, I think," I said.

She raised her head as if that would help her to sense it. "Ya may be right," she said. "It's kinda bumping."

And that was true, too, not that I'd planned it. Just a little luck for a change. Things were at last about to go my way.

It was about time, after all.

"Why don't I pull off up here," I said. "I can get out and check it." I gave a delicate cough. "I wish I didn't feel like I was coming down with a cold."

"If ya are, ya better not get your tootsies wet. I'll check it out for ya."

"How very thoughtful," I said.

I pulled into the turnout very carefully, just the way I had practiced it. Just the right angle. I stopped the car. Not a single automobile had passed us on the way up.

Good-bye, Ethel Ann, I thought.

Or maybe I said it aloud. She laughed. "I'll be right back, ya big jerk."

That's what *you* think, my dear.

I could visualize myself talking to the police officer, tears of sorrow welling in my eyes. "It . . . it was terrible, officer. I suppose my foot slipped off the brake—God knows how!—just as she was crossing behind the car. It struck her, and the railing—the railing there is so low! There was nothing I could do to save her! Oh, my sweet darling!''

And at that point I would break down in body-shaking sobs, the drizzle in the night air blending with the tears that flowed down my innocent cheeks.

As a plan, it was perfect.

The execution of it, however, was flawed.

In order to be sure that I struck her hard enough, I was going to have to do a bit more than let the car roll backward. I was going to have to put it into reverse and give her a good, solid bump.

Even at that, I might have succeeded had I not been overly eager. I should have waited until she got right in the middle, but I didn't. I let her take one step behind the car, and shifted gears. She saw the backup lights and stepped back to the side.

I got my foot off the gas and back on the brake, but the surface was extremely slick, possibly oily. The guardrail was no help at all.

I remember hearing it splinter, my foot still frozen to the brake. I remember the rear end of the car tilting out over the ledge and the hood rearing up in the air.

I remember looking out the window at Ethel Ann's horror-stricken face.

And that's all I remembered for quite some time.

When I woke up in the hospital, all I could think of was how cold it seemed and how thirsty I felt.

I tried to move, I think, but that proved to be impossible. I was encased in casts and had one leg suspended in some sort of medieval torture device. The pain was excruciating.

I fainted.

When I came out of it again, I felt better, though not much. There was a nurse in my room. I tried to say something to her, but I found I couldn't talk. It was as if my tongue had swollen until it filled my entire mouth. So I just lay there. Then I went to sleep.

I woke up more and more often, and the nurses and doctors seemed to be encouraged by my progress. Ethel Ann was there most of the time. I tried not to look at her.

One day she asked me how I was feeling. I surprised myself by being able to answer. After that we talked a little.

I had been in the hospital for three weeks. In another three I might be able to go home, if I behaved myself and was a good little boy.

"My itsy boogums will be good," she said. "I will take care wuv my itsy boogums."

It hardly bothered me.

I got better and was able to watch the tube. I watched all the game shows that came on, which meant that I got to see a few I'd missed because of work, like "The Price Is Right." I also got to see Donahue, and by the time I was ready to go home I knew I'd miss him when I had to go back to work, even if he was a little bit wimpy.

Then one day Ethel Ann came in crying. "What's the matter?" I said. "Have you talked to the doctor? He didn't say anything that he told you not to tell me, did he?"

And then an even more terrible thought struck me. "Ethel Ann— your father. He's not . . . he didn't . . ."

She looked at me and I could see that she wasn't sad at all. She was actually smiling, but the tears were running down her face and she was sobbing. "It's Daddy," she said. "It's Daddy."

I was out of traction by then, almost ready to go home. Just the casts here and there. One arm (the left) and one leg (the right), plus wrappings around my ribs (broken again, five this time). I sort of fell back in the bed in a collapse.

The old man was dead.

She was trying to keep a good face on things, but the tears gave it all away. He was dead, and that was that. If I killed Ethel Ann now, everyone would suspect me.

I tried to do the right thing. "I . . . I'm sorry," I said.

Ethel Ann wiped the back of her hand across her eyes and pulled at her nose with her fingers. "Don't be sorry," she said. "It's just that I'm so happy."

"Happy?" I said.

"That Daddy's doing so well."

"Uh . . . well?"

"Yeah. I was gonna surprise ya when ya got out of the hospital. He's been just gettin' better and better ever' day. Strong as an ox. I just found out he's gonna run in the Won-Ton Marathon."

"He's . . . going to run . . . in a marathon?"

She rubbed her face, which made it look redder than ever. "Ain't it great? It's like, you know, a miracle. The doctor says he may live another hundred years."

Something came over me. I don't know what. I just knew that I had to do it then, no matter what. I came off the bed at her.

At least that's what I tried to do. I remember the leg with the cast hitting the floor and skidding. I remember the sound of the bedpan clattering across the floor. I remember falling.

I remember Ethel Ann telling the doctor, "He was so excited about my news that he tried to get up. I didn't know it would make him do that, honest I didn't."

And the doctor saying, "It's not your fault; don't worry."

So I had to stay in the hospital for a while longer, and watch a bit more television. I got real good at "The Wheel of Fortune." Did a little more study for the bar exam with Judge Wapner. Ate hospital food.

Eventually I got to go back to the apartment. What it looked like after more than a month of Ethel Ann's care and hers alone, I can hardly tell you. There were piles of dirty clothes on the couch. The roaches had moved to the coffee table. There were coffee cups on top of the TV set. With cold coffee in them. Some of them had mold growing on the top of the coffee. It was yellowish, with green around the edges.

Ethel Ann shoved the dirty clothes from the couch to the floor and installed me on the hide-a-bed. "This'll be fun," she said. "We can watch a lotta TV."

And we did. And we drank brewskis. And we ate Budget Gourmet. Drank Diet Pepsi. Ate ice cream. And watched TV.

Finally all the casts were gone. I could walk almost as well as I had before. I could have worked at the shoe store, but I had long since been replaced. They were very sorry, but that was all.

One day when Ethel Ann was out for more junk food, I called Raymond. I named the movie where we'd met before and gave him a time. I told Ethel Ann that I had to get out for exercise and some fresh air.

"Is it the Glade I've been sprayin'? I could change brands."

I assured her that the house smelled fine. It smelled like a gymnasium built in a pine forest, but I didn't say that part.

"What, then? Exercise? That stuff'll kill ya."

I assured her that I wouldn't be long, and I went.

Raymond showed up on time. He was a little bit put out that the movie was *Crimes of the Heart*. "*Hon*estly, Diane Keaton should never have let herself go like that, even to get the part. And Jessica Lange? My dear, she should at least have used a little makeup."

I wasn't interested in his criticisms of the movie. I had Siskel and Ebert for that. And Harris and Reed. I had another thing entirely on my mind. I told him.

"Yes, it's really too bad that it turned out this way," he said. "It seemed like such a good idea at the time," he said.

"That's all you've got to say?"

"I'm sorry, dear boy. What else *can* I say?"

"How could you ever have come up with such a harebrained scheme in the first place?" I said.

"I've often wondered. I don't think I ever took it really seriously. I *did* hope to get the money, but I suppose that will never happen, not now. *C'est la vie.*"

"*C'est la vie?*"

"French, dear boy. It means—"

"I know what it means," I said. "What about me?"

"You?"

"Me. The man married to your sister. What about me?"

"Well," he said, "there's always divorce."

"Divorce," I said.

"I suppose she'd never agree to it. Well, one has to make the best of things."

I looked at him. It was dark, but I think he was laughing at me, quietly.

So I killed him.

It was quite easy, much easier than all my attempts with Ethel Ann. I simply stepped across him to the aisle, then looked back and bent down.

"That's a lovely ascot," I said.

He simpered. "Thank you. It's pure silk. You don't think the color is a trifle . . . much?"

"Chartreuse? Don't be silly." I reached out my fingers to touch it.

And before he knew it, I had it off, twisted around his neck, and tight, so tight that he could only gargle. On the screen, Sissy Spacek was trying to hang herself, and the two or three other customers were more interested in her troubles than in Raymond's. I sat in the seat behind him and slowly strangled the life out of him. Then I left him there.

When I got back to the apartment, Ethel Ann met me at the door. She had an envelope in her hand. "Do ya know what day this is?" she said.

"No," I said. "I don't believe I do."

"That's what happens when ya spend all ya time inside. I guess gettin' out is good for ya sometimes. Anyhow, it's a special day for us." She handed me the envelope.

Then I knew, of course. How sentimental. I hadn't really suspected her of being so sentimental.

She walked toward the kitchen. "I'll get us some brewskis to help us celebrate," she said. "Open it up. It's special."

I opened the envelope, though I already suspected what I would find inside. I was right. A duplicate of the valentine she'd given me exactly one year before.

I looked at the face on the heart, the downturned mouth, the tears.

I looked up at the apartment, the filth, the roaches, the coffee cups, the clothes in piles, the plates full of crusts and crumbs.

I opened the card.

"My heart cries for you."

I saw Ethel Ann heading toward me with the brewskis.

And cries, I thought.

And cries.

COLT .24

by Rick Hautala

Diary entry one: approximately 10:00 A.M. on Valentine's Day—
hah! What irony!

If you've ever spent any time in academic circles, you've no
doubt heard the expression "Publish or perish." Simply put, it
means that if you intend to keep your cushy teaching position, at
least at any decent college or university, you've got to publish in
academic journals. I suppose this is to prove you've been doing
research, but it also contributes to the prestige of your school.

My experience, at least in the English department here at the
University of Southern Maine, is that the more obscure and unread
the periodical, the more prestige is involved. I mean, if you write
novels or stories that don't pretend to art, you can kiss your tenure
good-bye. A good friend of mine here did just that—wrote and sold
dozens of stories and even one novel, but because it was seen as
"commercial" fiction, he didn't keep his job. After he was denied
tenure, a few years back, he and I used to joke about how he had
published *and* perished!

I have reason to be cynical. The doctor who talked with me last
night might have fancier, more clinical terms for it, but I might be
tempted to translate his conclusions about me to something a little
simpler: let's try "crazy as a shit-house rat."

That's crazy, all right; but just read on. I'm writing this all down
as fast as I can because I know I don't have much time. I'm
fighting the English teacher in me who wants to go back and revise
and hone this all down until it's perfect, but if I'm right . . . Oh,
Jesus! If I'm *right* . . .

Look, I'll try to start at the start. Every story has a beginning,
a middle, and an end, I've always told my students. Life, unfortunately, doesn't always play out that way. Sure, the beginning's
at birth and the end's at death—it's filling up the middle part that's
a bitch.

I don't know if this whole damned thing started when I first saw
Rose McAllister . . . Rosie. She was sitting in the front row the
first day of my 8:00 A.M. Introduction to English Literature class
last fall. It might have been then that everything started, but I've
gotta be honest. I mean, at this point, it doesn't matter. I think I'll
be dead . . . and *really* in Hell within . . . maybe four hours.

So when I first saw Rosie, I didn't think right off the bat: God! I want to have an affair with her.

That sounds so delicate—"have an affair." I wanted to, sure; but that was after I got to know her. We started sleeping together whenever we could . . . which wasn't often, you see, because of Sally. My wife. My dear, departed wife!

I guess if I were really looking for the beginning of this whole damned mess, I'd have to say it was when we started our study of Marlowe's *Doctor Faustus*. Your basic "deal with the devil" story. I didn't mention too much of this to the police shrink because . . . well, if you tell someone like that that you struck a deal with the devil, sold him your soul—yes, I signed the agreement with my own blood—you expect him to send you up to the rubber room on P-6. If I'm wrong, I don't want to spend my time writing letters home with a Crayola, you know.

I'm getting ahead of myself, but as I said, I don't have much time . . . at least, I don't think so.

Okay, so Rosie and I, sometime around the middle of the fall semester, began to "sleep together." Another delicate term because we did very little "sleeping." We got whatever we could, whenever we could—in my office, usually, or—once or twice—in a motel room, once in my car in the faculty parking lot outside of Bailey Hall. Whenever and wherever.

The first mistake we made was being seen at the Roma, in Portland, by Hank and Mary Crenshaw. The Roma! As an English teacher, I can appreciate the irony of *that*, too. Sally and I celebrated our wedding anniversary there every year. Being seen there on a Friday night, with a college sophomore ("young enough to be your daughter!" Sally took no end of pleasure repeating), by your wife's close (not best, but close) friend is downright stupid. I still cringe when I imagine the glee in Mary's voice when she told Sally. Hell! I never liked Mary, and she never liked me. Hank—he was all right, but I always told Sally that Mary was *her* friend, not mine.

So, Sally found out. Okay, so plenty of married men (and women) get caught screwing around. Sometimes the couple can cope—work it out. Other times, they can't. We couldn't. I should say, Sally couldn't. She set her lawyer—Walter Altschuler—on me faster than a greyhound on a rabbit. That guy would have had my gonads if they hadn't been attached.

But I'm not the kind of guy who takes that kind of stuff—from *anyone!* And, in an ironic sort of way, I'm getting paid back for that, too. If someone sics a lawyer on me, I'm gonna fight back.

Now here's where it gets a little weird. If I told that police shrink all of this, he'd bounce me up to P-6 for sure. I said we were reading *Faustus,* and that's when I decided to do a bit of—let's call it research. I dug through the library and found what was supposedly a magician's handbook—you know, a grimoire. I decided to try a bit of necromancy.

Look, I'm not crazy! I went into it more than half-skeptical. And I want to state for the record here that I . . .

Diary entry two: two hours later. Time's running out for sure!

Sorry for the interruption. I'm back now after wasting two hours with the shrink again. He ran me over the story again, but—I think—I held up pretty well. I didn't tell him what I'm going to write here. I want this all recorded so if I'm right . . . If I'm right . . .

Where was I? Oh yeah. Necromancy. A deal with the devil. Yes—yes—*yess!* Signed in *blood!*

The library on the Gorham campus had a grimoire. Well, actually a facsimile of one, published a few years ago by Indiana University Press. It's amazing what's published these days. I wonder if the person who edited that text—I can't remember his name—kept his job. I looked up a spell to summon the devil and— Now I *know* you're gonna think I'm crazy! I did it! I actually summoned up the devil!

Laugh! Go ahead! I'll be dead soon—in Hell!—and it won't matter to me!

I have a key to Bailey Hall, so I came back to my office late at night—sometime after eleven o'clock, so I could be ready by midnight. After making sure my door was locked, I started to work. Pushing back the cheap rug I had by my desk (to keep the rollers of my chair from squeaking), I drew a pentagram on the floor, using a black Magic Marker. I placed a black candle—boy, were they hard to find—at each of the five points and lighted them. Then, taking the black leather-bound book, I began to recite the Latin incantation backwards. Actually, I was surprised that it worked— my Latin was so rusty, I was afraid I'd mispronounce something and end up summoning a talking toadstool or something. But it worked—it *actually* worked! In a puff of sulfurous fumes Old Nick himself appeared.

Looking around, he said, "Well, at least you're not another damned politician! What do you want in return for your soul?"

With his golden, cat-slit eyes burning into me, I had the feeling he already knew—more clearly than I did at that moment. Anyway,

I told him. I said that I wanted an absolutely foolproof way of killing my wife and not getting caught. I told him I was willing to sign my soul over to him—yes! Dear God! In *blood!* If I could somehow get rid of Sally and be absolutely *certain* I wouldn't get caught.

I'm writing this, you must know by now, in a jail cell. I'm the prime suspect, but I haven't been charged with anything. I have a perfect alibi, you see, and there are other problems, too; but if you read the *Evening Express*, you'll know soon enough that I didn't get away with it.

What the devil did was hand me a revolver; he called it a Colt .24—a specially "modified" Colt .45—and a box of nice, shiny, brass-jacketed bullets. He told me all I had to do, after I signed the agreement, of course, was point the gun at Sally—he suggested I sneak home sometime before lunch someday—pull the trigger, throw the gun away, and make *sure* I went to work as usual the next day. If I did what he said, he guaranteed I'd go free.

Sounded okay to me. At this point, I was well past rationally analyzing the situation. I was under a lot of pressure, you've got to understand. My wife's lawyer had stuck the end nozzle of his vacuum cleaner down into my wallet and was sucking up the bucks. I'd been without sleep for nearly two days and nights running—I was getting so worked up about Sally.

And the capper was Rosie. As soon as she found out that Sally knew about us, she cooled off. Maybe—I hate to think it!—it was just the chance of getting caught that added to her excitement—her sense of adventure. Once we got caught, the thrill was gone for her. Could she have been *that* shallow?

I wasn't completely convinced this whole business with the devil had really worked, because . . . well, I must've fallen asleep after he pricked my finger so I could sign the contract, gave me the gun, and disappeared. I woke up, stiff-necked and all, flat on my back on the floor of my office just before my eight o'clock class the next morning. The candles had burned out, but in the early morning light, I could see the pentagram still there, so I knew I hadn't dreamed *everything*. I also had the gun—a Colt .24.

I'd been asleep— I don't know how long. Not more than four hours, I figure. I had started the summoning at midnight, like you're supposed to. I have no idea how long it took, but—at least for me—old Satan didn't waste any time with visions of power and glory, or processions of spirits. Nothing, really. At times, thinking

about it, I could just as easily have been talking to Old Man Olsen,
the janitor in Bailey Hall!

But, as I said, I also had the gun, and—damned if I didn't decide
then and there that I'd use it. I had my two classes first. But after
that, I was going straight home and point it at Sally and pull the
trigger—even if, then and there, it blew her out through the picture
window. I'd reached my limit which, I'd like to think, was considerably beyond what most men can stand.

So I did. After the second class—between classes I had time to
drag the rug back and gulp down some coffee and an Egg
McMuffin—I took off for home. Sally, as luck would have it, was—
Damn! Here they come again!

Diary entry three: more than an hour gone—mere minutes left!

This time the police came in again. Talk about being confused.
I think they'd like to charge me. But my alibi is solid and they
can't get my gun to fire. So they asked me to fill them in on my
relationship with Sally. They said that maybe it could give them a
lead on who else might have killed her. They said I'd probably be
released shortly. *Hah!* As if that might make a difference.

Well, as I was saying—Sally was home and her lawyer, old
Walter-baby—was there with her. I sort of wondered why he was
there—at *my* house. Maybe nosing around gave him a better idea
how to skin me to the bone. Or maybe getting into her pants was
part of his fee. But I couldn't afford to leave a witness, so whatever
he was doing, that was just his tough luck. One more lawyer in
Hell wasn't going to matter.

I walked in from the kitchen and nodded a greeting to the two
of them, sitting on the couch. I said something about having
forgotten some test papers as I put the briefcase down on the
telephone table, opened it, and slowly took out the gun. Keeping
it shielded from them with the opened top of the briefcase, I
brought the gun up, took aim at him and squeezed the trigger. Not
once—not twice—*three* times! Good number, three. A literature
teacher knows all about the significance of the number three.

Nothing happened! There was no sound—although I had been
careful to slip a bullet into each chamber before I left the office.
There was no kick in my hand. There wasn't even much of a *click*.
The only thing I could think was that maybe the Colt wouldn't
work for someone who wasn't part of the deal. So I pointed it at
her and fired off three more shots—with the same result. I do
remember smelling—or thinking I smelled—a faint aroma of spent
gunpowder, but I chalked that up to wishful thinking.

Sally and Walter ignored me, just kept right on talking as I gawked at them . . . so I slipped the gun back into the briefcase, shut it, and went up to the bedroom and shuffled around a bit, sounding busy while I tried to figure things out. I'd been packing to move out, but Sally—against old Walter-baby's advice, I might add—had said it was all right for me to stay at the house until the apartment I'd rented in town opened up the first of the month. Thanks, Sally. As it turned out, that was the last favor you ever did for me—except a day later, when you dropped dead!

So I left the house for my next class—with Sally and Walter sitting on the couch just as alive as they could be—feeling as though I'd been ripped off—set up or something by the devil. His gun was a dud, as far as I was concerned.

Back in my office about two that afternoon, I checked the Colt and was surprised to see six empty shells in the chamber—no bullets. Could I have been dumb enough to load the gun with empty shells? I didn't think so, but I tossed the empties and slipped in six new bullets from the devil's box. I was getting a little bit scared that I *had* hallucinated the summoning, but that still didn't explain where I had gotten the Colt.

By then I wasn't thinking too clearly, so I decided to test the gun right there in my office. I sighted along the barrel at one of the pictures on my wall—one of my favorites, actually; a silkscreen advertisement for the Dartmouth Christmas Revels—and gently squeezed the trigger. Nothing happened. Quickly, I aimed at my doctoral dissertation—now *there* was something else to hate—on the top shelf of my bookcase and pulled the trigger.

Nothing.

Again, aiming at the pencil sharpener beside the door, I squeezed the trigger.

Nada!

I pointed at the wall and snapped the trigger three more times, and still nothing happened. The tinge of gunpowder I thought I smelled couldn't have really been there, I thought . . . just my imagination, I guessed. But you shouldn't ever *guess* when the devil has your soul!

Again, though—and it struck me as really weird this time—when I opened the chamber all six bullets were spent. Maybe they were dummies or something—not really made of lead. Or maybe I was the dummy being led. I got the box, now minus a total of twelve bullets, and after inspecting them closely—they seemed real— reloaded, put the gun on the desk, and tilted back in my chair.

I'd been had, for sure, I thought, with rage and stark fear tossing me like a seesaw. I had signed my soul over to the devil for *what?* For a revolver that didn't even work!

Anyway, like I said, the next day at noon, Sally was dead. Our neighbor, Mrs. Benton, said she heard three gunshots from our house. Afraid that there was a robbery or something going on, she stayed home and, clutching her living room curtains to hide herself as she watched our house, called the Gorham police. They came shortly after that, and found Sally dead of three gunshot wounds to the head.

I, of course, didn't know this at the time. I was just coming back to my office, following a graduate seminar on Elizabethan Drama. I hadn't gone home the night before and had been forced to sleep— again—on my office floor, so I wasn't in the best of moods.

I spent the next couple of hours sitting at my desk, working through a stack of tests and pondering everything that had happened recently when there was a knock on the door. I scooped the Colt into the top desk drawer but, foolishly, didn't slide the drawer completely shut before I went to the door. Two uniformed policemen entered, politely shook hands, and then informed me that my wife had been murdered . . . shot to death by a Colt .45.

I fell apart—wondering to myself which I felt more—shock or relief. I hadn't done it, but *someone* had! The policemen waited patiently for me to gain control of myself and explained that they wanted to know where I had been in the past three hours. Apparently Mrs. Benton had seen fit to fill them in on our domestic quarrels. They also wanted to know if I owned a Colt .45.

If this whole story has a tragic mistake—for me, at least—it was not following the devil's advice to the letter. That's how he gets you, you know. I should have *realized* that! He had said that if I aimed the gun at Sally, pulled the trigger, and then threw the gun away, I'd never be caught.

But I didn't throw the damned thing away.

If you had asked me then, I suppose I would have said the gun was worthless. What difference would it make if I kept it or tossed it? I hadn't summoned the devil that night. I'd fallen asleep and, beaten by exhaustion and the pressure I was under, I'd had a vivid nightmare. I hadn't *really* summoned the devil. Stuff like that didn't *really* happen!

I gave the cops my alibi, and it was solid. When the shots rang out, I was more than twenty miles from my house, on the University's Portland campus, lecturing on Shakespeare's use of horse imagery in his history plays. You can't go against the testimony of a roomful of enthralled graduate students.

About then one of the policemen noticed the revolver in the desk drawer, and, eyeing me suspiciously, asked if they could take a look at it. Sure. There was no denying that I did own a Colt .45, but after they inspected it for a moment, I took it from them.

"Look," I said, hefting the Colt. "This sucker doesn't even work. It's a model or something." I opened the chamber, showed them that the gun was loaded, clicked it shut, and, with a flourish, pressed the barrel to my temple.

"See?" I said, as I snapped the trigger three times. "Nothing happens. It's a fake."

That seemed to satisfy them. They thanked me for my cooperation and left, saying they'd wait in the hallway until I felt ready to come with them to the hospital to identify the body.

But they had no more than swung the door shut behind them when shots rang out in my office! I was just turning to pick up my briefcase when the center of the Christmas Revels poster blew away. I turned and stared, horrified, as the top row of books on the bookcase suddenly jumped. I could see a large, black, smoking hole in the spine of my dissertation. Then the pencil sharpener by the door exploded into a twisted mess of metal. Three more shots removed pieces of plaster and wood from the office walls.

With the sound of the six shots still ringing in my ears, I heard the two policemen burst back into my office. They both had their revolvers drawn and poised.

"I thought that gun didn't work," one of them shouted, leaning cautiously against the door frame. He was looking at me suspiciously, but then his expression changed to confusion when he registered that the Colt wasn't in my hand. It was lying on the desk, where I had placed it as they left.

"Man, I don't know what's going on here," the other one said. "But you had better come downtown until we can check the ballistics to make *sure* this wasn't the gun that killed her."

I was in a state of near shock—I'm sure my face had turned chalky white because I felt an icy numbness rush across my cheeks and down the back of my neck. A sudden realization was beginning to sink in. It had been almost—*no!*—*exactly* twenty-four hours ago that I had aimed and shot the revolver six times in my office. Six times! And nothing had happened—until *now!*

This bit about the ballistics test had cracked my nerve. I mean, at this point I was convinced that it hadn't been coincidence. The shots I had banged off twenty-four hours earlier must have done in Sally. And I knew that, if the cops checked it out, the ballistics would match.

What about sleazy Walter Altschuler? Was he dead, too? With a sudden sickening rush, I remembered what the devil had said to me the night I summoned him . . . he said the gun was a Colt *.24!* A special, *modified* Colt .45!

I tried to force myself to appear calm. *Damn my soul to Hell!* I had pointed the gun to my head as a *beau geste* and pulled the trigger—three times! I remembered—now—that when I had done that, I *had* smelled a trace of spent gunpowder . . . like I had that morning at the house, when I had targeted Walter and Sally.

Then Joan Oliver, the department secretary poked her head—cautiously, I might add—into my office to tell the policemen they had a phone call. I fell apart completely, knowing what it would be. Walter Altschuler had been found dead in his car in the Casco Bank parking lot in downtown Portland with three .45 caliber bullet wounds in his head.

I'd been *had!* I signed that damned contract . . . in *blood!* And I *had had* that damned gun. And it *had* worked! And the devil *had* cheated me, but good, in the bargain.

So while sitting here in the cell, after coming to my senses this morning, I asked for some paper and a pen. If I'm wrong, I don't want to tell my story and be committed. But if I'm right, I want to get all of this down to leave a permanent record before those bullets from Hell blow my hea

FINE CHOCOLATES

by Jeannette M. Hopper

The department store is a kaleidoscope of red, pinks, gold, and chrome. Multiply reflected in the wall mirrors, the sparkles and filmy laces of this season of romance dazzle his eyes, make him take a step back just inside the door. The *haute couture* woman behind him curses with her black-rimmed eyes, touches her bleached hair. He turns, lowers his gaze, and mutters, "Pardon me."

He pats his back pocket beneath his long coat to make sure she hasn't lifted his wallet. Mustn't be careless; appearances can be deceiving, even here, in this lusty wonder-world of the rich.

He hurries past the frilly night-things, the fur-edged bedroom dressings and satin seductions, passing up the glittering jewelry cases that glow with fluorescent lights to make cheap glass look like diamonds to justify their prices. He passes the genuine crystals, as well, interested only in that warm-smelling corner of the store where love's true aphrodisiac awaits.

Chocolate.

Chocolate from France, from Germany, from Belgium and Switzerland. Chocolates in golden boxes, wrapped in velvet hearts with red cellophane to protect a virgin silk flower, or encrusted with penny rhinestones and sold for thirty dollars a pound. The heady aroma of roasted beans and distilled juices welcomes him. Add fruit, add rum, add whatever you will, but still call it chocolate, for there is no more enticing word in the universe: *chocolate*.

He buys five one-pound boxes and pays the wide-eyed woman with cash. She asks, "Would you like these gift-wrapped?" He shakes his head at her stupidity; he's paid extra for bows, silk, satin, and lace. She places the heart-shaped boxes into white cartons kept folded behind the counter. These she stacks in a plastic shopping bag, smiles, and says, "Have a nice day."

As he rides home in the back of a taxi, he thinks of the women to whom he'll give the chocolates. They're rich, these women, as rich as the candy nestled within the sensuous packaging. Like the gifts they'd soon receive, the women are exercises in false advertising. Cheap products decorated to appear high quality; paste jewels in platinum settings. They laughed at him when he tried to win their affections, turned up their remodeled noses at this mere city employee who *dared* approach their kind.

He'd show them! He'd prove that middle income does not mean *cheap*. He'd subdue them, make them crawl on their knees, *begging* his attention. Those who had spurned him would realize their error soon enough, once they'd received his expensive gifts.

He's spent the better part of his paycheck, and pays the cab driver the exact fare. Once inside his small apartment, he lays the shopping bag on his bed, removes his coat, and sits on the old mattress with one hand resting on his treasure. The scent of chocolate drifts to his nose even through layers of cardboard and fabric. He begins to sweat.

On his walls are posters and center sheets from his favorite magazines. Women of all shades grace his vision; he is not racist. To him, a woman is a woman is a woman, no matter what her color. The only quality he cannot tolerate is fatness. He abhors loose flesh, becomes sick at the very thought of touching spongy skin like that of his mother. Her bloated, white hands inflicted too much pain; her hamlike buttocks crushed the air from his lungs. The only female texture he longs for now is that of firm, unyielding flesh. The women who will soon receive the chocolates keep their bodies hard. He knows the risk in sending candy, but also knows that no woman, no matter how expensive her health club, can resist chocolates on Valentine's Day.

He slides the square white boxes from the bag and arranges them upon his bedspread. Five, a mystical number for head, arms, and legs. It's appropriate in his mind, since the heart is at the center of it all, just as the costly liqueur is at the center of each bonbon. Hearts of liquid cherry will soften the hearts of his frigid loves.

Five improves the odds, too; of the five, at least one is sure to surrender to his charms.

He uses a sharp knife from the kitchen to break the interior and exterior wrapping on each box, careful to avoid marring the delicate silk petals and satin ribbons. Plastic looks cheap, and he wonders why manufacturers insist on sheathing such fine chocolates in it. The woman should be able to lift the decorated lid and inhale deeply the sweet incense of the bean.

Now, with a fountain pen filled with red ink, he flourishes a note to each in his elegant hand. *My love,* he pens, his hand moving gracefully in wide arcs, *I ache for the touch of you, the smell of you, the very presence of your exalted body.* It is enough, he decides; not profane, not pleading. He must state his desire and let the hearts of the gift do the rest.

Before replacing the lids on their boxes, he lifts several pieces of candy from each, examining them for holes, cracks, and white spots. It is indeed fine chocolate, rich in butter and cream. It does not leak.

The hearts are back in their plain containers, and the containers stacked once more in the shopping bag. He calls the taxi company and waits on the sidewalk.

In the cab, he counts his money: enough left to make his rounds, but he will have to eat lightly for the next two weeks. The driver has reached the first address and stopped.

"Wait here," he commands.

He takes one of the heart boxes from its protective carton and climbs the stairs to the second floor. It's a fine building, new, and the carpet upon which he lays the pink velvet heart is clean. He rings the bell and leaves quickly.

The driver nods and grins as the car stops in front of the fourth address. "Got lots of girl friends, eh, bud?"

"Yes," he says.

As they slow at the final address, the driver whistles. "Damn, man! *You* got a woman living in this big, fancy place?"

"For now," he says, and nothing more.

He leaves the gold-and-white heart in the large delivery box attached to one of the marble pillars at the edge of the porch. As he leaves, he picks a perfect, white rose from a dwarf tree, one of many lining the circular drive, and inserts it in his lapel. The flower has adopted a few dots of red, like blood upon its tender petals, from a neighboring tree. He smiles.

Back home, he leans into the passenger window to pay the driver, who says, "Hey, happy Valentine's Day, man. And good luck with your ladies!"

He pauses, spotting the small snapshot taped to the dashboard, a young woman with bright eyes and dark hair. Impulsively, he gives the driver an extra five. "Buy something nice for *your* lady," he says.

Coat off, in his room, he lies on his bed and stares at the women on his wall. All recline languidly, faint smiles or pouts below smoking eyes. There's something in the way a woman's breasts fall when she lies on her back, he muses, something about the way her body smooths out, flattens, as gravity hugs to it her curves and hollows. His hand finds its way to the mound beneath his zipper, and he moans softly.

Two hours later he awakens to the beep of his alarm clock. The room is darkened, night having sifted through the cracks as he slept.

He drinks instant coffee, showers, shaves, and splashes his neck with good quality cologne. If his plan goes perfectly, he should be contacted by at least one of his loves tonight, and he doesn't want to smell cheap.

What will he do, he ponders, when she—whoever is first—arrives? He will caress her, whisper sweet words in her ear. The earlobes, so soft, are the only part of a woman he wants to be able to bite into. All the rest of her must be firm to the touch. Solid. Then, as she purrs in his arms, he will take her, and it will not be by force, because she will give herself to him freely. Chocolate does that to a woman.

The clock chirps the hour, and he shrugs on his coat for the third time today, thankful for the length that covers his anticipation. It's been a long time since he has held beauty against his skin, and his heart beats wildly at the prospect.

His bus is on time, and he drops the fare into the coin box. The bus driver cocks one eyebrow, recognizing him from many rides before, but questioning with his eyes the clothing. Other riders, some of whom also know his face, stare at his oiled and combed hair, whisper among themselves at his gleaming polished shoes, black bow tie, and the spotted white rose that now looks tired. He takes the flower from his lapel and drops it in his jacket pocket with the items already there. He will get a new rose from the florist near his stop.

Alighting from the bus with a jaunty step, he breathes in the cool night air, smelling . . . chocolate. Everywhere lovers have given bright boxes of candy to each other, and the air reeks with the odor of dark passion. The scent stirs him anew, and he trots to the florist, in a hurry now to get to the rendezvous.

The young woman at the shop wears a pink sweater and red skirt in honor of the day. She glances at him and smiles, knowing what he's come for, but asks, "Roses, or carnations?"

He answers, "One white rose, please."

She brings him a long-stemmed rose from a refrigerated case. He pays her, and as he exits the shop, snaps off the cold stem just above the bottom. It has no thorns.

A two-block walk lies between him and his destination, and he takes his time, luxuriating in his expectation. He passes jewelry stores along the way, their windows aglow with the same garish light of all jewelry windows, overbright blue to make the diamonds sparkle. The stones never sparkle as much once they're on a woman's finger, perhaps because of the guilt and fear that rubs off on them. His mother had demanded diamonds from his father, but they had grown dull from her neglect of the man. A sad lot in life, and one which has seemed, so far, to be hereditary.

But tonight would be different. He would prove that the key to inspiring love in a woman is not diamonds, or other costly treasures, but simple things, such as heartfelt declarations and fine chocolates.

He arrives early at his destination and sees one light burning from a rear window. As usual, he enters through the back door and hangs his coat in the employees' lounge. He finds the other man standing over a microscope, adjusting a slide while a purpled image on a video monitor jiggles. It becomes still, and the other man stands tall to stretch.

"Oh, hi. You're early," says the man. "Hope you don't mind if I go on. My wife's got something special cooked up—Valentine's Day, y'know." The man grins and shakes his head, taking in the figure before him. "Looks like *you've* just come from a hot date."

"No," he says, twirling the rose in his fingers, "looking forward to one."

A quizzical expression crosses the man's face, followed by a shrug of shoulders. "Well, see you, then," he says, leaving.

The glare from overhead lights is annoying, and he dims them. One round lamp at the far end of the room reflects off the chrome surface beneath it, casting a soft, blue glow through the entire chamber. The microscopes and other clinical equipment retreat into shadow; the tiled walls no longer glint with antiseptic sharpness; only the gleaming table stands apart from everything else. He shakes open a moss green sheet and spreads it over the steel surface, smoothing it carefully with nimble fingers. The rose, now in a beaker of water, adorns the head of the table.

From the pocket of his black suit coat, he pulls the wilted rose, brings it to his face, and breathes in its still-full aroma. Plucking the petals, he scatters them over the sheet. He draws the last two items from his pocket now: the slender, unmarked vial goes into the steam sterilizer, and the syringe is tossed into a bin with hundreds of others like it.

Lights down, bed made, he stares at the big, empty steel drawers lining one wall, and awaits his first lover's arrival.

THE VIRGINS OF VALENTINE

by *Edward D. Hoch*

The town of Valentine is nestled in the hills of northern Pennsylvania not far from the New York State line, about a four-hour drive from Manhattan. I know because I drove Simon Ark there on a blustery February weekend during the worst winter the East Coast had experienced in a decade.

"Is this trip really necessary, Simon?" I asked as I edged the car around a lumbering snowplow from the state Department of Transportation.

He sat beside me in the front seat, staring out at the snow. "It seems to be letting up," he decided, no doubt trying to raise my spirits.

I had to admit that the snowfall had lessened as we moved away from the coast, but I still wondered how I'd allowed myself to be talked into this expedition in the first place. My wife, Shelly, who never harbored any great warmth for Simon, had denounced it as sheer foolishness—driving over two hundred miles in a snowstorm to visit a graveyard in a Pennsylvania town no one had ever heard of.

Somehow, as Simon Ark's voice droned on, he made the journey seem both necessary and desirable. "My friend, we will not see such a conjunction of lunar and calendar events again for decades. Tonight is Friday the thirteenth, the first night of the full moon, and the eve of St. Valentine's Day."

"So we have to go to a cemetery in Valentine, Pennsylvania?"

"The only other towns named Valentine are in Nebraska and Texas, both too far south for a proper positioning of the full moon at midnight."

For as long as I'd known him, Simon Ark had been engaged in a tireless quest for Satan, seeking him on the voodoo beaches of Rio and in the burial pits of Bombay. Simon claimed to have been a Coptic priest in Egypt nearly two thousand years ago, and who was I to argue with him? Whatever he was, he knew a great deal about Satanism, witchcraft, and allied subjects. A decade ago my firm had even published a book by him which attracted a moderate degree of attention. Over the years Simon often called upon me to serve as his companion during periodic investigations into the strange—and occasionally Satanic—events in the world around us.

168

It was a role I accepted with mixed feelings, though I had to admit the company of Simon Ark was rarely dull.

By the time we passed through Scranton, heading northwest on Route 6, the snow had stopped. And when we reached the little town of Valentine in midafternoon, there were actually a few bare spots of grass showing through the mantle of white. The temperature was into the low thirties and some sun had broken through the clouds.

"You made our reservations?" Simon asked.

"At the Village Inn. There's not much choice in a town this size."

The Village Inn was a quaint little place on Main Street, freshly painted in an obvious effort at restoration. A sign in the shape of a large red heart was tacked to a pillar by the front steps, announcing in big black letters: *Welcome to Valentine! We'll Steal Your Heart Away!* Simon merely grunted at that as I helped him up the icy steps and into the lobby.

A fresh-faced young woman, short and small-boned, appeared from somewhere to greet us, wearing jeans and an old shirt. "You must be Mr. Ark and Mr.—"

"That's right," I confirmed. "From New York."

"Have you come for our Valentine's Day celebration?"

"More or less."

She smiled and gave us registration cards to sign. "I'm Kate Summers. We have a nice room reserved for you on the second floor, with double beds. It gets lots of morning sunshine."

"I'm sure it'll be satisfactory."

"You'll be with us two nights?"

"We expect so, yes."

She took out a fancy lighter and cigarettes and lit one as she studied our cards. "Come, I'll show you the room."

It was as homey as I'd expected, with bright flowery spreads on both beds. The big bay window looked out onto Main Street and I could see my car at the curb. "Do you have parking for guests?"

"It's around back. Turn right at the next corner and you'll see the driveway."

Simon Ark was testing out the bed nearest the window. "Tell me, Miss Summers—"

"It's Mrs. Summers. My husband Herb runs the place with me. You'll see him at dinner. We start serving at five."

"Which way is it to the Methodist church and the cemetery?"

"Oh, I'm afraid the church is closed now. The minister only comes through once a month to conduct services here, on the last

Sunday. Most people drive into Sayre where they have Catholic and Baptist churches.''

"We were only interested in the cemetery," Simon explained.

"Oh! Well, you drive straight out Main and it's on your left, about a mile. But I certainly never noticed anything special about that old place."

I cleared my throat. "We do tombstone rubbings sometimes."

"You'd better not go out there tonight. The place'll be full of teenage girls."

"What?"

"Here in Valentine we follow all the old customs," she explained. "Girls used to believe that they would eventually marry the first eligible male they saw on Valentine's Day. In England two hundred years ago it was customary for the braver girls to go to the local graveyard at midnight on St. Valentine's Eve. They would sing a prescribed chant and run around the church twelve times. Each girl was supposed to conjure up the appearance of her future spouse. Here in Valentine the boys don't leave anything to chants. They usually drive out to the cemetery themselves and manage to put in an appearance at the magical moment. Then everyone goes off to a party."

"That's quite a beginning for Valentine's Day," Simon admitted. "What happens tomorrow?"

"We have a little parade and the general store has a sale. The post office is kept busy, of course. Everyone wants a letter or card postmarked from Valentine on February fourteenth."

"It doesn't bother the girls that it'll still be Friday the thirteenth when they arrive at the cemetery?" I asked.

"Goodness, no! We're not superstitious here."

After she went back downstairs I started to unpack my overnight duffel. "I doubt if you'll have any success encountering Satan in a graveyard full of screaming teenage girls," I told Simon.

"Stranger things have happened, my friend. Virgins are often used at black masses where the devil is said to preside."

"We'll see."

Kate's husband Herb Summers helped serve dinner in the Village Inn's small dining room. He was a handsome, soft-spoken man around thirty, and it was obvious he was quite content to let his wife take charge of running the inn.

"I'm just the handyman around here," he explained with a pleasant smile. "It's all Kate's place. She inherited it from her dad. I always imagined I'd be a farmer and here I end up as an innkeeper." He glanced around at the empty tables and added, "Not much of one, though, at least in the winter."

"Doesn't anyone else come for your Valentine festival?" I asked.

"A few people drive in for the day, but we don't get many staying overnight."

We finished our dinner and went for a walk around the town. There were stores and a movie theater, though upon closer examination this proved to be shut down. A few bars dotted the center of town, and there was a small bank with a lawyer's office upstairs. Near the edge of the retail area was a farm implement dealer, and farther out in the growing darkness we could just make out the steeple of the Methodist church.

"Do you want to take a ride out there now," I asked Simon, "while there's still a little light?"

"That's a good idea."

It was after six by that time, and practically night, but we went anyway. I parked in front of the church, close to the graveyard, and we managed to avoid some of the deeper snowdrifts to walk where the ground was almost bare. We studied some of the tombstones.

"These inscriptions are all pretty old," I observed. "I wonder if the place is still used."

"It doesn't matter for our purposes."

"Suppose you tell me just what our purposes are, Simon. What do you think is going to happen here at the conjunction of the full moon, Friday the thirteenth and Valentine's Day?"

"It may be that Satan will walk, as on Halloween when that day precedes the feast of All Saints. If he is to appear anywhere, the graveyard in a town named Valentine seems the most likely place."

"Some doubt St. Valentine ever existed. It's merely a legend, Simon."

"These days some doubt that Satan ever existed, but it does not prevent the evil done in his name. If I were to see him now, striding toward us between the gravestones—"

"Simon! What's that?"

There was indeed someone out there in the night, outlined against the snow, moving toward us. A man dressed in black, wearing a full-length cape that showed flashes of a red lining as he drew near. A man who, God help us, even had a devilish little beard coming to a point beneath his chin.

"Stop there!" Simon Ark called out. "Who are you?"

"I might ask the same of you," the man answered, coming a bit nearer. "I'm Oliver Martin. I live in the next house down. I was out walking my dog when I saw someone in here.'' As if on cue, a large golden retriever bounded over a snowbank to join him.

''My name is Simon Ark and this is my friend. We're traveling through and decided to spend the night at the Village Inn. Valentine seemed a likely place in view of the date.''

''Sightseers, are you? Not many sights to see in a cemetery at night. Come, Rex, we're going home.'' He turned without another word and returned the way he had come, the dog following at his feet.

''Not very friendly,'' I observed, ''but then I don't suppose the devil has a sense of humor.''

''Appearances can be deceptive, my friend.''

''I suppose you're right. Satan would have had a black cat, not a golden retriever.''

''There is nothing more to be seen here. Let us return to the inn until it is close to midnight.''

''You're really serious about this whole thing, aren't you, Simon?''

''I am indeed. We will be back at midnight.''

We spent some time browsing in the Valentine general store until it closed at nine. It was more of a modern supermarket than a traditional general store, and scores of hearts dangled from the ceiling to announce the Valentine Sale. I bought a couple of magazines to read and Simon purchased a box of dog biscuits.

''Are you that hungry so soon after dinner?'' I chided.

''They might prove useful.''

We stopped in one of the bars along Main Street for a beer, sitting at a little table while a few men argued over the merits of some hockey players on the television screen.

''You think Oliver Martin will return at midnight?'' I asked Simon. ''Is that what the dog biscuits are for?''

''We'll see. I had imagined we would have the cemetery to ourselves at that hour, but if we must have virginal chanting and running about, who knows what else might turn up?''

The temperature had dropped back below freezing and the night chill prompted a return to our room at the inn for warm sweaters to wear under our coats. Kate Summers was not in sight, but Herb was behind the desk in the lobby. Simon struck up a conversation with him, the motive of which quickly became obvious. ''We were out by the graveyard and we met a man named Oliver Martin, walking his dog.''

''Martin is something of a town character,'' Herb Summers

explained. "He does have a sinister air about him. Some people think he looks like the devil, but he's harmless enough. He worked for a big electronics company up in Syracuse, but he moved down here with his wife a couple of years ago. They've been active in the town affairs, and in fact Amy Martin is the one who revived the custom of girls going to the graveyard on Valentine's Eve to conjure up visions of their future husbands."

"Is that so? It seems a harmless enough custom," Simon remarked.

"Keeps the kids off the streets. The boys usually drive out there too, and take the girls off to a party afterwards. Chaperoned, of course."

"By the Martins?"

"Yeah, how'd you know?"

"It seemed likely," Simon Ark replied.

We drove out to the graveyard at the Methodist church around eleven-thirty. Simon was quiet most of the way, but as we approached I could see a number of girls arriving, bundled in parkas and ski jackets, many with scarves wrapped around their heads and faces against the February cold. "There will be twelve of them," Simon said quietly. "Twelve virgins. The traditional number of witches in a coven."

"You're really convinced that Oliver Martin is the devil? After meeting the man for all of two minutes, Simon?" But even as I spoke I saw Oliver Martin approaching down the road, accompanied now by a tall handsome woman wearing an expensive white mink coat. The retriever trailed at their heels.

We got out of the car and approached them. Martin scowled in our direction and said, "You two back again? What are you, big-city reporters?" The promised full moon glowed behind him in the eastern sky.

I introduced myself and passed him my card. "A publisher, actually. But we're only driving through. What's going on here?"

"My wife will tell you. It's her project. Come, Rex!" He hurried along the road, leaving Amy Martin to make excuses for him. I suspected it wasn't the first time.

"He'll be back," she told us. "He just wants to exercise Rex. His bark is worse than his bite."

"Rex's, or your husband's?" I asked.

"Both of them," she answered with a smile.

Simon gestured to the cemetery, where more girls were arriving. "I understand this is an annual tradition."

Amy Martin laughed. "Only for the past two years. It's an old

English custom, and I thought it went well with the town's attempts to revive the traditions of Valentine's Day. The teenagers love it.''

"Just what do they do?"

"I wrote a little chant for them to sing, and then they're supposed to run around the church twelve times and see a vision of their future husbands. The boys arrive about that time to make sure the visions are of flesh and blood. Come along and watch.''

I could see a few other townsfolk pulled up along the side of the road as midnight approached, but the cold night air kept most of them in their cars. I assumed they were the parents of some of the girls. A few cars had their headlights on, but much of the cemetery and churchyard was in darkness. Just before midnight Oliver Martin returned with his dog and wandered around to the side of the church where his wife was passing out song sheets.

I did a quick count and told Simon, "Only eleven virgins. You were off by one."

Exactly at midnight the chanting began with a musical but slightly off-key rendering calling upon St. Valentine to lift the veil from the future and reveal the girls' true loves. A car pulled up by the church and two tardy virgins jumped out, running bareheaded across the snow to join the others. "Now it's thirteen," I chided Simon. "You're still off by one."

"Twelve times around the church," Amy Martin announced in a loud voice as the chanting ended, "and then you will see your future love!"

The girls set off, more at a trot than a run, conserving their energy. Oliver Martin stood in their path, counting off the laps as they passed him. Suddenly I realized we were not the only spectators who'd left our car to brave the cold. Herb Summers from the Village Inn had joined us with a tall, beefy man wearing a wide mustache. "Mr. Ark, this here's Sheriff Aikens. He keeps things lawful in Valentine.''

The sheriff shook hands with us. "Always happy to see tourists in for Valentine's Day. You be staying for the parade tomorrow?''

"We hope to," I said. I heard Martin call off the third lap.

"I suppose this seems silly to people from New York—''

"No, no," Simon assured him. "It is in rural America that the folk customs of an earlier period are preserved. Some say Valentine's Day is the date on which birds mate. It is a pleasant holiday, given over to love and romantic notions.''

Summers drifted away but Sheriff Aikens stayed to chat. "I been telling folks for years that we should do more to cash in on the name of Valentine. Before the Martins moved here we didn't do anything, except for the special postmark. Now we've got this thing for the kids and the parade and sale tomorrow. That usually brings them in from the surrounding towns. Hell, if Punxsutawney can become famous every Groundhog's Day, I guess we should be able to do the same on Valentine's Day!''

Oliver Martin was already up to lap number seven and the girls were still running through the night. To me it looked more like an exercise class than a Valentine's Day ritual. But presently I saw the lights of two more cars arriving down the line, and several teenage boys piled out of each. I had to admit the thing was being well orchestrated.

''Lap number ten!'' Martin called out as the girls ran by in a group, a few stragglers trailing some feet behind.

The boys were creeping along the road, staying behind the parked car so they'd come into view just as the girls finished their laps. Sheriff Aikens left us, saying, ''I'd better keep those kids in line.''

As the bevy of teenagers rounded the Methodist church for the last time, they converged on Oliver Martin. He held up his hands, signaling the end of the event. At my side Simon started forward, disturbed by something I couldn't see. ''That fiend!'' he muttered.

''Do you still believe he's the devil, Simon?''

''Don't you see what he's done? Don't you realize—?''

One of the girls screamed, and the tight little circle around Martin suddenly parted. There was another scream, and another, and then blind panic. The boys had run forward on cue, but no one was paying the least attention to them. All eyes were on Oliver Martin, who'd toppled over onto the snow-covered ground. His black cape had fallen open and as we hurried forward I could see the knife protruding from his chest.

Sheriff Aikens was no small-town bumpkin, and I had to admire the manner in which he immediately took charge. The state police were notified, an ambulance was summoned from the volunteer fire department, and he started taking down the names of everyone who was on the scene. ''We don't get many murders here in Valentine,'' he told us as he copied down our names and addresses. ''I guess this'll put us on the front pages if nothing else will.''

Amy Martin had remained remarkably composed during the moments after her husband's death, but now I noticed her in tears as some of the other women led her away. The golden retriever, Rex, was forgotten for the moment, and Simon Ark found a use for the pocket full of dog biscuits he'd brought along.

Most of the girls were near hysteria in the moments after the

killing, and there was only one to whom the sheriff could speak.
She was a bit taller and older than the rest, an eighteen-year-old
named Laurie Enright. She wore a red down ski jacket and
earmuffs, and was pretty enough to have modeled the garments in
a magazine ad. ''I don't know what happened,'' she told the sheriff
while Simon and I stood nearby. ''We ran up to Mr. Martin, just
as we did last year, and crowded around him. All of a sudden he
gasped and his body seemed to stiffen. One of the girls screamed
and I felt him falling over, right on top of me.''

''Did you see the knife then?''

''Not till he was on the ground. Then everyone was screaming.''

''Who would want to kill Mr. Martin?'' the sheriff asked.

''I don't know.''

''Did any of the girls ever talk about him?''

''Not really. Jennifer thought he was really sinister, but that was
about all.''

''Jennifer?''

''Jennifer MacDonald, over there.''

''Oh, yes,'' the sheriff agreed. ''I know her.''

But Jennifer was in no state to be questioned at the moment, and
Sheriff Aikens wisely arranged for her mother to bring her to his
office first thing in the morning. Then he turned his attention to
Simon and me.

''You fellows are the only strangers here. I got to consider you
as suspects.''

''We were twenty feet away when he was stabbed,'' I pointed
out. ''How could either of us have done it?''

''The knife could have been thrown just as the girls crowded in
around Martin. The pressure of their bodies would have kept him
upright for a few seconds. In the darkness no one would have
noticed.''

''There was enough moonlight to see that,'' I argued.

''Well, you're planning to stay around tomorrow anyway, aren't
you? Come down to my office in the morning and we can talk about
it. I'll need statements from everyone here, and I'm not going to
get anywhere with these hysterical girls tonight.''

The Valentine celebration had turned to horror, and as Simon and
I returned to our car we could still see groups of girls comforting
one another as anxious parents attempted to locate their daughters.
The ambulance had arrived and so had the state police, and photo-
graphs of the body were taken before it was covered and moved
away. The quiet graveyard seemed alive with flashing red lights and

the crackle of police radios. I saw Herb Summers grab hold of Rex's collar and lead him down the road toward the Martin house.

"I guess he wasn't the devil after all," I told Simon as we drove away. "Only a mortal human like the rest of us."

"But perhaps one who engaged in devilish pursuits."

"Why do you say that? And what was it that so upset you the instant before he was killed?"

"Didn't you realize what you were seeing, my friend? After circling the church twelve times, the virgins were supposed to have a vision of their lover, their future mate. Yet they all flocked around Oliver Martin. He was the first male any of these impressionable young girls saw after their chanting and running. And don't you think Martin arranged it that way?"

"You make him sound like a Svengali with some sort of harem, Simon. I think you're letting your imagination run wild."

"We shall see, my friend. If one of those girls stabbed him, she must have had a reason."

We were up in the morning after only five hours' sleep, awakened by a loudspeaker in front of the general store playing "My Funny Valentine" and other suitable love songs. Obviously the celebration was progressing in spite of the murder. Simon and I had the dining room all to ourselves for breakfast, served with a preoccupied frown by Kate Summers.

"Herb told me what happened last night," she said. "It's all over town this morning. God, I can't believe it!"

"The sheriff wants a statement from us," I told her. "We're on our way over there now."

"You know, just about midnight I looked out the back window here and saw that full moon, and I knew something awful was going to happen. It was a premonition."

"Did you know Oliver Martin well?"

"Hardly at all. I'd see him around town, but I probably spoke more to his wife than to him. Amy's a lovely person, always wanting to help people."

"She seemed nice," I agreed. "I understand this business at the cemetery was all her idea."

"That's right. She got it going two years ago, shortly after they moved here. She was supposed to be in the parade this morning, too." She walked with us out to the counter as we talked.

"What time does that start?"

"Around ten o'clock." She finally managed a smile. "It won't take long. A parade in Valentine's not like New York City."

We reached the sheriff's office around nine-thirty. A state police investigator was with him and they were questioning the MacDonald girl and her mother. A half dozen other girls were in the waiting room with their parents. Most were red-eyed and silent.

When the sheriff saw us waiting he excused himself and ushered us into an adjoining office. "He can handle the interviews alone. After the first two, I could see they're all going to be the same. The girls saw nothing and they know nothing. It's as if Oliver Martin was struck down by the hand of God."

"Perhaps he was," Simon speculated.

Sheriff Aikens showed us a plastic evidence bag with the murder weapon inside. "Since when does the hand of God wield a wooden-handled boning knife with a five-inch blade?"

"Fingerprints?" I asked.

"None. And we'll never be able to trace it. It probably comes from a set of kitchen knives that most any home might possess."

"Did he die instantly?"

"Right to the heart. Probably didn't live more than a few seconds."

Simon looked thoughtful, picking up a list of the girls to be interviewed, as if the names themselves might tell him something. I glanced over his shoulder and read along:

Catherine Brophey
Shannon Cinelli
Kathy Clark
Laurie Enright
Julie Foley
Christine Hawkes
Jennifer MacDonald
Jamie Morey
Lisa Russo
Yvonne Sojak
Kristan White
Amanda Williams

I wondered what had happened to all the Marys and Janes I grew up with. Simon grunted and returned the list to the desk.

"Of course, everyone was wearing gloves out there last night," the sheriff said, "so the lack of fingerprints is no surprise."

I tapped the evidence bag with my finger. "This boning knife couldn't have been thrown with any sort of accuracy."

"Possibly not," Sheriff Aikens agreed, "but we'll try it out. I find it hard to believe one of those girls killed him."

We dictated our statements, describing what little we'd seen. When we left the sheriff's office there were still several girls waiting to give their statements. They all shared an expression of fear and bewilderment.

Outside, the parade was starting. A float decorated with valentine hearts led the way, with a small boy in woolen underwear pretending to fire cupid's arrow at a pair of young lovers. This was followed by a carload of town officials and a high school marching band. A few more cars and trucks completed the parade. Kate Summers had been right. A parade in Valentine didn't take long.

"Seen enough?" I asked Simon.

He nodded. "Let's drive out to the Martin place."

"It might be a bad time to intrude."

"Sheriff Aikens is a smart man, but he's out of his depth here. He clearly needs our help."

"Against Satan?"

"Against a clever murderer."

We drove out Main Street to the house next to the cemetery. I pulled in the driveway and the door was opened at once by Amy Martin. "Oh!" she said, frowning at us. "I was expecting the funeral director. I have to go over the arrangements."

"We're sorry to intrude at such a time, Mrs. Martin," Simon Ark said. "If we could just have a word with you—"

She studied us for a moment and then said, "All right. Come in." Again she seemed in control of herself, as she had been immediately after the murder.

The house was large and richly decorated. I could see she took pride in it. Simon and I took seats in the living room and she sat opposite us. "It's about your husband," Simon began.

"You're dressed in black. Are you a priest?"

"I was once, a long time ago. But then, your husband dressed in black, too. What was he?"

"Only a poor deluded man."

"Mrs. Martin, was Oliver having an affair with one of those girls?"

The audacity of such a question to the grieving widow startled me, but perhaps Simon had a better insight into her feelings than I did. She hesitated a few seconds and then replied, "I think he was having an affair, yes, but I never dreamed it was with a high school girl. I still can't believe that. There was some evidence recently—mysterious phone calls at night, little notes that he managed to hide before I could read them. You get to know the signs, especially if you've been through it before. When we were living in Syracuse he was quite friendly with his secretary. I guess I thought he'd grown out of it at his age."

"Did you accuse him of it?"

"Yes. We had a stormy session about two weeks ago. He told me he'd already broken it off, but of course I had no way of knowing if that was true."

"Did he mention her name?"

"No. He told me nothing about her."

Simon Ark drew a deep breath. "Did you hate your husband enough to kill him, Mrs. Martin?"

"Yes, I think I did," she said after a moment's consideration.

"Did you kill him last night?"

"No, Mr. Ark, I did not."

Simon stood up to go and I followed his lead. "Thank you for your frankness."

"Will there be an end to this nightmare?"

"I believe so, very soon."

On the drive back to the Village Inn, I asked Simon, "What will you do now?"

"Perhaps I will buy a valentine at the general store. Have you sent Shelly one?"

I had to admit it had slipped my mind during the preparations for our trip. When we returned to our room I telephoned the florist we used back home and ordered a dozen long-stemmed roses delivered to my house. "Thanks for reminding me, Simon. I'm in enough trouble for taking this trip in the first place. Now what? Do you still want that Valentine?"

"No, no. We will relax a bit this afternoon, and return to the cemetery after dark."

"Are you still expecting the devil to appear there?"

"Either the devil or a murderer. You might telephone Sheriff Aikens and invite him to join us."

Simon's vagueness with the sheriff was a problem, but finally he agreed to join us at the cemetery just after dark. We sat in his car, which was parked behind the Methodist church, where it couldn't be seen from the road. When we first arrived, Simon had walked out a bit to where the tracks of the previous night's runners came around the corner, and dropped something on a bare spot of ground. I couldn't see what it was.

When he returned to the car, Sheriff Aikens asked, "What are you up to? What's this all about?"

"A theory I have, nothing more. We may unmask a murderer, or we may lose a night's sleep. Only time will tell."

Around eight o'clock a carful of teenage boys came by to inspect the murder scene. They stayed about ten minutes and then drove off. Another car came about an hour later. We could see there was a boy and girl in that one, but they didn't get out. By ten o'clock we were all a bit discouraged. "I could be questioning those girls again," Sheriff Aikens grumbled. "Or getting some sleep."

"Did you get anywhere with them today?" I asked.

"No," he admitted. "One of the young ones, Julie Foley, thinks she saw the flash of the knife in the moonlight, but with everyone clustered around she couldn't tell who was holding it. The other girls didn't see a thing until he started to fall."

"Were any of them especially friendly with him?"

"One of the seventeen-year-olds, Amanda Williams, had spoken to him a few times on her way home from school, but that was all."

We heard the barking of a dog on the road, and the sheriff slipped out of the car for a look. He came back to tell us, "It's Mrs. Martin walking Rex, but she stayed out on the road."

We settled down to wait some more.

I was half dozing when Simon touched my shoulder lightly. "There! It's the beam of a flashlight moving along the ground!"

I felt Sheriff Aikens grow tense beside me as a small figure in scarf and ski jacket came into view. "What's she looking for?" he whispered.

"Something she thinks she dropped last night, when she stabbed Oliver Martin. Come on!"

Simon Ark slipped noiselessly out of the car without closing the door behind him. We followed along. The figure with the flashlight had just reached the bare spot when the beam of light must have picked up whatever Simon had dropped earlier. She bent over to retrieve it as we moved in.

"Hold it there, miss," the sheriff said.

She whirled around, her face still covered by the scarf, and ran for the road. We were after her in an instant, and Sheriff Aikens grabbed her around the waist, spinning her off her feet. The scarf fell away.

"Let me go!" she shouted. "Damn it, let me go!"

It was Kate Summers from the Village Inn.

* * *

We went down to the sheriff's office after that, while Simon Ark explained it all. "My friend and I counted thirteen girls last night," he said, "but there were only twelve names on your list. That simple fact told the whole story. The killer had mingled with the girls and then escaped in the darkness and confusion after the murder. Dressed for winter, with scarves around some of their heads and faces, it was easy enough to pass undetected while they were running around the church. The fact that the killer chose to escape rather than stay and identify herself told me she wasn't a teenager. She was someone who would have seemed out of place with the others, which is why she couldn't stay."

"It could have been a man or boy," I pointed out.

"True enough, though the one necessity was that the killer have small stature. That pretty much eliminated men, and a boy probably would have been noticed by the girls around him, especially during the chanting that preceded the run. Also there's the question of motive. If Oliver Martin really had broken off an affair with one of the women in town, that might have given her a motive to kill him. A spurned love, especially on Valentine's Day in a town like this, might have been too much to bear."

"But why Kate Summers?"

"Remember earlier today at breakfast when Mrs. Summers mentioned seeing the full moon out the back window at midnight? We saw it rising in the eastern sky at about that same time, out at the cemetery. But our room at the Village Inn, facing Main Street in the front, is on the eastern side. Kate Summers herself told us it got the morning sun. If the front of the inn looks east, the back must face west. She couldn't have seen the moon out the rear window at midnight. She was lying."

"Why would she lie about a thing like that?" the sheriff wanted to know.

"She was trying to establish her presence at the inn around midnight, the time of the murder. I suppose she saw the full moon in the western sky much later, when she returned from the cemetery. By placing the time at midnight she implicated herself. Then when I really looked at her, I saw a short, small-boned woman who could easily double as a teenage girl. This was even before I saw your list with only twelve names on it. On a hunch I stole her cigarette lighter which she'd left on the counter, and I dropped it out at the churchyard tonight. She was so preoccupied this morning I took a chance that she wouldn't remember when she'd last had it. The lighter was distinctive enough that she couldn't take a chance on having dropped it in the snow while running around the church. She came out tonight to search for it, and we had her.''

The sheriff nodded. "She's with her lawyer now. I think she's going to make a confession.''

Later, as we drove out of Valentine and headed back toward New York, I told Simon, "There was nothing very romantic about this Valentine's Day.''

"I disagree," Simon Ark said. "After all, my friend, she killed Oliver Martin because she loved him too much to let him go. And she stabbed him through the heart. In its own way it was a fitting Valentine's Day crime.''

HOME FOR THE HOLIDAY

by Susan Casper

Margaret Dixon heard the rattle of the front door. She put down her coffee cup and walked to the front hall. The morning mail was lying in a heap on the welcome mat. She picked it up and walked back to the kitchen table, and sat down to shuffle through it. One bright red envelope attracted her eye, and she pulled it out of the stack, and held it up.

A valentine.

She eyed it with shock and a sense of foreboding. Who would send *her* a valentine anymore? She used to love Valentine's Day, back when Michael was little. It had always been their special day; a day to do things together. A day for trips to the zoo, or later, when he was older, a day for him to take Mom to dinner. She put the valentine down, picked it up tentatively, then laid it down again. Later, she told herself, when she was more composed.

She put more coffee on the stove to perk, but the apple green chairs and brightly painted walls of her kitchen no longer cheered her. Despite the early morning sun that streamed in the unshuttered window, the room seemed dull and gray. Even the coffee was flat and tasteless.

The phone rang, startling her. She didn't want to answer it, and she didn't know why. It was probably only Laura Freeman, calling to invite herself over for tea. But she didn't want to speak to anyone. It was as if some great calamity would come crashing through the wires. Seven . . . eight . . . nine times it rang, and seemed to get louder with each ring. When it stopped, she relaxed, releasing the breath she had not noticed holding. "What's wrong with you, today?" she asked herself, and the words echoed dully through the large empty house. She was twitchy and nervous, so unlike herself that her very fright scared her even more.

Last night she hadn't been nervous or uneasy. She had spent a normal evening watching TV, mostly sitcoms, then gone to bed. And then . . . *she'd had the dream!* She sat up straighter, shivering, remembering how the dream had woken her sweaty and screaming in the middle of the night. There had been a valentine in the dream, too. She remembered it clearly now. The house was done up for a party. Balloons and streamers hung on the wall. The pieces of furniture were those of her childhood, but strangely distorted, and oddly arranged. She was wearing a blue dress, very outdated, that she might have worn as a young girl. The phonograph played, but she couldn't quite make out what—"The Ohio Waltz," perhaps. None of the guests had arrived yet, and she paced the floor impatiently. When the doorbell rang, she ran to it eagerly, but no one was there—only a valentine in a big, red, heart-shaped envelope, left on the mat by someone. She picked it up, noticing the odd cold slickness of the paper, and carried it inside. When she got back to the living room with it, all the guests were there, talking and laughing. All eyes turned to her as she entered. She ripped open the envelope, and it began to bleed. The blood cascaded down over her hands, staining her pretty blue dress, and forming a pool on the rug. Like yards of dark ribbon unwinding, the flow of blood continued . . . until, shaken and pale, she woke up in her bed.

She trembled at the thought of it. How odd that someone should send her a valentine *today*, after she'd had that terrible dream last night. Perhaps she had *known* it was coming. Perhaps the dream was some sort of premonition. An omen. Or maybe she was just getting old. Old and crazy, and completely alone. She looked at her hands, seeing the wrinkles and age marks. She didn't usually think of herself as old. She imagined herself feeble and wandering aimlessly through empty rooms, lost and afraid until she died. Dead and alone in the big old house she'd been born in. And nobody even to care. "You are a foolish old woman," she told herself mockingly, taking a sip from her cup. "Open your mail."

The envelope lay there in front of her on the table. With renewed bravado, she picked it up. It felt perfectly normal, not preternaturally cold or slimy or slick. One thing she was certain of: it contained only paper, nothing more. But in spite of that, the hairs on her spine tingled and her fingers shook. Viciously, she ripped the envelope open and pulled out the card inside. It was a valentine, all right. A plain red heart covered with tiny white flowers. Under a printed sentimental poem, in a thin scrawl, was written:

> Be home for our special day. All my love,
> —Michael.

Anger like liquid fire spread up her neck and into her face. Tears filled her eyes. How cruel! How unutterably cruel! She licked her parched lips, feeling dazed and confused. The valentine slipped unnoticed from her fingers. Without even thinking of where she was going, she walked up a flight of stairs, down the hall, and up another flight. The phone was ringing again downstairs, but she ignored it. She paused for a moment with her hand on the doorknob, then slowly opened the door.

The room seemed to glow in the morning light. The bed was neatly made up, but the pale golden print on the blanket had faded. The Ann-Margaret poster was peeling off the wall at one corner, but that was the only damage the years had done. His books and his records still lay where he had left them. She stepped carefully over his vinyl boots and eased herself into the chair. Oh Michael, Michael! She leaned back against the desk, knocking over a photograph. Agitated, she set it upright again. Nothing must be moved— nothing. She sat staring at the picture. It was a picture of Michael and Cannonball. They had looked so cute there on the lawn, little Michael and the huge St. Bernard. She had used up a whole roll of film. She replaced the snapshot carefully. There were other pictures around, and she looked at each thoughtfully, bringing back the memories she had exiled all this time. Michael, dark and beautiful, with the wonderful flashing blue eyes. The solitary, sometimes brooding child, playing soldier in the backyard. "Mommy, I'm gonna be a hero someday!"

"Yes, dear," she whispered to him across the years.

She remembered the way she saw him last, with his spotless uniform and brightly shined buttons. He had given her a big jaunty grin and said, "Take care of yourself, Mom. I'll be home before you know it. I'll expect you to have dinner waiting." And she had ached for one more chance to tousle his hair, to give him a big hug and kiss.

But Michael never came back. Instead, there had been that cold, impersonal telegram, the sealed, flag-draped coffin, and rain drumming on the freshly turned earth. No chance to see him or kiss him good-bye.

The doorbell jerked her out of her reverie. She sat for a while, not wanting company, not wanting to give up the feeling that somehow Michael was near her again. The doorbell rang again. With a sigh, she forced herself to go down to answer it. Laura would be good for her now, calm her down. She pulled open the door, saying, "Laura," then stopped, openmouthed.

A young man stood there. He had close-cropped hair and his smartly pressed khaki uniform had brass buttons that shone in the sunlight. She gasped and fell back, going white. "Mom?" he said. "Mother? Are you all right?" She stared at him wide-eyed, the word *no* forming silently on her lips. It couldn't be. It just couldn't be. But it was. She reached out and touched him, feeling his arm, the material of his jacket.

"Michael? Michael, is that really you?" She felt weak and dizzy and her heart was racing. Had she conjured him up? Could this be happening, could this possibly be real? He looked just the way she remembered him last, but here he was touching her, kissing her, talking to her. "They said they would tell you. Poor Mama, such a shock. I was sure they had let you know. It was a mix-up. It was someone else who got killed, but they mistook him for me. I was a prisoner of war. They just released me a little while ago. It was all a terrible mistake, but it's all over now. Everything's all right." He put his arm around her thin shoulders and she led him into the house, still staring at him in dazed wonder.

"But how are you? How did they treat you? Are you all right? It must have been dreadful for you," she stammered. Then she smiled. "Never mind now. Come into the kitchen and I'll fix you something to eat. You can tell me about it later. For now, it's enough that you're here." She wrapped her arm around his waist, hugging him, and walked with him into the kitchen, bright-eyed, smiling, no longer alone.

Mrs. Freeman came over at three o'clock. She was a little worried that she had not been able to reach Marge on the phone; she knew that her friend hadn't been feeling well lately. When nobody answered the door, she let herself in. It was never locked. She walked through the living room, calling. How odd that it hadn't been dusted yet. She walked down the hall to the kitchen, where they spent most of their time. Marge was sitting at the kitchen table and for a moment Laura thought that she was only sleeping. She was sitting nearly upright in the chair, head tilted slightly back, an unopened valentine in her hand.

NO HEARTS, NO FLOWERS

by Barry N. Malzberg

I am sitting in my accustomed spot in Stendahl's, just across from
the entryway, which gives me command of the vistas of the room,
to say nothing of the vistas of the inner self which like Stendahl's
warming cuisine open up whole layers of possibilities, an accustomed spot which, I should note, enables me to note every one of
the clientele as they exit and enter, to say nothing of large portions
of the room itself when I hear, from a table adjoining, lines so
shocking and devastating in their impact that they—instantly, as it
turns out—cause me to shift from inner to outer landscapes. "Let
us presume," this speaker is saying, "that on this sixty-first
anniversary of the St. Valentine's Day Massacre we commemorate
this most famous and interesting act by its very replication in the
downtown reaches of Brooklyn. This will send a powerful and
unanswerable message to our enemies, of whom, I must remind
you, there are more than several."

This pronouncement, in its offhand audacity—not to say its
dreadful implication—catches my attention at once and I crane my
neck netherwards, then to portside to see who might be the utterer
of such profoundly unsettling plans and sentiments; the voice itself
is nondescript, a voice such as might be heard in Stendahl's at any
time of day or (more usually) evening ordering one or another of
the specials or speculating upon local politics, but my view is
blocked by several riotous diners at the next table, to say nothing
of the late afternoon sun, pouring in through the slender windows
of Stendahl's and setting up a brisk and diverting clatter of light.
I am therefore unable to isolate the voice and am forced to half
stand at the table, distend my limbs into something approaching a
crouch while I incline my head in the direction of the voice, only
to find that there are so many diners of indistinguishable appearance and absorption that I am unable to accomplish this task. "A
presumption," I hear someone say, "that does not need to be
empirically verified," and then once again the sound, closes over
and I am unable to isolate the speaker. Let me make it clear that
Stendahl's at this time is more than ordinarily crowded; it is difficult enough to isolate one's waiter, to say nothing of one's
companion seen across the table, and that this dereliction is not,
then, in the least unexpected and unusual.

"Do you hear that?" I say to my companion, the beauteous and accomplished Baby Jane Harrison, who at that very moment has abandoned the last scraps of her meal and is fetchingly tearing her napkin into small pieces in front of her; what Baby Jane Harrison and I share is a passion for her physique and a series of small tics which for me drive toward attentiveness, for her tend to result in the breakdown of small objects she may have in hand. "Someone over there is talking about another Valentine's Day Massacre in downtown Brooklyn."

"I wouldn't know anything about that," Baby Jane Harrison says. I tend to write these reminiscences in the present tense, not only because the crisp style of the local chronicler which I fancy myself to be is best suited by that method of attack but because, like so many denizens of Stendahl's, to say nothing of Baby Jane herself, I seem to live in a kind of enforced and eternal present, a mode devoid of consequence and barren of history, a pretty good paradigm, one might say, of the twentieth century itself as it closes upon its termination, a century which has much to teach us about the failure of consequence and the damaging of memory. My taste for the present tense, however, does not exclude *all* knowledge of the past, which is why I am able to react quickly to intimations of the St. Valentine's Day Massacre, a celebrated misunderstanding in a suburb of Chicago many decades ago filled with iron and flying teeth and somewhat legendary in its paralyzing effect upon subsequent myth, legend, and politics.

"I do not wish for another St. Valentine's Day Massacre," I say to my lovely companion, forty-two years old but possessed of a slender youthfulness and a powerful sexual obsession that would be the pride of a woman not three-quarters of her age. "Let me run this to the source." I stand and, facing in the direction of the overheard confidence, prepare to set upon the speaker with stately and insistent feet, not seeking confrontation itself so much as witness. My intent, I think, has something to do with making identification so that latterly I may seek the authorities; it has to be understood that my entire motivations here are testimonial rather than confrontational. I am not the scribe of the waterfront for nothing; *scriptor* is not action as I have had occasion to point out often in the context of my weekly musings and jottings. "I will run it to the source," I repeat.

Standing, however, is accomplished with somewhat less ease than I had hoped, Stendahl's borscht and blintzes weighing more heavily than I might have initially expected, and as I turn my head avidly in the direction of the overheard confidences I find myself suddenly

and distressingly locked in place by an enormous, oncoming belch.
The belch racks me, doubles me over in focused consternation
(Baby Jane Harrison looks at me with an indifference only partially
masked by concern), and as I attempt to deal with the inner man
I am rudely, then consecutively, pushed out of the way by a series
of bodies making graceless exit from Stendahl's; first one, then
three or four bodies made enormous by satiation brush by me in
an unfocused blur of grumbling, divestiture of crumbs and belching
(Stendahl's menu is of indiscriminate impact) and I find myself
crumpled inconsequently in my seat, subsumed by these enormous
and implacable forces, stunned, and at a loss for identification.
Baby Jane Harrison, holding a last wedge of unforked cheesecake
in her lovely and tapering left hand, reaches over to pat me with
her right, her fingers lying damply but lovingly on my forehead.
"You're so clumsy," she says with the same mixture of concern
and distance, her eyes focused on some distant imagined point
which may have to do with tangled sheets and orgiastic, random
cries of necessity compounded by cheesecake. "I don't know how
you can be a reporter, a press agent, someone who makes his living
by going around, if you can't get around. If you follow what I am
saying," she adds and grants me poised and distressing laughter.

The afternoon does not quite end at this point, to be sure, to say
nothing of the night; in the nature of such things it goes on and on
but these subsequent events, even the raging and final argument
which I have with Baby Jane Harrison over certain practices and
demands and presumed inadequacies, which marks the permanent
interruption of our often temporarily interrupted relationship, all of
these undiscussed, undramatized events can be seen as irrelevant to
the main business of the events described earlier. These events have
to do, of course, with my unplanned, undesired auditing of the
terrible Valentine's Day Event, the Sweetheart Killings (as the press
so fetchingly calls them), which occur three days later, on the actual
holiday that is to say, and of which I have had such unhappy
foreknowledge. The nature of these slayings, the nature of the
actual Sweetheart herself, draped in a series of obscene poses, semi-
dead over the hood of a 1979 Pontiac Le Mans—all of these are
too well known, too accurately reported in the daily press to neces-
sitate graphic description. It is only necessary to say that it is
dreadful in the extreme, distressing in the main; it is one of the
more horrendous debacles in a city and a century which have not
shown themselves averse to splendid verifications of the bestiality
of the race and I am thinking upon these very factors and impli-

cations on the morning of the following day in Stendahl's, seated in a considerably less crowded version of that restaurant in which I had sat some days ago, reading the accounts in the local press and feeling all the fingers of injustice *tap-tap-tap*ping at my consciousness when Stendahl himself comes over and, nodding at the papers and at my own attention says, "Didn't you say something about that a couple days ago?"

I look up at Stendahl. He is a wide person in his early fifties, the original means of introduction to Baby Jane Harrison, if truth be known, and also one who has done me other favors, extended various courtesies in return for my own frequent usage and mention of his establishment in my column. I am, as has been pointed out, *scribendi* rather than activist and command a certain small cachet in that regard, even though a weekly is not a daily.

"I know you wrote something about it," Stendahl says. His face exudes cunning and incomprehension by turns. "Didn't you say something about a plan?"

"This is correct," I say. Part of my unease at this time is due to the sudden loss of Baby Jane Harrison and the shocking nature of her accusations, but another part of it has to do with recollection that I had incautiously and synoptically made reference to the overheard lines of conversation in the column that had come out just yesterday, lines that were, I hasten to note, written in a jocular and satiric manner as is all of my stylistic output. Jocularity and satire keep the belly full and *Avoid difficulty* has always been my motto, but as I look at Stendahl, even wider in the great morning light and expanse of his restaurant, and as Stendahl looks at me, it occurs to me that it is possible that out there might be a population of hundreds of thousands of wide persons in the world who are capable of, as they say, missing a point. "It was an oblique reference," I say. "Quite subtle and glancing. I will have another Danish if I may and—"

"It was not oblee enough," Stendahl says. He leans very close. "There are two persons who would like to see you. They are waiting outside the checkroom and they look very determined."

"Tell them I am not here," I say. "It was found necessary for me to take the healing breezes of Rockaway. I am at this very moment in the Rockaways, chartering a very large fishing boat."

"I am afraid that is not possible."

"I am aboard the fishing boat, catching fluke amidst various bouts of seasickness. I shall return next month after I am thrown overboard and drown. I will be found in a state of vast attention—"

"This humor," Stendahl says, "strained at best, was borne only for the sake of commerce. There is no commerce. There are two gentlemen waiting for you by the checkroom who have not followed me in here only because I have made most dignified persuasion and pleading. I have been given one minute to produce you after which—"

"It was a jesting reference," I point out to Stendahl. "I merely said that there was a Valentine Day's greeting in the works; a celebratory valediction of a greater event, that is all. I tied it in with the cuisine at Stendahl's, a valentine to the gastronome. No harm was intended."

Stendahl's hand upon my shoulder is enormous. It is remarkable how definitive and grandiose doom can be; good news and beneficence arrive with a wispy and effeminate aspect. Bad news carries a rifle and kicks down doors. "I have in order to demonstrate my own good faith and lack of collaboration," Stendahl says, "volunteered to produce you," and produce me he does, lifting me from the table with an almost perilous ease and guiding me toward the vicinity of the checkroom, which in happier times (as when I would exit with Baby Jane Harrison or earlier admirers who appreciated the journalistic power I could invoke and were eager to share with me their own attestations of communications) had always struck me as such a benign and pleasant place. It was not so pleasant now, graced as it was by two men of indistinguishable stature and bellicosity who, as Stendahl led me netherwards, brightened to my appearance with a mutuality of attention.

"A glancing reference, gentlemen," I pleaded, abandoning all amenities, even as Stendahl abandoned me, leaving me to their devices and retiring to his manager's post, which he had located somewhat to the left and several yards below the surface of his eating establishment, "made in the purest good humor, made only as a nostalgic reference to a historic and nostalgic event, an event that formed the basis as you may recall of the famous *Some Like It Hot* with Miss Marilyn Monroe! A reference to olden times, gladder times, easier times when retribution arrived in the form of gunfire and only funny-looking people with accents gunned one another down. Surely you can understand—"

But they could not, I regret to say, understand any of this, or perhaps I am failing to see the situation in its full implication because, making up in action for what they lacked in verbal attestation, they seized me with hands even more determined than Stendahl's and led me out quickly; little Borough Park breezes kicked Borough Park litter into the air as I was impelled by them into an enormous green car that bore a shocking resemblance to a 1979 Buick. One of them sat next to me in the back, the other most determinedly sat in the driver's seat and started and began to move the car as if he had a personal grudge against it. "Publicity, gentlemen!" I shouted. "It is a simple matter of publicity! I write about those I know; those in turn protect me and show their consideration in small ways! I wish to live simply, with determination and panache. Don't you have anything to say to me?" I ask desperately. The pleading, plaintive tone of my voice is somehow repellent; there is, after all, a certain point past which one (no matter the degree of self-love, self-absorption) needs to hear someone or something else.

"For Heaven's sake, gentlemen!" I say, "it might have been ill inspired, but it was innocently meant! It was a mistake. No harm was intended. The police have no suspects and thousands of people eat at Stendahl's at one time or the other." All desperately logical elements, as you can see. The eminence of logic cannot, however, overcome other imminence, an aphorism I tell myself that I should have put in print a long time ago since there now does not seem to be that easy, indeterminately extended future in which to air all of my thoughts to the world.

"That is not the point," the driver says. It is the first indication of human speech and I fall upon it gratefully, just as the Buick can be said to have fallen gratefully upon the patches and ruts of the attractively entitled Gowanus Parkway. I lean forward, eager for further transaction. "Not the point," the driver repeats.

"Then what *is* the point?"

"Enough, you," my companion in the backseat says and presses a grip that might be a manacle, "it is time for quiet."

"There is enough point for you," the driver says. "It means—"

"And you too," my companion says to the driver. "Shut up with the mouth, please, before I lose my temper."

This appears to be enough for the driver. It is certainly enough for me. This is the first hint of individuation; the companion appears to have been selected for the violence of his temper, the dreadful possibilities he can invoke; it is a theme with which I am not unfamiliar, my ratcheting and doomed consciousness flickering back again to certain recent discussions with Baby Jane Harrison, and then all too soon we are stopped in front of a large warehouse-appearing building and I am being propelled toward the door. "What is this?" I say uselessly. "It isn't necessary to do this; I get the point—"

"You move," my companion says, giving me a thrust far deadlier and concentrated than any stab from Stendahl's cheesecake (inspired by several old Russian recipes granted the owner by his sainted grandmother, or so I have written in happier times) and departing the 1979 Buick with ancillary speed and valedictory despair, I find myself inside the enclosed spaces of the warehouse, being moved hither and after by what appear to be more than the usual complement of arms and legs. The interior of the warehouse bears a doomed resemblance to my recollections of the spaces in *Some Like It Hot* where Marilyn Monroe's friends found themselves in so much unanticipated trouble. The difference is that my troubles are *not* unanticipated; a scribe has a definite, darker, even lunatic vision, as I have had occasion to contemplate, and at some level I must have known that my literary inclination and my big mouth would get me into some kind of apocalyptic jam, *apocalypse* being a word which I have waited more than fifty-four years to use in its proper context and which *Improve Your Word Power* would definitely indicate is now not inapropos.

I am conveyed up levels, through surfaces, around and about stairs and at long last am deposited in a spacious room where I am, redundantly, frisked here and there, checked out for the usual complement of genitals and the expected paucity of firearms and I am then propelled into a smaller room where I find myself looking at a face of which I have heard and of which I have seen pencil sketches in the dailies from time to time but which I have never, up to this point, actually witnessed. It is an interesting and complex face with the whole history of the century written, as they say, upon it and, never having thought to see it in this world nor having wanted to see it, I find myself transfixed. Thoughts of various kinds wend their way in and out of my fading consciousness while I stand before the face which at length adds arms, legs, a blue suit, an expression of poignancy and interest and becomes, no less than the driver or my companion or Baby Jane Harrison or me, simply a person.

"I have called you here," the face says superfluously. "It seemed to be necessary."

"It was a foolish thing," I say. "I was just making banter. I have to fill out this column, two thousand words, once a week. It is how I make my living."

"It is a terrible living."

"I agree," I say.

"How much you make, this column?"

"Two hundred dollars."

"Terrible," the face says again. "A grown man, a man your age—"

"But it pays off on both ends," I say hastily, pointlessly. "I mention things, I get concessions. I say good things about Stendahl's, Stendahl gives me a table, gives me things to eat—"

"Kickbacks for mentions, then. I know about that."

"Not exactly. I mean, I don't *have* to say good things. I could say bad things—"

The face gives me a perfect, an implacable smile. It is the kind of smile my father gave me the last time I saw him, when we had the final disagreement. It is the look Baby Jane Harrison gave me and gave me until she finally stopped giving me and began to take stringent action. It is, at last, a look which must be accepted.

"All right," I say. "So there were considerations. But if I couldn't say good, I *didn't* say good."

"Hah."

"Well," I say, thinking about this, allowing these last few precious moments of my extinguishable but irreplaceable life to at least permit some thought and consideration, "that's what I wanted to think, anyway. A man has to have his pride. You have to have principle somewhere."

"You know my name?" the face said. "Sure you know my name. Is Bruno. You call me Bruno?"

"I had no names in the column. It was just a little item, 'overheard from all over,' that's all."

"You don't understand yet," Bruno says, "I *like* you. I like your column; you have a good way with words. You, how you say it, light and bright and right on the money." He reaches a hand toward me. "St. Valentine Day's tribute, that was funny," he says, "that's a nice way to put it."

"I don't understand," I say. Consternation and bemusement chase terror through the core of my being in their old accustomed way, but there is a certain quizzicality as well. I am terrifyingly alert to my moods, a factor not beloved by Baby Jane Harrison. "What do you want?"

"What do I want?" Bruno says, his stern and patrician face assuming an aspect of near cordiality, a benignity that oozes through all the spaces of what I had erroneously thought of as darkness, Bruno being from this angle a genuinely engaging and blissfully communicative fellow, "I want you to come to work for *me.*"

"What's that?"

"You a good writer," Bruno says. "We need a writer. What

we're going to do, we start a newsletter or maybe you get your own paper and you can do nice things for us, like you do for Stendahl. I should have thought of this a long time ago. We are not—how can I put this?—so up to date in some ways as we are in others." His hand shakes my own, absently but with force. "Writing!" he says. "Communications, jokes, the light and bright side! That is what I mean; that's the way to go. You come with us, we make you happy. Two hundred dollars a week for a talent like yours? We do better."

I have had reversals and rereversals in my life; I am not uncognizant of that long-elusive opportunity when it comes. My father and Baby Jane Harrison said that I would never manage, it would never come, but how little they knew. I look at Bruno and smile and it is a smile of greeting as if to the whole world, the world in this warehouse opening to me like a huge and important flower, a flower like musk, like desire.

"*Five* hundred," I say.

Bruno embraces me. "My valentine!" he says.

His valentine.

Zecharia Sitchin's

The Earth Chronicles

BOOK I: THE 12TH PLANET
39362-X/$4.50 US/$5.75 CAN

This revolutionary work brings together lost, antediluvian texts, ancient cosmologies, and newly discovered celestial maps to reach the shocking conclusion that we are descendants of a superior race from the 12th planet.

BOOK II: THE STAIRWAY TO HEAVEN
63339-6/$4.95 US/$6.50 CAN

The mysteries of man's pursuit of immortality and afterlife with the gods is researched through the astounding conclusions based on names, places, and monuments whose true meanings have been lost for centuries.

BOOK III: THE WARS OF GODS AND MEN
89585-4/$4.50 US/$5.95 CAN

Mankind's earliest records reveal a startling new theory of human origins—and of the "gods" who destroyed the first civilization!

CHARLOTTE MACLEOD

*America's Reigning
Whodunit Queen*

PRESENTS

"Murder among the Eccentrics of Boston's
Upper Crust"* with
**Art Investigator Max Bittersohn
and Sarah Kelling**

THE FAMILY VAULT	49080-3/$3.50 US/$4.50 Can
THE PALACE GUARD	59857-4/$2.95 US/$3.50 Can
THE WITHDRAWING ROOM	56473-4/$3.50 US/$4.50 Can
THE BILBAO LOOKING GLASS	67454-8/$2.95 US/$3.50 Can
THE CONVIVIAL CODFISH	69865-X/$2.95 US/$3.75 Can
THE PLAIN OLD MAN	70148-0/$2.95 US/$3.95 Can

"Mystery with Wit and Style and a Thoroughly Engaging
Amateur Sleuth"**
Professor Peter Shandy

REST YOU MERRY	47530-8/$2.95 US/$3.95 Can
THE LUCK RUNS OUT	54171-8/$2.95 US/$3.50 Can
WRACK AND RUNE	61911-3/$2.95 US/$3.50 Can
SOMETHING THE CAT DRAGGED IN	
	69096-9/$3.25 US/$4.25 Can
THE CURSE OF THE GIANT HOGWEED	
	70051-4/$2.95 US/$3.75 Can

Mystery magazine   **The Washington Post*

By the year 2000, 2 out of 3 Americans could be illiterate.

It's true.

Today, 75 million adults...about one American in three, can't read adequately. And by the year 2000, U.S. News & World Report envisions an America with a literacy rate of only 30%.

Before that America comes to be, you can stop it...by joining the fight against illiteracy today.

Call the Coalition for Literacy at toll-free **1-800-228-8813** and volunteer.

Volunteer Against Illiteracy. The only degree you need is a degree of caring.

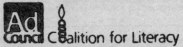

Ad Council · Coalition for Literacy